ABOVE

BELOW

PALMETTO
PUBLISHING

Charleston, SC
www.PalmettoPublishing.com

ABOVE BELOW
Copyright © 2023 by Maianna von Hippel

All rights reserved

No portion of this book may be reproduced, stored in a retrieval system, or transmitted in any form by any means–electronic, mechanical, photocopy, recording, or other–except for brief quotations in printed reviews, without prior permission of the author.

Paperback ISBN: 979-8-8229-0753-9
eBook ISBN: 979-8-8229-0754-6

ABOVE

ABOVE of LOVE BELOW

BELOW

Marianna von Hippel

For Vali
Love Forever

I

He hurtled along, rushed and pushed, flying through fields of matter, spinning in pools of color, nearly crashing into rocks, or maybe stars, but just before impact always veering off to fly further. He was caught up in a river of force, swept along like a spider trapped in a flood. He was being sucked back in, into the womb, into the Universe that holds it all. Then suddenly, mercifully, the motion, sound, and brilliant light ceased.

ABOVE

Now that his mind was no longer being assaulted beyond the point of generating a single idea or even a beep, he could at least resolve, by gratefully acknowledging a lack of sensation, that he did still have a mind. He almost dared to wonder what state he had entered or become.

He was sitting in a field. Startled, he realized that it looked like the field in the old John Wayne movie he had been watching the night before on the Late Late Show. It was a patch of land filled with long grasses and in the distance were purple mountains and a lush green valley with a glistening river wandering though. *Is this Wyoming? Or some part of Europe?* He asked himself, looking about. *Maybe I was in a plane crash and somehow landed in this field and am now waking up, dazed but alive....* He heard laughter in his ears, but he didn't see anyone laughing, there was no one. He thought again, *dazed but alive*, and again the laughter, like a radio broadcast inside his head.

To counter his confusion he tried to take a deep breath. It gave no relief. He had no body, just clothes over a vacuousness. Upon further inspection, he realized that the clothes too were just a mirage, but they were a mirage of his clothing, his favorite green shirt and best jeans. This recognition jogged his memory. *I was walking to the Little Red Store. Heard a truck behind me. It was so loud that I turned to look. An enormous blue and yellow truck was racing towards me. I tried to run. It struck me. No breath. That's all. Then this....*

An announcement: NEWCOMERS IN THE FIELD, a short silence, AMERICANS. A tinny rendition of The Star Spangled Banner filled the air. It sounded scratchy like an old record. He suddenly noticed a man sitting quite close to him. He was rubbing his eyes but then stopped and looked over at Harry and with a half wave of his hand called out, *Sinclair, from Cincinnati.* He was wearing a business suit, impeccable except that most of the buttons seemed to have been ripped off the shirt. He appeared to be waiting for a response.

Harry Miles, ah, from Boston.

Do you know what's going on here? Did they say 'Americans'? They played 'The Star Spangled Banner'. Is this a foreign country? I work for Standard Oil, Acquisitions and Development. At first I thought this was Newfoundland. I'm going there tomorrow.

He vaguely patted at his flapping shirt which caused a shimmer of air and color. *Jesus! I have no substance!*

I know. I thought maybe this was Europe but I guess it's further....

A voice distracted them. *Hello, hello, I'm Florabelle.* A sweet old lady in a flowered dress was coming towards them. She wore a straw hat abloom with roses and tied with ribbons that streamed down behind her. Upon closer observation, Harry realized she was not walking but wafting.

Hello my dears. Two Americans, isn't that nice!

Sinclair tried to extend his hand but it wouldn't move. He stared at it for a moment, amazed, and then decided to rely on his voice for forcefulness. *Sinclair, from Cincinnati. I never have time to really enjoy life* (the old lady giggled) *my work keeps me on the go. As much as I'd like to stay, could you direct me to the nearest airport? My wife says I drink too much and now I think she's right. I can't even remember how I got here. All I remember is being at a meeting in New York, going to a Broadway show and then having dinner at Sardi's. Steak… I was choking on a piece of steak….*

The old lady was nodding encouragingly.

I don't remember anything after that….

The old lady moved closer to Sinclair. *We looked over your file from this lifetime and we need you in Processing. Ramsey, your Archangel, is so excited to have a soul with your skills as we've been getting a lot of drunks and deadbeats lately. Let me talk to your friend here and then we'll get you both checked in and settled.*

She wafted over to Harry. He had begun to see how thinly shimmering was the illusion of the familiar. Florabelle hovered next to him. He observed her closely. A feeling like warmth was flowing towards him.

LaMont Peterson I presume? Her face evolved into a semblance of a smile.

No, actually, Harry Miles.

Her smile disappeared. In fact, as he stared, her whole face disappeared. It reappeared in a moment.

I know you have an outstanding sense of humor, Mr. Peterson, as well as, I must say, an awful lust for violence.

You mean LaMont Peterson, owner of Pinball City?

Yes, residing at 36 Banks Avenue. You've done quite enough fooling around already, Mr. Peterson, or should I say lying and cheating and yes, even murdering! The only reason we're not sending you right back as a cockroach is that we thought it might fix you up quicker to put you in Surplus Guidance. You will be watched closely and sent down the minute your attitude is less than sincere. It's such a waste, Peterson. That high I.Q. of yours won't matter in the life of a cockroach.

Hey, lady, I know LaMont is a jerk-off. I lived next door to him. He seduced my wife and now I'm divorced. Make him a cockroach already! An uncomfortable realization was coming over Harry.

The old lady became quivering light but soon reappeared accompanied by a tall man with disheveled sandy-brown hair. He had bulging muscles and was wearing a Harley shirt. Florabelle turned to Sinclair from Cincinnati and said, *this is Wayne. He's a junior guide in Admissions. He'll help you get settled. I have to go to Accounting with LaMont or Harry.* She sputtered a little. It made tiny breezes.

Harry felt himself pulled away with Florabelle and in a timeless moment he was in a place as familiar as a vague dream. He was aware of being held near the old lady by some force.

It's a mistake. Who the hell was on duty in procurement? We got the guy's neighbor.

Having got the drift of it, yes, he was dead, but it had been a mistake, Harry tried to express himself. He struggled to break into the conversation but it resumed with no notice of his attempts.

So what about this guy? How's his record? Maybe we were supposed to bring him in anyway?

The old lady appeared next to him.

You are Harry Miles of 42 Banks Avenue?

He did everything he could to send an affirmative response. She disappeared again. Harry found that he could tune in but couldn't orient himself. It felt like a dream where there was no border between oneself and all else.

He's been good. Movin' right along. Passed all the tests. We had him set up for a wonderful love affair leading to marriage. Two kids, two cars, American dream stuff. Wait a minute! He was gonna make some changes. He's a Walk-In!

Oh God, we zapped a Walk-In? What do you do in a case like that?

Get the manual!

Erred procurement – In the event, mumble, mumble, *if the funeral has not yet taken place and there is room in circumstance to create a resurrection, it can be done....*

Quick! Check the Be Registry. He would still be on it. Read out the tape. Start with last night.

AMBULANCE TO MAPLEVILLE HOSPITAL. CRUSHED SKULL, INTERNAL INJURIES, PROFUSE BLEEDING....

He tried to see if his body was intact. Nothing seemed to be missing.

TRANSFER TO MASS GENERAL HOSPITAL. POLICE TRY TO FIND RELATIVES TO NOTIFY....

His thoughts joined in this collage. *I live alone. Both of my parents are dead. My father's cousin in New Hampshire is the closest, or Aunt Sally and Uncle Fred in New Jersey....*

VITAL SIGNS DISAPPEAR, CPR ADMINISTERED THROUGHOUT AMBULANCE RIDE. MASS GENERAL EMERGENCY ROOM RESIDENT ASSESSES INJURIES AND PRONOUNCES HIM DEAD ON ARRIVAL. POLICE PRESENT EMERGENCY ROOM STAFF WITH ORGAN DONOR CARD FOUND IN HIS WALLET.

Oh no! What time was that?

10:26 p.m.

What time is it there now?

5:16 a.m.

Go on with the tape!

EMERGENCY ROOM INTERN OBTAINS PERMISSION TO REMOVE KIDNEY. PERFECT MATCH FOR A MAN IN RENO, NEVADA.

Ok, that's it. Even if we could beat the funeral, no kidneys and I'm sure if you read on he would have no eyeballs, no liver, no heart and lungs, all that stuff would be gone....

Harry felt sick. What barbarism, at least his soul seemed to be intact. It was only slightly heartening to find that the state of the physical body did not seem to affect the soul.

The old lady was back. *I'm sorry Harry. It's too late. There is no opportunity for resurrection. Even we, here, cannot set all things right.*

Harry grumbled. *It ain't a question of setting things right, lady. It's a question of not fucking them up to begin with.*

Florabelle ignored his outburst. *You will be trained as a Guide and given the responsibility of being a Primary Guide. Usually the job of Primary Guide is only assigned to those who have worked their way up to Level 6. As a Primary Guide you can complete your own karma from this lifetime and therefore start at your intended level in your next Earth lifetime. A Primary Guide directly affects an Earth person's thoughts and actions. It's a heavy responsibility because it calls for constant awareness of your own values and then exacting consideration of their influence on your Earth person's value system.*

Harry was taking it all in but also feeling a sense of finality and loss in the realization that he would not be returning to his life.

Can I see what's happening with the people in my life? How they are doing without me?

I didn't know you were close to anyone at this point, Florabelle replied.

Harry felt sad. *My life didn't matter*, he muttered to himself.

She seemed to have heard him, *no, you were good, Harry. It was all just beginning for you. You were a Walk-In. That's what makes this mistake even worse. You were slated for love and happiness and to make a great contribution to the world. You were going to invent a water filter, a screen made of the white of egg. We'll send you back as soon as we can but first you need to wind up the karma for that life. As a Primary Guide you can probably get through it in less than a year.*

What's a Walk-In? Harry realized that no speech was necessary, thought was transmitted directly.

You do not recall it at this moment but you were here with us recently. After his wife left him and he lost his job, Harry Miles was so depressed that he wanted to be released so you were sent down to take over his life but you only lasted six months. That's why you have adjusted to being back so quickly. Sinclair will be down in Admissions for days. He's still trying to take a pee and all that. He was caught wandering in the periphery and said he was looking for a phone. He keeps asking about you as his claim to being alive. You may need to go down there and help him. She tuned out for a moment and then transmitted, *now he's having a fit. Somehow he got back to the Arrival Dock and discovered that the grass and mountains are fake. Oh God, now he's flailing around and put his leg through the mountains. It was only paper. He still has some body force because he hasn't acknowledged his state. The Admissions Guides are all Juniors and they're not getting through to him. We'll have to zap him back as a rodent,* (here she cackled, quite in contrast to her demure demeanor). *You'd better come help.*

They appeared at the Arrival Dock. Sinclair was a mass of movement. He was half transposed, shuddering in jerky spasms and somewhat shimmering. As soon as Harry arrived he calmed down.

I thought you got away! Oh Jesus, they got you too! How far did you get?

Harry sent him some soothing vibrations, suddenly recalling how to transmit the forces. Florabelle was right. Harry had been in ABOVE recently. He was disappointed by this flash of remembrance. He had really looked forward to this trip to Earth. He was going to get a chance to be a good guy, rich and famous, all the bennies.

Sinclair awkwardly wafted closer to Harry. *Hey dude, ah Harry, tell me how you got away. The two of us can make a plan. I was really getting desperate....*

Harry sent him more soothing energy. He and Florabelle communed. Should Harry tell Sinclair like it is or should he pretend to be his partner in escape to the end of a slower adjustment? They decided to go for the truth at the outset. In a flash Harry remembered that he had worked in Admissions. He was good, brought the new arrivals into submission and positive action quickly. Florabelle showered him with warmth acknowledging his realization. Harry swung into the role.

Sinclair, I have come to understand what has happened to us.
Sinclair was avidly attending.
It may not sound reasonable to you at the moment, Sinclair, but the truth is we are dead and the only way back to life is to do good work here.
I know about good work, Harry, but are you sure we're dead? Sinclair sounded scared.
Yes, but it's all right, Sinclair. It's not horrible, just different.
Sinclair was calm because Harry was calm and Sinclair was not the type of man to demonstrate a lack of control especially when confronted with someone who was handling the situation well. He had aspired to being a statesman.

2

Florabelle wafted off to meet LaMont Peterson. He was lying in the field, flailing and cursing. Behind him the paper backdrop was being battered by the breezes, ripping little by little until a great triangle of it floated away. Florabelle called out in an authoritative tone, *cool it, Peterson. These two* (two large men appeared next to her, both wore tuxedoes and sported the body builds of bouncers) *will escort you to Admissions. Do you know where you are, Mr. Peterson?*

He was sputtering and protesting. They started to drag him off. Florabelle wafted along, glaring at him. *You're DEAD, Peterson! You are lucky to be here at all. Souls like you usually go directly to Rodent Recycle.*

He sputtered. *To what?*

Rodent Recycle, instant rat....

Florabelle lashed into him, perhaps partly because she thought his evil deeds were somehow responsible for Harry's premature return. *Don't worry, Peterson, you'd be a fine rat and you'd be with all your friends.*

Peterson had turned into a mass of splotchy flashings in resistance to his bondage between the two men.

When I get outa here, lady, you're gonna pay!

Florabelle laughed a surprisingly masculine belly laugh but then responded sweetly.

I'm afraid those techniques don't work here, Peterson. This is what you could call a re-conditioning center. You were thought to have characteristics worthy of your salvation as a human so you've been assigned to Surplus Guidance. You're gonna hafta give a damn, Peterson. That's your only way out of here… pretty bad, huh?

Peterson responded with a low growl. Harry wafted over to him.

Hi LaMont, strange place to meet up with ya.

Hey, Miles, they screwin' wid you too?

No, I guess you reap what you sow. I got a promotion. This round I'm the rich bastard and you're the unsuspecting nerd.

Florabelle communed to Harry, *now, now, vengeance could get you put back a grade or two.*

Harry straightened up. *Think about it, LaMont. Here's your chance to show you got a heart. Your soul ain't worth a damn without a good heart.*

Hey Miles, you goin' into songwritin' now?

Florabelle took over with Peterson. *LaMont, we've assigned you to Surplus Guidance. That's our fastest growing department. At first we kept guidance work strictly to family and friends but that meant doubling up and sometimes even tripling and we've had some pretty tragic outcomes like that fire in Newark last week, six little kids burned to death! They were left alone in an apartment and the space heater blew up. The mother's guide was working with a nephew who was chasing someone with the intent to murder. It's real active in some of these families so we've created the Surplus Guidance Department to lower the ratios and create an opportunity for soul development for people like you who need to learn to have a heart. You can't just waft around up here unless you want to be here forever. You gotta get points to move on.* Florabelle snickered. *When you get adjusted you'll be fine. Everyone likes it here, no laundry, no shaving, no painting the house, but a hundred years without sex is more than most people can stand. I never liked sex. I'm here permanently, Grade 10, Spiritual Civil Service.*

LaMont interrupted. He was sputtering and his limbs were jerking, only vaguely responsive to his wishes. *A hundred years! You gotta be kiddin'!*

Florabelle led them to Surplus Guidance. They passed through some gates that appeared to be painted to look pearly and entered a huge area where many vaporous souls were leaning over what looked like computer screens. Rows of what appeared to be servers surrounded and cut through the space in straight lines. A hum filled the air as many communications mingled. A woman appeared next to them. Florabelle directed her thoughts to her. *Madeline, I have a new volunteer for you.*

Peterson could be heard muttering, *not exactly....*

Florabelle continued, *LaMont Peterson, he's in dire need of reconditioning. His last life was a series of evil deeds....*

Hey, wait a minute. I worked at the Knights of Columbus kids' fair!

He got no response. Florabelle just raised her ghostly eyebrows and sent him a look of disdain. *Madeline, put him on a city kid, a quick mover and give him lots of supervision. Left on his own, I'm afraid he'll have the kid pilfering and murdering in no time.*

That bad, huh? Madeline shook her head.

Oh yes! His file is thick with reports of gross deeds.

Peterson spoke up. *You ain't gonna put me wid no black people are you? I don't think I could stand it.* He accompanied this statement with a weak wave of his hand.

Florabelle tittered. *We're all the same color here, LaMont. Madeline, give him someone who will put him in a state of soul searching but put someone on him. Don't trust him for a minute. Any problems, call Rodent Recycle and have him picked up.*

Harry had allowed Sinclair to wander along because Harry knew that the best way to get through to him was to have him observe a scene with a person to whom he could feel superior, LaMont Peterson produced the desired effect.

You said I was assigned to Ramsey in Processing? Sinclair asked contritely.

Mr. Sinclair, (even as a spirit he was not someone to be addressed on a first name basis) *you certainly have become compliant! We do allow a final viewing of your life scene. Actually, we encourage it. You can learn a lot by seeing how you are missed. Some people aren't missed at all. It can be quite shocking.*

Sinclair looked somewhat aggrieved and concerned but indicated that he would like a final viewing. They brought him back to the field which was now surrealistically surrounded by blowing tatters of paper. Off to one side was a chapel-like structure. It looked like a Hollywood prop. Harry was confused. *I don't remember any of this. Either Reception has really been dolled up or I just forgot.*

No, it's all brand new. That's why it's such a shame that Sinclair ruined the backdrop. We didn't think it needed to be substantial as usually no one even moves around over there. They're always dazed and we bring 'em right to Admissions. John Wayne designed the Reception area for us.

I should have guessed, Harry murmured. The John Wayne movie he'd watched the night before on the Late Late Show was still a vivid memory.

Sinclair was ushered into the chapel by a young man wearing nondenominational vestments. At the front, where you would expect an altar to be, was an instrument panel. The priest-type sat at the controls. He motioned for Sinclair to sit down in the front pew. Harry hovered in the doorway with Florabelle. It appeared that Sinclair was off and running, adapted, but Harry silently agreed with Florabelle that he should wait until she delivered him to Processing. Sinclair gingerly sat down on the edge of the pew. A huge screen stretched across the front of the chapel. The priest punched a few buttons and a picture came into focus on the screen.

Sinclair gasped. *Oh, it's Heidi, my wife. Where is she? In church? No, it must be the funeral home. Oh, she looks so sad, but gorgeous.* He glanced around for a moment, a flash of pride passing over his face. The scene became a wide shot and Sinclair could see many other people. *Oh, the twins, Clarence and Clara! They're only fourteen. Oh, Clara looks like she's been crying for hours. My poor dear! But I had lots of life insurance. They shall never want. Oh, look, my Aunt Cora. Just like a mother to me. Oh my dear, dear, Auntie Cora!* Uttering little clucks and moans, Sinclair moved his attention from one mourner to the next until he had surveyed the entire crowd.

With a considerate, *ah, hmm*, the priest asked if there was anyone, or anyplace else that he wanted to tune in on. Sinclair glanced around uncertainly, somewhat furtively, and then mumbled, *yes, I had a secretary, ah, a couple of years ago, um… she left our employ but we've, ah, kept in touch, Barbara Dooby. Do you need an address or what?*

No, the name is enough, B-A-R-B-A-R-A D-O-O-B-Y? The priest spelled it out.

Sinclair confirmed the spelling and a picture came up on the screen of a youngish woman reclining on a sofa, weeping. She appeared to be clutching a pin-striped shirt. *This is all I have of dear Sinny. Oh, oh… I should never have had that abortion, oh….* She began to weep even more profusely and with her arms clutched around herself she rocked back and forth on the couch.

Sinclair gasped and muttered, *I should have left her something.*

The priest asked, *anyone else?*

Sinclair seemed to have settled into a morose mood tinged with embarrassment. *No, I guess I'm ready to get to work. Which way to Processing?*

A man appeared. He was dressed in black coveralls. The word **ZOOKEEPER** was printed across the back of them. Florabelle introduced him to Sinclair.

This is Lester. He'll take you to Processing. We're grateful to get a soul with your fine skills.

Sinclair sighed with pride and his mouth twitched as he tried to speak. A few garbled sounds came out.

Florabelled communed, *just think it, Sinclair. Expressed words are not feasible here. The language of thought is universal. No, it's not a mistake. Lester always wanted to be a zookeeper. We're indulged in little ways here. Despite the uniform, he **is** taking you to Processing. We don't have a zoo. Arrivederci, Sinclair.*

Florabelle and Harry wafted off.

Come into my office, Harry.

They entered a pink zone filled with images of leaves and flowers and even the hum of bees.

I don't remember any of this, Florabelle.

Ya, it's new. We just got a new SuperArch. He's into mood. He says it creates an environment that supports the development of the soul. He keeps telling us that souls resist change and stagnation is an ominous force in the universe. We got a memo stating that we were required to make a scene for ourselves and he was going to check them out and give prizes. A lot of us found it annoying. Well, Harry, I think I'd better clarify things for you, reorient you so you can get on with your assignment. A buzzing interrupted her... *God damn! I fucking work all the fucking time, nobody gives a shit....*

Florabelle's crass mutterings awed Harry. She looked like such a sweet little old lady! She was distracted for a moment, in tune with other levels, other conversations. Then she brought her being back to Harry.

Your story is damned unusual, Harry. Most of your history is as a South American jungle boy and some North American Indian lifetimes also. One of your more memorable lifetimes was in Peru. You lived in Lima, a poor kid from a large family. You shined shoes in the street. One day the earth opened in front of you. An earthquake split the land and nearly an entire school fell into the chasm. You didn't run but instead dragged over some boards and made a ramp to save many of the children. It was extremely fucking heroic, Harry! You were only eight, and a small kid at that. You arrived here a few years later. Unfortunately, you had perished under the wheels of a truck at age eleven but you were covered with stars. We were all impressed. We decided to train you for a promotion. You were a frigging hot shot, Harry. You picked the image of the Lone Ranger. We called you Lone. You learned real quick and had one hell of a persuasive personality. Cornelius Vanderbilt wanted to send you down as a tycoon. When you were working in Admissions we had no problems like this morning with Sinclair. You brought 'em in and had 'em straightened out in no time. You remember now, Harry?

Harry nodded. There was a look of dawning consciousness on his face.

After some years of impeccable service we gave you a choice of what country you wanted to go to for your next lifetime, a rare privilege, Harry, very few of us get to choose. The Assignment Committee won't even hear requests. But you were one of our wonder boys … anyway, predictably, the Lone Ranger chose the United States so we sent you down to the Kempers, a nice-enough couple in New Jersey who were yearning for a baby. In an unfortunate exercise of blind free will, you were again flattened by a truck at the tender age of nine. You were studying the revolution of the wheels from a little too close, felled again by your overwhelming curiosity. We were delighted yet exasperated to see you so soon again and with little faith in your ability to contain your youthful exuberance we sent you down as a Walk-In so your talents could come to some fruition. I don't know what it is with you and trucks, Harry. As soon as you came out of the jungle you met your fate every time under the wheels of a truck. Even as a jungle boy you always perished in dramatic ways. Once you were swept over a giant waterfall. In another lifetime you invented a technique to fell a row of trees at one time but were yourself duly fucking felled at the end of the row. Do you realize, Harry, in over thirty lifetimes you have never made it past the age of twelve!

Harry grinned slightly, twinges of recall passed through his mind.

So the Assignment Committee got smart, tired of your unfulfilled Earthly promise, and put you on the Walk-In list. That's why it is all so unclear to you, Harry. Your last stay here was very short. You didn't even get an assignment. We just kept you in the fucking freezer so to speak.

Harry thought, *this is really odd, such a dear old lady swearing so lustily!*

After ascertaining our error, I met with the Destiny Committee this morning. We did it. We grant you that, Harry. But what is it with you and fucking trucks?

Harry shrugged.

Shit, I was a sailor and finally a captain and I always went down with the ship. But it was fucking appropriate, Harry, and I always made it to a decent age. Do you realize you have never even fathered or mothered a child, Harry!? Anyway, the Committee decided we were just fighting the tide and you need to live out this karma here, get it over with once and for all. Because we need you, Harry. You gotta get over of this goddamn blip. It's worked for others. Being a Primary Guide lets you observe the machinations of free will in someone else. We picked you a smart woman. Her name is Julia. She's somewhat misguided in her use of free will and energy but we hope that with your guidance she can provide the world with the water filter we had in mind for you. She's a powerful soul and well placed: good family, good health, good education, attractive, intelligent, but she wastes a lot of energy on the vagaries of love. It's a problem that has dogged her throughout her lives like the trucks have dogged you. We tried to stabilize her with religion but she's as flighty with that as she is with love. If you can guide her out of the vagaries of love we know that her gifts are substantial and critically needed on Earth. Your success with this assignment will ready you to unloose your skills on the world. Get the picture, Harry? I wanna make one thing perfectly clear, **don't** *get her run over by a goddamn truck!! You are to guide her and watch the exercise of her free will and heal your own overexuberance while earning points as a Primary Guide. You could get as far as a Grade seven, Harry, maybe even an eight if you do this right.*

Florabelle was again distracted. She muttered, *fucking asshole,* and then communed to Harry, *you look like a goddamned mess, Harry, get yourself integrated. I'll be back in a while. John Wayne is down at Reception ranting about the damage. He wants us to rebuild in wood and stone. I don't know how that asshole got so much clout up here. Everybody loves those goddamn American movie stars. I'll be back soon to take you over to Guidance. Get yourself together!*

Harry indicated acquiescence. He was vibrating irregularly with parts of his image appearing and disappearing indicating conflict and ambivalence, hardly an appropriate posture for someone who hoped to attain Grade 7 or perhaps even Grade 8.

When Florabelle returned Harry was evenly shimmering, his image finally uniform.

Thank God, at least you've got yourself together, Harry. I like you, boy. Wish I could have gotten you as my assistant but you're in the fast lane. Let's go.

Harry ascended with Florabelle. Her billowing pink dress was buffeted by the breezes. Harry rose right behind her. For a minute they looked like a Chagall painting.

Get off here, Harry.

As if traveling on an elevator, they stepped out.

Harry, what image you want this time? Lone Ranger again?

No, I think I'll be Albert Einstein. He was such a great man, a great face.

Suit yourself but are you sure you don't want to be a broad for a change? It's pretty sexist up here. You be a broad and you'll always get a seat and you'll never be put on the cloud repair late shift when the ranks get low.

Naw, anyway, I like being outdoors.

Florabelle snorted, *outdoors?* She guffawed. Her only feminine attributes were her name and her garb.

Florabelle and Harry wafted through a pinkish blue corridor of slightly shifting clouds and came to some intricately designed wrought iron gates. Passing though, the sense of hubbub was immediate. It was a vista of little semi-circles of wrought iron garden chairs arranged in clusters. Most of the chairs were occupied and many figures milled about. Harry picked up fragments of conversations as they passed by.

Don't let him do it!

Watch out for the elephant!

That man isn't good enough for her.

Everyone seemed to be kibitzing. Guidance work appeared to be a shared activity. They passed a group of six who were dressed as Bolivian soccer players. Florabelle commented, *a family into soccer.* They overheard, *pass it! Pass it! Oh hail, a goal!* The whole group cheered. The little gatherings seemed endless. They stretched as far as the eye could see.

Quite an operation! Harry commented.

Florabelle grunted affirmatively. They approached a counter. Florabelle addressed the image behind the counter who appeared to be Mickey Mouse, ears and all. *Hey Mick, how's it goin'? Got a new one for ya. He's gonna be a Primary Guide.*

The mouse-type leaned across the counter to stare at Harry for a moment and then opened a large registration book.

Country of assignment?

Florabelle answered for Harry, *USA*

Family name?

Harry said, *Harry Miles.*

Florabelle cut him off. *No, Harry, he's asking about the family you are being assigned to. No Mick, scratch that. Miles was just his last cover. He's not going to relatives and anyway the Miles weren't relatives. He was a Walk-In.*

Oh.... Mick looked at him with new regard.

He's assigned to the Frenns. I think the grouping is listed under given name James.

Mick went through the register, turning pages. *Here, Frenn, James, F-2.*

Harry glanced around wearily and noticed that there were pennants hanging on tall poles at regular intervals. They were flapping in the breeze. There were letters on them. He could see a row of L's and M's.

Mick was writing in the register. *How bout the image? You gonna stay like that?* His tone indicated that he was not impressed with Harry's current image. The original Harry Miles had assuaged his depression by eating non-stop so even though Harry Miles, the Walk-In, had exercised and dieted diligently for the six months of his occupation, he was still quite gourd shaped.

Harry said, *Albert....*

Florabelle cut him off again. *Lemme caution you, Harry. This is not a routine guide assignment. When you clear up this karma you'll probably be sent down at a moment's notice. There might not be time for an image change so whatever you pick at this point you might be stuck with for another lifetime. It's possible that you'll be a Walk-In again but you might just be sent down 'As Is' if there's nobody placed in a likely spot who wants out at the time. It's a new category we've just created. Things are such a mess BELOW that we're sending down extras whenever we can. It's less time consuming than preparing the Walk-Ins. You don't have to take on an existing life and then slowly change it. We call them Drop-Ins. They just appear with a likely story. Perhaps an engineer returning after years in Saudi Arabia, or a nun coming out of the convent after 22 years, stuff like that. What I'm trying to tell you is that the Albert Einstein image might be a little limiting. He's an older guy. It might make employment difficult and he might be still using the image if he's still up here.*

Albert Einstein, whoa, you got some heavy images, boy, Mick mumbled while adjusting his Mouseketeers hat. *How bout Donald Duck, Goofy, something light and fun?*

Hey Mick, give us a minute. Florabelle pulled Harry over to the side. *Think about it Harry. What type ya wanna be. It would probably be best if you'd be some kinda universal type. You know you're going back soon, unless you fuck up, so be a little splendid Harry, youthful. Ya wanna get some action when you get back there. You've never been a stud. Hey, you think I'd choose this rig if it wasn't a long term assignment?* She fluffed her dress.

All right then, how about Clint Eastwood? Can I look like him?

Mick started turning pages. Florabelle wafted about nervously and shook her head which caused ripples in the cascade of ribbons that flowed down her back from her hat. *Wait a minute Mick. Listen to me, Harry. That's fine as a general idea but Eastwood's an older guy too, and he's not dead yet so that could be a problem. But how about the Eastwood look but younger, and with green eyes and brown hair. Still tall and handsome and all that....*

Harry wearily nodded in agreement

A vapor appeared to descend and after a moment it lifted and Harry emerged a young Clint Eastwood clone. He appeared to be about thirty-five. Mick looked him up and down and sighed, *another jock....* He made an entry in the registration book and then closed it. The large pages cascaded down like the shuffling of a giant pack of cards. Mick wrote F-2 on a piece of paper and pushed it across the counter. Florabelle picked it up and handed it to Harry. *Think you can find it all right, Harry? The numbers are along the sides, the letters go across the top and bottom.* She pointed to the flapping pennants. *It's like a map, Harry, or ya wanna be called Clint?*

I don't care. Harry was tired. It had been a full day, with dying and all.

It's like a map, Harry, Florabelle repeated.

Ya, I can figure it out, no problem.

Good fucking luck to ya, Harry and drop by Admissions if ya get a free moment.

3

Harry followed the pennants to the perimeter. It seemed to take forever. He passed many little gatherings, thoughts and fragments of thoughts hummed. It reminded him of Coney Island in August. He'd been there once. The little clusters merged into a scene that stretched out in all directions. He could feel the emotion build and then subside as he moved past each group.

Harry noticed that there was a central point to each gathering. The wrought iron chairs surrounded a raised circular glass plate. Everyone was holding what he had assumed were walking sticks but then he saw them being held over the glass and stared into like telescopes.

When he reached the end of M he started along the perimeter towards 2. It was an arduous journey. With great apprehension, he turned in at 2 and moved along to F. There were a number of clusters at the intersection of F and 2. He approached the closest group and asked, *Frenn's?* They seemed an idle bunch. Their telescopic sticks leaned against their chairs. They appeared to be a family dedicated to ballet as all of them were dressed in dance regalia. They indicated negative to his inquiry. Three young girls were doing slow plies.

Harry moved on to the next group. It was a bunch of women in formal wear, two men in tuxedoes and a boy dressed like a clown. Harry diffidently asked, *Frenn's?* The boy looked up and then shook his head.

The groupings were not in a straight line as there was a wide swath under the F flags. Harry approached a group slightly off to the left, *Frenn's?* He asked. A man of medium height with gray hair and a dignified appearance nodded in acknowledgment. He wore a charcoal gray suit with a blue dress shirt and bedroom slippers. The slippers seemed oddly appropriate.

Are you from Central Casting? He asked Harry.

Harry vibrated in dissonance. *No! I am a Primary Guide assigned to Julia, F-2. Family gathering named Frenn.* He tried to transmit this in an authoritative tone. The suggestion that he might be from Central Casting struck him as an insult. The old man tilted his head solicitously, perceiving the sense of insult radiating from Harry. He transmitted, *new arrival? All we mean by Central Casting is those spirits who keep the works going up here, the level 10's. They're here forever, like Florabelle. Did you meet her?*

Harry relaxed a little. *Yes, I met Florabelle, but no, I'm not a level 10. Is this the right family cluster, Frenn's?* It had been a long and confusing day and Harry had no energy left and just wanted to get to the right place and not feel so adrift.

The old man studied Harry intently and then made a welcoming gesture by shifting his posture slightly. *James Frenn here. You've come to the right place.* He turned and motioned to a small gathering of spirits off to the left, *Iris, Hugo, Dinah, Sonny, come here.* The spirits drifted closer. There were two women who looked quite similar, both had dark eyes and black hair and wore lovely, vaporous lavender dresses, perhaps sisters. Then there was another elderly man in a blue suit and a young man in a ski outfit. They stared at Harry. *James, is he a relative?* One of the sisters asked.

James addressed the small assemblage. *This...* he gestured forthcomingly to Harry, *ah... what was your name again?* Harry started to reply, *Har...* but then realized that he could take this opportunity to change his name. He quickly considered, *Allen, Arnold, Arthur, Beasley, Bill, Bob, Brent…* they all sounded awful so he abandoned the alphabetical progression and concentrated on evoking names of men he admired. James shifted from one foot to the other, arm ashimmer, outstretched.

Jimmy Carter, Harry finally said.

To James the name apparently had only the significance of a label. He quickly introduced the family. The other older man was Hugo. The two women, Iris and Dinah, were mother and daughter in their last lives BELOW. The young man in the ski outfit was called Sonny. James was obviously the head of the family. He explained to the others in a kind, patient tone, *Jimmy has come to us as a Primary Guide for Julia. You may remember we put in a request, oh, quite a while ago….* He leaned over Iris and said quietly, *you may have forgotten, dear, but we all felt at a loss with Julia. Sonny, this means you can go back to watching over your parents and your brothers full-time. Dinah, that gives you one less, but of course we'll have to help Jimmy for a while.* There was a murmur of agreement as they all scrutinized Jimmy, looking him up and down. Sonny muttered to Hugo, *I can't see anyone in our family wanting to look like Clint Eastwood.*

Hugo muttered back, *Clint who?*

Sonny continued in an undertone. *I know it's a look-alike 'cause Eastwood doesn't have brown hair, it's gray, and he's still alive. I'm sure we would have heard if he wasn't. And what about the name? Jimmy Carter was President of the United States a while ago. Don't you think that's a bit of a reach?*

Jimmy who? Hugo asked.

James glanced at the source of this low level transmission and sent a quieting look and then extended his arm out to Jimmy in a welcoming gesture.

Come, sit down…. He moved towards the semi-circle of chairs. They all sat down but Dinah was left standing. *We need another chair*, James noted. *I'll put in a request as soon as we finish the formal introductions. Dinah, sit here*, he patted the arm of his chair and she perched there. James turned to Jimmy. *Can you tell us a little about yourself? This is the first time we've used a rental guide.* Immediately, James could feel the heat of anger radiating from Jimmy. *No, Jimmy, my boy, it's a small joke in the language here. Whenever we get particularly frustrated in our guidance efforts, we threaten to go on vacation and hire a rent-a-guide. Ah, I guess that doesn't sound any better. I say, Jimmy, you wouldn't be Jewish by any chance would you?*

No, actually, I haven't been religious. Let me explain. In my past lifetimes I haven't gotten very old or been in many civilized places. Way back, in Egypt, I partook in some rituals but my strength of mind is more from action than from thought. As Jimmy spoke, he wearily realized that the process of his acceptance was not going quickly or well. The Frenns seemed to be a genteel but withholding bunch, except for Dinah, she was smiling warmly. Jimmy then wondered how he could feel so tired when actually disembodied, perhaps weariness was a soul measure.

A number of conversations sprang up in the semi-circle of Frenn family. James called them to order again. *We have all guided Julia. I had her for the years before any of you came up, of course with your help, dear*, he patted Iris gently. She looked to be a bit of a lost soul. Here it seemed an ironic condition. James continued. *During the early years we had at least twenty Earth persons to look after. They never allow those ratios anymore, but of course things have become so much more complex.* All the Frenns murmured in agreement. James continued. *Perhaps we should all briefly recount our efforts to guide Julia. You see, we've never gone out of the family before, so it's a new experience for us. You must be top drawer or Mick wouldn't have sent you over. We know there are great expectations on us and we've decided that Julia has the largest amount of uncommitted energy. She's fairly seething with unrealized potential.*

A man wearing Grecian robes drifted over. Hugo turned to greet him and then introduced him to Jimmy. *This is Amesbury. He's been an advisor to us for some years ever since Sonny arrived. Sonny is so outgoing. We have better relations with the neighbors now. Amesbury's family has dwindled to a couple of dried up middle-aged men, committed to bachelorhood and the accounting profession. There's nothing much for him to do as these aging boys seemed to have inspired no malice so there is very little protection needed. Amesbury checks on them whenever conditions on Earth are unstable, storms, wars, disasters....*

Amesbury interrupted. His robes swayed grandly as he explained further. *The others in my family group have moved on to different assignments. It got to the point where we were all moldering. For years we tried to set up the boys for marriage and job challenges but they steadfastly plodded around all obstacles and temptations. Once we sent over identical twins, gorgeous girls. There was a blizzard going on and the girls were stranded and had to stay overnight with the boys. These guys are even blessed with good looks and the girls were interested but Ed and Fred told them to go into Ed's room and the boys locked themselves in Fred's room and at the crack of dawn they called the police to come get the girls. We really tried.* Amesbury heaved a ghostly sigh. *I've become an uncle-type to some of the neighbors. I've enjoyed Julia, she certainly is feisty. What's happening with that boyfriend of hers, that big one that she's so madly in love with?*

Sonny joined in. *I was on her before,* he held up his telescopic stick. Jimmy tried to send the thought, *what's that stick thing for?* He apparently succeeded because Sonny flinched and communed, *we hear you, turn down the volume! It's called a wand.* Embarrassed, Jimmy's image flashed.

So, is Julia OK? Dinah asked Sonny, a worried look on her beautiful, oval face.

Actually, she was seriously down. If there's any flooding in her basement now it's strictly from tears. She found out that her boyfriend is moving in with another woman.

The little gathering seemed to involuntarily shift to the central table. When Jimmy got closer he could see that embedded in it was a large monitor. The Frenns approached as one with their wands held in readiness. Amesbury murmured to Jimmy, *newcomer, we're serious about this guidance business, tremendous responsibility. I'm a rarity here. I can afford to leave my monitor for hours, or even days as we have general announcements over the PA system, typhoon in India and that sort of thing, but most families have to keep someone on the monitor at all times, like a sentry.*

Sonny was looking through his wand into the monitor. *Uh oh, speak of the devil, all's quiet except for Julia. She is definitely not crying anymore, seems on a homicidal bent.* The family clustered around the monitor, peering through their wands.

She's on Storrow Drive! Dinah exclaimed. *It's icy and it's dark... she's driving too fast... whose car is she driving?*

They all stared intently into the monitor. Amesbury pulled a spare wand from a pocket in his voluminous robes. He handed it to Jimmy and they joined the others at the monitor.

4

BELOW

Julia was on Storrow Drive, just past the Hatch Shell, heading out of town. Suddenly she veered towards the high speed lane, tightening up to a burgundy Mercedes. She was making desperate motions at the wheel, driving erratically. She sped up and then suddenly put on the brakes. The Mercedes, which was now behind her, nearly hit her and honked furiously. Julia sped up, changed to the center lane and just as the Mercedes pulled up on the left, nearly adjacent to her, she pulled into his lane. He swerved and crashed into the guardrail, to the tune of screeches of scraping metal and breaking glass. She straightened out her car and drove on, staring straight ahead. The Mercedes managed to keep driving. It came up beside her, honking non-stop. The driver furiously signaled to her to pull over. She nodded compliantly.

The first exit was the one by Boston University. She pulled off and he followed, having hugged her car all the way. She had been watching his face in her rearview mirror. His eyes and mouth were set in straight lines. With an irate grabbing motion his hand had loosened his tie and undone the top button on his shirt. She felt her face flush in anticipation of his rage. Catching a quick look at herself in the mirror, she nervously fluffed her hair and then pulled into a parking lot and turned off the car. She waited.

As he walked the few steps between their cars, she saw, beyond his approaching body, a face in the back window of his car, a little face. It was hard to tell if it was a child or a small grown man or woman.

For God's sake, lady, do you even have a license?

She unrolled the window a little.

You drove right into me! Pushed me into the guardrail! It was you or the guardrail! He was looking for a little credit. *Do you know how much that car COSTS!?* He irately pointed at his car and then wiped his palms on his plush suede jacket, obviously exasperated.

He's handsome, she thought, *but pampered rich. For the sake of exercise he probably plays tennis and mixes drinks.* She raised her hands in a gesture of innocence. *There must have been ice on the road. The car just took off on me. I'm not used to these, ah, unresponsive lummoxes. I drive a BMW myself, would never have had the problem if I were driving my own car. It's being fixed, wheel alignment, tune-up, I keep it in top form.* She could tell that she had slightly engaged his fancy car mania, and continued. *This heap is a loner. Well not really, it's just an old junker that the guy's 13 year old nephew works on. I'm embarrassed to even be seen in it. They don't usually lend it but it's all they had and I was desperate, had to get to an important meeting and my car wasn't done. You know how busy a good foreign car place can be....*

His wronged attitude slipped. *Which place is that? My mechanic just jacked his rates up to the goddamn sky, but he is good....*

A place in Watertown, all foreign cars, actually mostly Mercedes....

His eyes picked up a new level of interest. He seemed happily engaged in a fruitful conversation but then he caught sight of his broken headlight and his dented fender. *Would you look at that? I could cry....*

She nodded somberly and fumbled in her purse, saying she would write down her license number and insurance company. He groaned and walked over to his car with his hand extended, to feel the damage. She got out of her car to write down the plate number of the old Ford Fairmont. She reversed the numbers and added a fake phone number. *This car is obviously defective. It must be twenty years old! I thought the steering was loose, now I know! I just have to get to Kenmore Square. This thing is ready for the junkyard!*

Seeing her full length, a decent body, expensive coat, classy leather boots, attractive, his mood seemed to widen to encompass her, a fellow aristocrat trying to survive in this stinking barbarian society. He walked towards her, one arm held out to sweep her along as a fellow conspirator.

I would be home with my feet up in front of the fire if it wasn't for having to drive this goddamned little bitch back to the city. My wife hired her to cook at the party and then clean up and watch the kids while we went for a midnight sauna. This dumb bitch announces, he was speaking out of the corner of his mouth, *she has to go home. Says her mother is sick… and I mean before the dishes, dinner barely served, and you know what, she had the nerve to ask for full pay. Of course I didn't give it to her… I don't think her damn mother is sick at all!*

Out of the corner of her eye Julia saw the little lady going through the guy's glove compartment. She leaned closer to him. *I know. I don't trust anyone anymore. People are so-oo awful!* Over his shoulder she saw the little figure hop over the seat into the back. *You must know how sorry I am about this.* Julia pressed the paper into his hand and gave him a sexy look. He responded with a wink and put his arm around her shoulder.

Since I have to go to Kenmore Square, I'll take her. Why don't you hurry back to your party. She put her hand on his forearm. He seemed genuinely grateful and sent her a long look and said, *I'll be calling you.* He turned towards his car and beckoned impatiently to the little figure in the back. She got out, a small spidery person. *She'll take you the rest of the way!* He yelled and pushed past her. He uttered a nasty grunt as he got into his opulent car and whizzed away.

Hey kid, get in. Julia had decided upon closer inspection that the little person was a young woman. She held open the door of the moose Fairmont.

You goin' over Shawmut Ave way? That's where I live.

Sure.

My name is Tracy. She put on the seat belt, fumbling with it. *I ain't never worn one of these before but since you already had a little accident... what the hell.*

They pulled out onto Storrow Drive again. Tracy tuned the radio to Kiss 108. Julia spotted another Mercedes, a little creamy job. *Look at that fucker*, she murmured under her breath. Tracy was snapping her fingers and dancing to the music under the constraints of her seatbelt. The Mercedes zoomed by, must have been doing 75, easy. The roads were clear, an ebb in traffic. Julia stepped on it. The Fairmont's speedometer quickly climbed to 80.

Hey, what! Is this some kinda derby? Tracy had stopped bouncing and snapping her fingers and was owlishly peering out the window. Julia pulled out in front of the Mercedes. *I think the accelerator gets stuck*, she muttered through clenched teeth, and then she jammed on the brakes. The Mercedes smashed into the giant Fairmont rear. There were shatterings of glass and resounding barks of metal. Julia sped up, pulling away. Tracy's eyes were huge, her hands raised, fingers spread as if to take off.

Signal him to pull over, Trace. I've had enough of being banged around.

They pulled over by Mass General Hospital. The Mercedes never got off Storrow. It sped by as Julia and Tracy idled at the curb.

Oh well, guess he knew he was responsible, a rear-ender.... Julia sighed and turned off the car. *Let's check out the damage.*

They went around to the back of the Fairmont. A scrape, a dent, but not even a broken tail light.

This car can take it. Julia admired it anew. She gave one of the back fenders an affectionate pat. It was a big old Ford station wagon from Rent-A-Wreck, green with faded fake wood paneling on the sides.

Jesus, Julia! Two crack-ups, ain't that enough? Your drivin' always this bad? And both Mercedes! Can you beat that!

Hey, Trace, how bout we pick up a bite to eat? Oh, I forgot, your mother's sick. You gotta get right home.

Naw, I just got sick a bein' out there with those rich folks. I could see the writin' on the wall. They was usin' crystal an a diffren plate for each course. I don't mind cookin'. I even went to cookin' school. I just hate dishes.

You seem awful skinny for a cook.

I love to eat but it don't stick on me.

Julia checked her wallet. *Hey, how bout I treat us to a steak?*

Tracy looked around for a moment as if gathering an opinion on the offer. *Sure, great, love steak'n fries....*

They drove to Kenmore Square and parked and then walked the few blocks to Ken's Steak House. They were seated without a wait and in ten minutes they each had a plate of steak and fries.

Trace, wanna hang around with me tonight or you got something you have to do?

You lonely or something? You ain't queer are ya?

No, no. I'm just hanging around and you seem like a good person to hang around with....

What do ya have in mind?

Thought maybe we could just drive around.

*Oh no, no way. You got bad drivin vibes. I kin tell. My brother Sammy, he's the same way. My daddy won't let him borrow the car no more at all! He even cracked up in a taxi las week. He 'tracts accidents. A bus hit the cab, nearly cut it in two. Jus down the street from the house. I heard the crash and ran out. Sammy was layin' in the street, blood streamin' outa his neck. He was tryin to get up. I yelled, 'Lay still, Sammy! It's a gold mine!' This lawyer came up to me in the emergency room. It **is** a gold mine! He's talkin' fifty thou or more!* Tracy rubbed her hands together gleefully and then stuffed a big chunk of steak in her mouth.

An old man and an old lady were sitting at the next table. He got up. His napkin fluttered to the floor as he rose and after establishing in a loud voice which way was to the Men's Room, he tottered off. His suit jacket hung over the back of his chair. Tracy quietly moved her chair closer to the old folks' table and in the blink of an eye, almost invisibly, she leaned over and drew the old man's wallet out of his jacket pocket. Julia didn't know whether to look or not. It felt like a moment that should be ignored. Tracy thumbed through the wallet and removed some bills and then deftly slid the wallet back into the pocket. The old lady never noticed a thing. In fact she was busy stealing the old man's French fries. She carefully spread the remaining fries around his plate. Julia giggled and murmured, *a conspiracy of women.*

They finished eating and the waiter brought the bill. Tracy held out a twenty. *I pay for myself. Don't like womin's payin for me....*

Tracy suggested that they go to a movie. She said she just didn't have the stomach for driving around with Julia any more.

Julia ordered a cup of coffee. *Trace, lemme talk straight... you don't know my last name and you don't know where I live an' I don't know that stuff about you. So lemme tell you what I'm up to. If you're interested and you want to hang around with me, fine. If not, we'll just fade out of each other's lives. Simple. Ok?*

Tracy, chewing her last fry said, *shoot.*

Well, I could explain it all in terms of my unhappy childhood. Both my parents were ill. I was the youngest child and nobody noticed that I was even alive. But that's real boring, historical crap. It's not that my parents were mean or anything, they were just sick. Wait a minute... lemme start again. I'm really a very rational person. I take care of my responsibilities. I'd do anything for my kids. I'm frugal but generous....

Tracy interrupted, *you right, this be boring big time!*

Ok, well listen. It's like this. I hate Mercedes. They're always cuttin' me off, stinking up my life with their goddam smelly diesel fumes. I hate em!

Oh Jesus! You some kinda psycho? You just escape from a bin or somethin'? What are you talkin' about! Everybody loves Mercedes!

Cool it, Trace. Listen, lemme try one more time. I hate Mercedes.

Ya, I got that part. Tracy rolled her eyes. *An you look like a well-dressed, together broad. Who'd know by lookin at ya that you're looney tunes?*

I rented the Fairmont this weekend so I could wreck some Mercedes. I've been wanting to do it for a long time and I finally got it together. When I get mad enough I get organized. I just figured out that my boyfriend is a loser and my kids are driving me crazy. But don't get me wrong. I totally love 'em. I'd die for 'em. But I needed to express myself. Get my licks in. You know they got those damn Mercedes by cheating the hide off the rest of us. It's like my own personal little revolution. You get it now, Trace?

Ya, sorta. You hate Mercedes and you're out to bust a few.

Exactly!

Well, I ain't got nothin else to do. I'll go along. My thing is to pick pockets. I'll get us some money and we can go to the dog track. You sure you know how to do this right? I don't wanna get hurt in no accident. If we get stopped, I'm walkin'. Don't know ya at all. Just hitchin' my way home.

No problem. Trace, I've been drivin' for twenty years and I've been thinkin' about this caper for a while. I got it down.

When they emerged from the restaurant the night had gotten darker and colder. It was foggy and there was a light ice drizzle but the traffic on Storrow was still moving fast.

The rich folks should be heading west to their estates. Let's see what we can find. An' check for cops with me, Trace.

Past the Harvard Bridge. Nothing. Julia aimed the moose Fairmont over into the right lane. A car zoomed by, expensive sounding motor, but not a Mercedes sound.

You want a Jag, Julia? Tracy was getting into the co-pilot role.

Naw, they don't do much for me.

Hey! You want a Porche?

Naw, my thing is strictly Mercedes.

They cruised along, all the way to Fresh Pond, went around the rotary and headed back intown.

We could try Memorial Drive but I'm not after the old fart professors. I'm after the doctors and lawyers… they all live in Weston. I think I'll go over to the Pike. No, wait a minute. State Police, toll gates, too tight. How about Route 2? A lot of those fuckers live out in Concord and Lincoln.

It's up to you, boss. I ain't never been further than Mattapan, Tracy said.

A new white Mercedes purred by in the fast lane. A distinguished mustachioed man was driving. He had his arm around a blonde. They were laughing. Julia hunched over the wheel, the alert posture of one stalking prey. *This is it. Probably his secretary, heightens the embarrassment factor.*

Tracy quickly tightened her seat belt. Julia floored the moose Fairmont. There was a moment of silence and then a great roar and heave forward. She pulled alongside the Mercedes and with another great roar passed it and then she suddenly veered into the fast lane. The Mercedes reacted like the other ones had. It smashed into the guardrail. The sounds of shattering glass and screeching metal were becoming an old refrain.

Julia pulled back into her lane and then slowed down to check out the scene in the rear view mirror. The man was glaring at her but the woman had covered her eyes, perhaps she was crying. Having pulled his car back onto the road he turned his attention to her. They got off at the next exit. Julia heaved a contented sigh. *Three down, Trace.* She took one hand off the wheel and stretched. *I'm feeling lots better already. Another few and I'll be my contented self again. You need a release, Trace….*

Tracy looked bored.

Hey, Trace, like everyone's got to get the poisons out….

Duh, Julia, cut the crap. Don't bother me wid dat shit. You're on a bash. Talkin' it up don't make it right. It ain't right, it ain't wrong, it ain't nothin more than a bash. Shut up or I'll be so bored that I'd rather be wid my mama watchin' TV.

Tracy sat back and popped a piece of bubble gum in her mouth and started chewing loudly in time with the music. A slow and soulful song came on. Tracy said it was Linda Hopkins and turned it up even louder. The pent-up adrenaline seemed to drain out of Julia. Suddenly she wanted to go home to her little suburban house, blessedly free of children for the weekend. After Good Sex and being Madly in Love, being Home Alone was third on her Mighty Pleasures list.

Trace, I think I'll call it a night. Gas gauge is going down and I don't feel like filling up this sluggard again. Where can I take you?

Tracy sat up and peered out the window. They were on Fresh Pond Parkway just above Mass Avenue.

Drop me at the corner. My aunt lives two blocks up from here. I'll see if my cousin Tyrone wants to shoot some pool. She flexed her fingers. As Julia pulled up to the corner the light turned red. When she stopped the car, Tracy hopped out. She slammed the door and waved as she ran off. Julia headed home.

5

ABOVE

The Frenns heaved a collective sigh of relief. Everyone except Sonny wafted away from the monitor. The crisis seemed to be over. Looking around, Jimmy noticed that Sonny was the only one wearing earphones. They appeared to be plugged into his wand. His wand and Amesbury's were bigger and gold colored. The others were a dull black.

I'll just watch till she gets home, Sonny communed. *She had planned to go by the cemetery to see her mom but that was when she thought it was going to be a balmy, moonlit night. Considering the weather, I'm sure she'll go straight home and smoke a joint and go right to bed and we can put her on the beeper.*

The rest of them drifted back to their chairs. James sat down next to Jimmy.

You see what we're up against, Jimmy. But actually, that's the most blatantly dangerous thing she's done so far.

So is that how you guide someone? You watch and worry?

No, Sonny was on the transmitter. You saw he was wearing earphones?

Jimmy indicted that he had noticed that.

I'll let Sonny tell you what he was doing. He'll be over in a minute.

Sonny called out, *she's in the garage. I'm putting her on automatic with the beeper.*

What's automatic? Jimmy asked.

That's just having the family channel open to the positive healing forces in the universe. It's usually sufficient input to balance the ever present malevolent energies that abound. The beeper goes off if she leaves the house or even if she opens the front door. It's a spiritual alarm system. We call it Honeywell. I've heard that's the name of an American Company but I don't know anything about it. I just figure it means we watch our honies well. James uttered a ghostly laugh.

Sonny joined them, taking the last empty chair. James asked him to explain how he was guiding Julia.

That was a hairy situation. I didn't bother to work on her thought pattern. I just tried to preserve her physical intactness. It's sort of like a video game in a situation like that. I tried to hold off that first Mercedes and once I understood what she was doing I threw a vapor over her car in case the Mercedes' guys had guns. I made her hard to see. That's really low level guidance work, simply manipulation for survival. The real skill in guidance is in values management. Damn, I hope this isn't a new trend with Julia!

After a moment of worried silence, Amesbury offered, *let me take Jimmy for a while. He can practice on my nephews, Ed and Fred. Lots of room for error there.*

The consensus was that it was a good idea. Feeling somewhat restored and nearly in a state of being back, Jimmy fondly remembered Sinclair from Cincinnati and vowed to look him up someday.

Jimmy and Amesbury wafted off to a neighboring site. It was true, Amesbury was alone. There was only one wrought iron chair and a stillness in the air that had substance, the weightiness of unflurried time.

Amesbury described the guidance process. He went on and on and finally declared, *it's easy Jimmy. You'll see. Just watch me and follow with your wand.* They both stared down into the monitor.

It's very dull, Jimmy. They never say anything interesting although sometimes their conversations with the mailman on Saturday are funny. He's curious about them because they never get any letters. He often complains of the heat or the cold and asks to come in for a drink of water. Ed occasionally invites him in for tea although Fred usually complains that it's his Saturday to do the dishes so the extra work is on him.

Amesbury and Jimmy peered down through their wands. Ed and Fred were just arriving home from work. They discussed who would open the mailbox and agreed that it was Ed's turn. The only mail was an ad from K-Mart. Fred insisted that since Ed got to open the mailbox, he, Fred, got to read the ad first. Ed didn't protest. They hung their raincoats in the coat closet and had a little chat about how it hadn't rained. Ed said twice that it had looked like rain that morning. They consulted a chart on the refrigerator door and it was Ed's turn to cook and it was Tuesday so it was macaroni and cheese and canned peaches for dessert.

Jimmy looked up from the monitor. *God! This is boring!* Amesbury nodded and rolled his eyes.

Is there a way to get a close-up shot? Jimmy asked.

Amesbury pointed to a small lever on the gold wand and demonstrated that it controlled the movement of a tiny pointer. He explained that you set the pointer on what you want to see and that segment would be enlarged to fill the entire screen. He told Jimmy to put the pointer on the kitchen cabinet. Fred was getting out a can of peaches. The screen was suddenly filled with boxes of minute rice, macaroni and cheese, RiceARoni, canned peaches and canned green beans. Then, with no warning, a brown curtain came across the screen and nothing was visible.

Oh no! What happened? Is it broken? Jimmy was horrified, afraid he had done something to the monitor.

Amesbury laughed. *No, Fred just closed the cabinet door, that's all. Watch, I'll bring back the whole picture.* With a twist of the little pointer knob the view of the entire kitchen was restored.

Ed, the Tuesday cook, put on an apron and studiously read aloud the instructions on the side of the macaroni and cheese box. Fred was picking dead leaves off the pretty red impatiens plant on the window sill. He then sat down at the kitchen table and read the K-Mart flyer.

It's incredibly boring to watch but what a comfortable little existence! They have each other for company and a nice little apartment. Jimmy effused to Amesbury.

Actually, they own the building. It has four apartments and they get income from two. They give the basement unit to the Grimes. Mr. and Mrs. Grimes used to work for the twins' aged mother before she passed and now they take care of the boys' building in exchange for the apartment. Mrs. Grimes is a marvelous baker. She leaves goodies on the boys' front hall table nearly every day. Let's look. He moved the pointer to the left edge of the frame and held it there. The view in the monitor became a slow tracking shot down the hall. He released the pointer knob when the scene shown was the front door and the table next to it. Sure enough, there was a large plate of cookies.

It looks like a sweet, relaxing life to me, Amesbury.

Yes, I suppose so. But certainly not very inspiring and that does seem to be the point of life. Look at their auras. He tracked back to the kitchen and then moved the bottom most segment of the wand a quick turn to the right. Now there were circles of colored light surrounding both Ed and Fred. Amesbury explained, s*ee how the colors are all muted, like pastels, really only hints of color. That signifies little engagement with the world. You see that kind of aura around people who vegetate in nursing homes.*

You mean the colors should be darker and brighter?

Exactly. Let me think. Where can I take you to demonstrate a vibrant aura? Let's go back to Fenn's. Julia's aura is all the demonstration you will need. She has produced some startling hues.

Amesbury and Jimmy wafted back to the Frenn's site. Sonny was on duty. He was alone. All the chairs were empty.

Amesbury asked Sonny, *is Julia asleep? I want to show Jimmy what a vibrant aura looks like.*

Jimmy suddenly remembered his assignment and tried to evoke a proper attitude of concern. *Did she go to sleep? What's the story? The big boyfriend who just moved in with another woman, does he have a Mercedes?*

No, he's from the country. He has some kind of truck.

What kind, a twelve wheeler? Jimmy's tone was very interested, hopeful.

Naw, just a little blue pick-up. At least at the moment but you never know what he's going to do. That's part of his unfortunately captivating charm. Maybe he'll arrive in an eighteen wheeler next time. Who knows.

Jimmy responded with heightened interest. *Maybe it's not over with this guy?*

What makes you say that? It's got nothing to do with what he drives! The fact is she can't afford, or we can't afford for her to be saddled with another undeveloped type. It'll be the vagaries of love all over again. Are you into trucks or something?

Jimmy remembered Florabelle's warning and put the images of trucks out of his mind.

They were interrupted by a neighboring soul. A svelte blond in a mint green cocktail dress wafted towards them. She inquired, *is Dinah here? My daughter is ruining my grandson. We need to borrow Dinah for a while.*

Sonny transmitted that the rest of the family had gone to the Lottery. The blonde asked that he give Dinah the message that her presence of mind was needed at the Finlayson's, F-12, as soon as possible. She wafted away, a cool vision in green.

Sonny explained that he couldn't switch the monitor to Julia right then as he was busy protecting his parents who were on a perilous canoe trip down a rain swollen river in Colorado. *And anyway, she's asleep*, he said.

Amesbury suggested that they go back to his site. As they wafted along Jimmy muttered, *I don't remember there being a Lottery up here. That new SuperArch sure is worldly!*

He thinks competition is good. He says it's the antidote to stagnation. Twice a week we have lottery drawings. Each soul can pick one ticket with any six numbers. It's usually jammed. Those who win can bestow the opportunity to win a lottery on the Earth persons they are guiding. There are games of chance in every country in the world. The Faulkners won last week and they went through the most complicated manipulations to get their Earth people to buy a lottery ticket. No one did, so the lottery win went to waste. So few people follow their intuition. If only they knew what we go through up here to give them opportunities!

Amesbury tuned into his nephews again and then took off the earphones and gave them to Jimmy.

My nephews aren't very exciting prospects but at least you can get some hands-on experience. There's only so much that can be explained.

Jimmy felt no sense of weight from the earphones but was immediately aware that he had tuned into a vast world. The energy waves were so apparent. Amesbury handed him the gold wand. Jimmy placed it on the monitor and found himself seemingly in the room with Ed and Fred. They were discussing brands of tuna fish. Ed insisted that Bumble Bee was the best. Fred said he was sure that Aunt Dora once said that Three Diamonds was the only clean brand. Ed responded prissily, *that was thirty years ago.*

Jimmy muttered, *this is asinine.* In a moment he heard Fred say, *this is asinine? Is that what you said?*

Ed stuttered, *no, no. I was just wondering if it was still true about Three Diamonds being the best. God knows, in her day Aunt Dora was never wrong.*

I heard it Ed. I'm not deaf you know! Fred retorted angrily.

Amesbury tapped Jimmy on the shoulder. *Jimmy, that was you who said 'this is asinine.' That's how we guide. We influence by our thoughts and judgements. I have only scanned these boys for years. Haven't said or done anything since I set them up with the twins. Of course I give them disaster protection,* but the other levels, it's just not worth it. Their resistance is such that the only effect is disharmony. They never do anything. They just feel miserable and are mean to each other and get sick. You should see what colors their auras become. Actually, you can probably see it now. Shift the bottom section of the wand one jog to the right.

Once again circles of light appeared around the boys only now the dominant color was a sick greenish brown with reddish traces around the edges. It evoked a gagging sensation.

If you're gonna start picking on me, I'm going to bed. Fred complained.

Amesbury continued, *you can see why I gave up. I wasn't able to unbind them and I caused them mental torment to no good end. Fred even developed migraines and Ed became seriously constipated. Five years ago I got a consult from the Destiny Committee and they said I had tried everything and it was obvious that these two cannot go back together again. Their interdependence has proven to be non-productive but they told me not to hassle them anymore, to just let them complete this lifetime in relative safety and peace. The Committee speculated that the twins must be filling some previously unfulfilled need. We often lie to ourselves in our Earthly stoicism and denial. We maintain that we have lived through something, really integrated it, and in fact we have just pushed it aside. When we come up against it in another lifetime there may be no context to resolve it so we live through it as a monotone. I would guess that Ed and Fred are adding to their basic security level. However, that's certainly not what they stated on the contract they filed before they left here. They declared that they needed to be twins in order to have double the physical presence for the task of solving the toxic waste problems on Earth. There are extensive investigations into proposals to go back as twins just to avoid what has happened with Ed and Fred. Are you following me, Jimmy?*

Sort of… my reaction to the boys' tuna debate was conveyed. A Primary Guide has impact as if his reactions were expressed, in this case by a third party in the conversation.

Yes, therefore your reactions must always be studied when you are on Guide duty. That's how you make progress. It is more than the effect of a third person partaking in the conversation. You are like the voice of God heard inside their minds, or in this case Fred thought the voice was Ed's.

So the crazy people who say they hear voices and are locked up, maybe they really do hear voices?

Yes, they do. But they are also crazy, or labeled that because they are in a suspended state and cannot tell whose voice is whose as they don't even recognize their own voice. Word gets out up here that they have no discrimination and we still have some undesirables who harbor sadistic tendencies and relish picking on these poor unfortunates, sending bogus messages. If they are caught doing it, they are sent beyond the periphery for a period of meditation and some chanting of our basic Commandments. You remember the Six Commandments don't you, Jimmy?

Sort of, but I may have confused them with the Earth Ten. There's still some sorting going on in my thoughts.

Let me repeat them and then I will leave you to chant for a while. It will orient you and bring you in tune with the random forces for general support.

1. *Thou shalt not overwhelm any Earth person's free will*
2. *Thou shalt not persecute any Earth person.*
3. *Thou shalt not use spiritual forces to play jokes on Earth persons.*
4. *Thou shalt not inflict any direct retribution on Earth persons from other family groups.*
5. *Thou shalt not kill. All death orders come from the Destiny Committee.*
6. *Thou shalt report any contact with Evil Forces.*

You should also chant the Credo. Repeat it with me so we can be sure you've got it right.

They shout together, *I WILL FULFILL MY RESPONSIBILITIES AND ACTIVELY PROMOTE MY SOUL'S GROWTH.*

I remember it, except for the word 'actively'.

Yes, the new SuperArch put that in. He's a real bugger about constant performance. He says the intensity and production of Evil Forces is greatly increasing and we need to process souls more quickly and get them back down there. Please excuse me, Jimmy. I've got to check in on a couple of friends now. I've become extended family to a number of groups. I'll be back in a while. You can wait here or go back to Frenn's and I'll see you there later.

He vanished.

6

After a period of chanting, the Credo and the Commandments became familiar again. Amesbury was right. The chanting obliterated the remnants of Earth-bound thought that had cluttered his soul. Jimmy was now fully acclimatized.

He went back to Frenn's. No one was there. He sat for a moment, self consciously waiting and then took up the gold wand and checked the monitor. It was on Julia. She was sitting in front of her wood stove staring into the flames. Then she got up and moved out of sight and in a moment came back with a large knife in her hand.

Jimmy started to panic. It looked like suicide. He felt less than competent but considering the extremity of the situation, he grabbed the earphones and prepared to try to intervene. As he watched, Julia put a salami on a cutting board and hacked off a big piece. Jimmy laughed and murmured, *Sweet Jesus*, and took off the earphones.

BELOW

The, *Sweet Jesus*, was transmitted and Julia stopped chewing and echoed, *Sweet Jesus?* She wondered, as she had many times before, if she should join a church. She vowed again to follow her plan, never yet enacted, that she and the kids would visit a different church every Sunday. The town had seven churches and two synagogues, perhaps one would interest them. The problem had always been how hard it was to get up on Sunday morning. Julia shook her head and decided to go to bed. Being somewhat of a mystic, she thought she might get answers in her dreams.

ABOVE

Jimmy carefully put down the gold wand. Some of the functions of a Primary Guide were now quite clear to him. No one was back from the lottery yet and he was sure that Julia would just go to sleep so he decided to wander around and introduce himself to the neighbors. He cut across F and wafted down the E aisle. Two young girls looked up at him and waved. They were wearing dirndl dresses. Jimmy said, *Hello,* and they countered with shy greetings. Jimmy introduced himself and his family group, *the Frenn's, right across the way.* The girls told him they were from the Essenberry Family and added that most of their people were from Nebraska.

The next family grouping seemed absorbed in their guidance duties. They were gathered in a tight bunch around the monitor. Jimmy wafted closer to see if he could get the drift of it. There was talk of divorce and infidelity. An old woman turned away from the monitor muttering bitterly about the state of morality in the world today. She nearly bumped into Jimmy who was hovering on the fringes of the group.

Bad day? He asked. She looked up at him but transmitted no sense of recognition. She was a proper lady. He introduced himself and then she said, *I just can't cope with the choices. My granddaughter can give up her affair, get divorced, have an abortion or continue as is, lying to everyone. I don't see a good choice in the bunch. Maybe I should get assigned to a family in a* developing country. I could feel good about helping to locate clean water or bringing in new technology to increase the rice harvest.

Why don't you? Jimmy asked. *There seems to be ample coverage here.*

Yes, I know. But Larry, she pointed to an old man who was holding forth to the group, *he wants me around. We've never been separated. We've even managed to die together, plane crashes, train accidents, and once we had simultaneous heart attacks.* She was obviously proud of their togetherness and as if reminded, she turned away from Jimmy and wafted back to the group

Jimmy moved on. He greeted a gathering of young men dressed as hockey players and asked, *are you a team?* They replied affirmatively and the one closest to Jimmy explained, *our bus went over a cliff on the way home from a game. We had won. We decided to stay together up here. We support our Canadian teams.* Jimmy nodded and moved on.

The next cluster looked like the Mahjong crowd. They were all middle-aged women dressed in apparent chicness. He nodded and passed by. The next group appeared to be a large farm family. They were wearing work clothes, overalls and straw hats, and many generations seemed to be represented. In the fragments of conversation he heard someone addressed as Grandpa and an old man then said, *Son, if they don't get rain, they'll have to sell the farm.* A little girl cried out plaintively, *no, no....*

Jimmy introduced himself to a young woman standing at the edge of the crowd. She quickly identified herself as from the Easterly family but said she couldn't stop to chat because they might lose the family farm. She drifted back to the huddle around the screen.

Jimmy then approached a woman sitting alone in a wrought iron chair. She radiated loneliness. There was an empty chair next to her. He stopped on the path beside her and she gestured for him to sit down. She said, *Hello*, and introduced herself as Mamie Esterbrook. He introduced himself and inquired, *are you alone?*

She radiated distress. *Arthur, my husband, went down to Admissions to meet our son, Burt. He's always been a willful boy and we couldn't stop him from jumping into the quarry. He was at a company picnic and we couldn't get through to him to keep him from this stupid, daredevil stunt. He's a fool when he's drunk!* She sobbed. *Actually, Arthur and I were at the lottery. We didn't think anything could happen. Who gets killed at a company picnic? We hoped to win him a chance on the Megabucks. He really needs,* she sobbed again, *needed the money.* She looked at Jimmy quite desperately, guilt now radiating from her. Jimmy attempted to be consoling, not knowing quite what was the appropriate response. She seemed inconsolable so after a kindly moment, he said goodbye, promising to come back and visit again.

Jimmy was frightened by the story of Burt jumping into the quarry and killing himself. He suddenly remembered that there was no sentry at Frenn's and Julia did seem to be an unpredictable type. Wafting quickly down the path he was relieved to see that the Frenns had returned from the lottery and Sonny was on the monitor.

Is everything all right?

With what? Sonny asked.

With Julia, of course.

She's fine. Just checked on her, sound asleep. Right now I'm on my parents. I'm trying to get my mother to check the oil in her car. She has ruined two engines in the last few years. She just can't seem to remember and unfortunately she's good at driving over rocks and puncturing the oil pan.

Jimmy sat down in the one empty chair. James looked up, *Jimmy, that chair is for you. It was delivered while we were gone. And, we want to apologize for not giving you a really warm welcome. We were told that our name had reached the top of the Primary Guide Assignment List but nobody said we would get one so soon. On the way back from the Lottery we ran into Florabelle and she sends you her best regards. She said we are very lucky to get you. She asked me to tell you to drop by her office sometime. So, Jimmy, did Amesbury explain the particulars of guidance?*

Yes, I think I understand how it works.

OK, you can be on Julia tomorrow. It will be Sunday down there. She usually doesn't do much on Sundays but it's hard to predict. We'll be here to help you.

A protective murmur rose from the family. At first Jimmy thought it was a signal of his acceptance but then he realized that they weren't quite willing to leave their Julia in the hands of a stranger. James, sensing the tension, suggested that Jimmy waft around for a while. *Perhaps some of your old friends are here.*

Jimmy retorted that he had already been wafting. James then suggested that Jimmy might enjoy visiting Sunset Productions.

Jimmy stared at him, perplexed. *Sunset Productions? What? We got real businesses up here now?*

The SuperArch is into adding trappings to the planet too.

I thought the true Earthly challenge was to see beyond the trappings?

Yes, yes, that's right. But Sunset Productions isn't some rinky dink factory of plastic junk. It is quite literally what the name implies. The SuperArch is concerned about the general drop in world-wide church attendance and the consequent lack of opportunity to reach our Earth people in a meditative state. Over the last decade there was a marked rise in the numbers of those embracing Eastern philosophies and religions but it turned out to be a fad. It had appeared to be a genuine movement, meditative postures, sitar music and all that but their minds were filled with visions of personal glory, money making schemes, diets and other Earthly junk. The new SuperArch decided that since fantastic sunsets always cause Earth people to stop and momentarily contemplate, we would add to nature's glory for the purpose of creating some meditative moments in which to send down universal positive messages. A lot of artistic types are assigned to Sunset Productions. There's been some trouble with unbounded enthusiasm in some new arrivals from the Acid Generation. They manufactured a sunset last week with a preponderance of bright green and a religious sect living in Nepal thought it signaled the end of the world and they all killed themselves. But generally we've seen good results. The point of manufacture is off on a diagonal from the corner where A and 1 meet. Why don't you stop by. You look like an artistic type.

Sonny was heard to mutter, *not really....*

Since there was time before Julia would rise on Sunday and the prospect of idly sitting around with the Frenns seemed to be somewhat tiresome, Jimmy decided to investigate Sunset Productions. Indicating that he would return in time to assume his duties, he wafted down the F aisle towards the perimeter.

At the juncture of A and 1 Jimmy found a wide and high corridor. It was a tunnel formed of strips of vapor, colored in sunset hues. The pinks became streams of orange which faded into lavenders and aqua blues. Wafting through was an extremely pleasant experience. The corridor ended and the view was reminiscent of a Japanese print. A wide vista with small figures scattered about, bent into working postures. The vats of dye were dots of color. The little figures were painting the piles of vapor with wide, mop-like brushes. An announcement came over the PA, *SUNSET IN JAPAN.*

How appropriate, Jimmy thought.

Groups of little figures approached the colored mountains and then trudged to the far side carrying overflowing baskets of color. A director shouted commands.

Three bushels purple... twelve bushels pink... six bushels blue... six bushels aqua... four bushels light blue.

In response, the figures at each mountain of color loaded up bushels and dumped them over the edge. Looking away from the scene for a moment, Jimmy suddenly noticed a spiral stairway leading down. He wafted down the stairs and it soon became obvious to him that the sunset manufacturing took place on a giant slab. As he descended he could see the falling vapors. They made beautiful trails of color as they streamed down to the Earth clouds below. Jimmy was quite mesmerized by the ribbons of glorious hues cascading from heaven to earth. Then he began to wonder. *No one has called this place heaven. What is it called?* He made a mental note to ask. His Earth vocabulary had once again jarred his orientation.

A figure appeared next to him. *Hello, I'm Emmanuel, front office staff with Sunset Productions. Can I help you?*

No, no, I'm just a new arrival working in family guidance. My family suggested that I come down here and have a look. Quite an operation!

Yes, it's been running well lately. We have a lot of talented souls here. Any questions I can answer for you? I'm kind of an all around type, a sometimes tour guide.

In his role as a newcomer Jimmy felt comfortable asking Emmanuel what he would definitely have hated to ask the Frenns for fear of appearing even more woefully inadequate to them. *Ah...ah*, he stuttered, *can you please remind me what it's called up here? I know it's not heaven, or is it?*

Emmanuel chuckled at the mention of the word heaven. *It's just called Home but some refer to it as the Other Side, some call it The Great Beyond, and you might hear others say the Pie, like pie in the sky. They're just slang terms.*

Oh, yes, Home, of course. As soon as he heard it, Jimmy remembered.

SUNSET IN CHINA was announced. Then there was a crackling, the universal PA crackle followed by the message, SPILL OF PURPLE, EMMANUEL REPORT TO COLOR BARN. Emmanuel pointed to a row of benches facing the view. They were exquisite in the complexity of their wrought iron designs.

Gaze from there, my good man. It's a wondrous and soothing experience, ideal for the newcomer.

Jimmy wafted over and settled on a bench. He watched the little figures scurrying amid the mountains of colored vapor. *It's a floating island...* he mused. A little shudder snapped him into the realization that he was having Earth-bound thought again. It was simply a cloud. In a moment of regret he tuned into a well of sorrow, a homesickness for Earth. He had been having the beginnings of a really good time. He remembered the pretty new secretary at work. *Maybe she was the one they picked for me*, he murmured. The definitely human swell of passion swept over him.

A voice yelling *Halloo*, cut into his fantasies. He looked up and was shocked by the vista before him. His musings had taken him so far away. Then he saw a little girl sitting on a nearby bench. She was wearing a party dress, party shoes with little white anklet socks, and a blue straw hat with a wide, white ribbon around the brow. She was pulsing with little flashes, the badge of a newcomer. He looked down at his own image. He too was a mass of little flashings. He warily thought of returning to Frenns, to the task of Primary Guide, flashing like an ignorant new arrival.

The little girl was trying to wave, her arm slightly flailing. He wafted over to join her, a patriarchal sense of responsibility settling upon him. He sat down on the bench next to her. *Are you alone?*

She shivered and indicated yes.

How can that be? He asked. *Didn't someone meet you at Admissions?*

Yes, my grandmother met me and then she dropped me off here. She had to finish a bridge game and said it would be good for me to sit here for a while. She was my mother in many of my lifetimes. I remember her style, 'It would be good for you, dear....'

Jimmy was relieved that she seemed to be somewhat oriented to where she was. At first glance she appeared to have perhaps stumbled over a park bench on Earth and been catapulted here to this park bench, a little girl who had truly lost her way.

Jimmy was curious. *Were you the same little girl you appear to be now, when you were BELOW?*

She gazed down at herself, at her ice blue dress of the finest dotted swiss. *No, I was very ugly. This is what Cynthia Smith looked like. She sat next to me in school last year. It took me a long time to get Mick to understand the image I wanted.*

What happened to you?

My father was driving us to the train station to pick up my mother. We were late because my sister Beverly insisted on doing her hair over again. My father was furious. He had been taking care of us for two weeks while my mother went back east to help her sister. He could hardly stand us for another minute! He was gunning the car out in the driveway and when Beverly finally got in, he drove off like a madman. He thought he could beat the train across Willamette Ave. I guess the rest of 'em made it OK. I don't see none of 'em here.

Hortensia, COME!

They looked up to see a dignified lady signaling from the top of the spiral stairway. The little girl obediently got up and wafted towards the woman.

Jimmy was alone again. He scanned the vista briefly but his mood had settled into a fatalistic groove and he just wanted to get on with it. Enforcing integration in his image, he returned to Frenn's.

A shimmer ran through the group in response to his reappearance but then everyone went back to what they were doing. Iris and Dinah were conversing and James and Amesbury were off to one side, also engaged in conversation. Sonny wasn't there but Hugo was on the monitor. Jimmy joined him.

How's it going?

Oh, fine. I was just checking on a friend in France, a great soul. I'm ready for my waft now. Are you taking over?

Yes, I guess so.

Hugo handed him the wand and wafted off. Jimmy called after him, *how do I get from France to Boston?*

Oh, don't worry, just click on it. You are hooked into your assignment automatically.

Jimmy placed the wand on the screen and put on the earphones. After a moment of blank screen and static, the scene on the screen was Julia's bedroom. It was dark but he could see the outline of her body under the blanket. The clock beside the bed said 9:46. Jimmy sighed. The remembrances of Earth were so acute. He thought, *how nice to be snuggled in bed on a Sunday morning.*

BELOW

Julia sighed and mumbled to herself sleepily, *how nice to be snuggled in bed on a Sunday morning.* She stretched and then curled up again, settling in for another nap. *I'll get up by eleven*, she murmured. She reluctantly rose at 11:30, dragging herself out of bed against a chorus of inner protest. She had a cup of coffee and a donut and breathed a contented sigh, enjoying the quiet house.

Still yawning, she went to the front door to bring in the Sunday paper. It was a stroke of good luck that it hadn't blown all over the lawn. The paper boy made his rounds in the pre-dawn hours to satisfy all the avid early risers and Julia's late risings had sometimes caused the neighborhood to be battered by blowing sheets of the Boston Sunday Globe.

She thumbed through the paper, shifting the sections into her prioritized piles. The Help Wanted section came up all too soon. Guilt washed over her. Months ago she had promised herself, and others, to become gainfully employed. Her deadline had been January first and that had come and gone. It was the end of May.

The kids were all in school and she really needed the income. She hadn't worked regularly for a year. She'd done publicity posters for a couple of fundraisers and she still had the calendar assignment from the milk company. She loved that job. It entailed studying pictures, really portraits, of cows, in order to select the twelve Big Babes of the Month. But none of her little jobs paid much, only allowing her to squeak by. No new clothes, no airplane trips and such. Her father railed that she should teach in a public school, *isn't that what you're trained for? Don't you have seniority after six years of teaching? Or if you don't want to do that why don't you go back to counseling. There are lots of troubled people in the world.*

Pop, I'm thirty-seven years old. I've spent my life working hard, teaching, helping people, raising the kids, taking care of my husband while I had him. Don't misunderstand me, Pop, I don't want him back... but listen Pop, it's time for me to find myself.

Oh, grow up, Julia!

But Julia couldn't bear the thought of her life again being owned by a job. She wanted to invent her own life. One that was fun and worthwhile. Brainstorms came to her, ideas for businesses to fill here-to-fore unnoticed gaps in the industrial grid. But none to date had flourished. She had a predictable cycle. It usually started with a newspaper ad. One recent failure had offered her services as a counselor. The ad read:

> **SKILLED/EXPERIENCED COUNSELOR WILL HELP YOU FIND RESOURCES TO SOLVE YOUR PROBLEMS. ALL TYPES OF PROBLEMS CONSIDERED. SEND A LETTER DETAILING THE SITUATION AND $25 FOR INITIAL ANALYSIS. BOX 668, MIDDLETOWN**

Julia realized that she offered no telephone number for those seeking further information about the service before committing twenty-five dollars. But she thought there were enough people to whom twenty-five dollars was a small price to pay to be able to unload the stories of their troubled lives, and besides, she hated answering the phone.

There was not a single response. She attributed it to the generalized laziness, the passive on-line mentality nowadays. People wouldn't make the effort to write a letter so she decided she needed a website but then soon forgot the whole thing because she was always overtaken by another harebrained scheme.

She searched for a pen or pencil as the words came to her. The headline would be in large type. **JULIA'S PERSONAL SERVICE**. As most services were highly impersonal, she though the word PERSONAL in big letters would stimulate the reader to go on to the fine print.

IS YOU DAUGHTER OR SON AGING AND WITHOUT PROSPECTS FOR MARRIAGE? I CAN GUIDE HER/HIM TO THE ALTAR FOR A REASONABLE FEE. I HAVE AN ESTABLISHED TRACK RECORD AND GUARANTEE SUCCESS WITH COMPLETE CONFIDENTIALITY SEND LETTER DETAILING SITUATION TO BOX 668 MIDDLETOWN.

Julia leaned back in the kitchen chair and stared at the ceiling, a slight smile on her face. She imagined her post office box stuffed full of letters but then her ex-husband Harvey's voice floated into her mind. *Oh God, Julia, not another ad! You're an embarrassment with your stupid ads.* The flaws of this employment aid were notable and her enthusiasm was momentarily dampened. *But,* she rallied herself, *this time I'm not asking for any money up front so I can pick and choose among the letters and avoid the truly hopeless cases.* She put the copy on her desk to bring to the newspaper office in the morning and sighing contentedly, she sautéed some vegetables and folded them into an omelet for a solitary and leisurely Sunday brunch.

7

ABOVE

Jimmy looked up from the scope. His ominous feeling of weighty responsibility had slightly diminished. By Earth time it was 2 in the afternoon and Julia hadn't done anything even mildly outlandish, in fact she had required no intervention at all. Glancing about, Jimmy saw that Sonny had returned. He was sitting in a chair and appeared to be reading a newspaper. Jimmy stared at him questioningly.

It's the Sunday Globe, Sonny explained. The SuperArch arranges delivery somehow, picks it up on the Internet I guess. But you'd be surprised how few up here are interested. I enjoy it and I feel that I have to keep up because I want to go back soon and I don't want to be at a disadvantage.

Jimmy nodded to indicate that he understood

I love the Sports Section.... Sonny was radiating a happy glow.

Jimmy felt that familiar Earth pull, really an ache and said, *so do I, and Automotive too.* He wafted over to Sonny asking, *do you think I could leave Julia alone for a while?*

Did she have any plans to go out?

No, she wants to stay in and relax and anyway, it's raining buckets down there.

OK. She'll probably just read the paper and take a nap. Put her on the beeper. Here, I've finished Automotive. You can have it.

Jimmy eagerly accepted the paper and was quickly caught up in the text. He and Sonny melded into a little bubble of worldliness, their minds awash with stories from the Sunday Globe. Sonny was so enraptured that Dinah had to practically dance a jig in front of him to get his attention.

Your cousin Edward is going to have a baby, or his wife Mary Ellen is. Do you want to be it? I can't guarantee that it will be an easy childhood. Edward is deeply engaged in his law career and Mary Ellen could be a real stifler. You would be wearing a heavy wool sweater in June and you know how Earth-time can drag.

Sonny's eagerness to go BELOW was apparent but you could also detect the operation of good sense. *Do you know if there are any other opportunities coming up soon in the family?*

Nothing I'm aware of at the moment, Dinah replied.

Jeez, it's eighteen years Earth-time no matter who you get for parents. Maybe I'll put myself on the Walk-In list and forget about going back as a baby in the family. I don't know.... He radiated sadness. The phrase, *I miss my mom and dad,* came through in a tiny, nearly indiscernible voice.

Dinah sent him solace as she murmured, *I know, I know....*

I guess you came up at a young age, Sonny? Jimmy asked.

Yep, 18.

Was it erred procurement or what?

No, I made a mistake. I had no problems. My life was wonderful! I was skiing down the side of a beautiful mountain in Nevada, 26 inches of powder. I thought I had become the wind. During my last two years on Earth I left my body all the time. I broke the rules. You're not supposed to vacate your body unless you're in bed, but I'd been lucky. My luck ran out. Actually, that's an unfair statement. I left my body as it hurtled down a mountainside and I didn't get back in on time. My vacant body didn't know to turn and it sailed over a cliff at an incredible speed. I know I was irresponsible, a misuse of my understanding and a tragedy for my family.

Dinah nodded and sent waves of love to Sonny. They looked like little lines of pink surf.

So my job here is to match my deep understanding with wisdom. I guess I'll take the Walk-In test. You can do that now, even if you haven't arrived here with enough merit. I'm a young soul but I learned to harmonize and synthesize very quickly but I was out of balance so I got myself killed. I wasn't recalled or anything like that. That plagued me at first, thinking I was recalled. It's embarrassing to be so out of whack that you get recalled at an early age. Recall is a terrible committee to work on. It's nearly impossible not to make value judgements. Sometimes you actually lose points!

An alarm sounded. It was a stream of piercing beeps. Jimmy shimmered in shock. Dinah and Sonny scurried over to the mnitor. In a moment Sonny reported, *it's Julia, her boyfriend just arrived. I guess they're back together again.*

Jimmy approached the monitor and in a tone conveying as much authority as he could muster, yet tinged with resignation, he said, *I'll take over. I'll keep you posted. Feel free to make suggestions.*

He began to describe the action below.

She's asleep on the couch. Doesn't seem to be disturbed, guess she's used to his late night arrivals. Apparently the door wasn't locked.

That's right! She never locks the door.... Dinah sighed worriedly.

Jimmy continued his narrative. *He sure is tall. Now he's leaning over the couch and kissing her. Well, she seems thrilled. Her aura has turned a brilliant primrose pink. He seems to be taking off his clothes.* Jimmy slipped on the earphones. *Oh, my God! What an erection!*

BELOW

The boyfriend thought that Julia said, *Oh, my God! What an erection!* He grinned and murmured, *you like?*

ABOVE

    Jimmy took off the earphones and asked, *is it all right to watch this?*

    Sonny giggled, *well, it's not illegal. But you can probably assume that nothing dire will come to pass and just put her on the beeper.*

    I think I'll do that. Jimmy sighed deeply. He was filled with a very Earthly longing.

BELOW

    All too soon Julia heard the children's voices and the scuffling and banging sounds of them dragging their gear up to the front door. Elias called out, *Mom, mom!* A pounding on the door was accompanied by Todd's newly lowered adolescent voice, *Mom, the door is locked!* Then Laramie's high-pitched giggle came through the mail slot. *Is Mac here? He must be. His truck is here. HI MAC!*

    Julia and Mac flew into motion. Mac laughed affectionately and called out, *Hi Laramie.* Julia angrily pulled on her sweatpants and sweater. *Just a minute guys, just a minute!* Under her breath she muttered, *there's never enough time.* Mac folded up the couch and pinched her ass playfully as she went by to open the door. The kids and their gear tumbled in.

    Greetings all around and three different stories about the week-end were told simultaneously. Mac listened to Laramie's plaintive sounding tale. Elias captured Julia's attention with a fishing story. *You shoulda seen it, Mom!* Todd took a couple of seconds to realize that no one was listening to him. He dropped his battered suitcase on the floor and asked, *what's to eat?*

    The next morning, Julia woke up grouchy. Mondays were not her favorite day. The kids were usually overtired and cranky. Often, at least one of them tried to stay home from school. That day Elias got first try. The other two kids observed his progress to see if there was any leeway in Julia's mood that would indicate she could be convinced of an epidemic.

    Mom....

    Yes, Elias....

I feel sick.... This statement was accompanied by a feeble snuffling. There was no immediate response. Laramie stopped chewing her toast to assess the situation, but upon inspection it was clear that Julia seemed to be getting mad, not concerned.

Goddamn your father! You come home sick and exhausted and I have to miss work to take care of you!

All three kids asked in a chorus, *you got a job, Mom?*

Almost, I just have to put an ad in tomorrow's paper. I expect to be working by the end of the week.

Todd, the oldest, remembered having been through this before and muttered with a mouth full of cereal, *not another one of your ads, Mom.*

His newly lowered voice sounded a lot like Harvey's and Julia responded with a steely look in her eye. *Don't give me any grief, boy!*

Seeing that she was somewhat evil tempered, Elias didn't pursue the cause of being sick. The three kids picked up their lunches and school bags and went out to wait for the bus. Elias kissed Julia sweetly and whispered in her ear, *good luck, Mom.*

The ad didn't get into the paper until Wednesday. On Friday Julia checked her post office box and there was nothing. On Saturday there were two letters. Julia could hardly contain her excitement but stuffed them in her pocket as she dashed off to get Todd after his swim meet and then cut across town doing 50 by the dump to try to be on time pickimg up Laramie from her karate class.

Julia then rushed home to prepare for an invasion of twelve ten-year-old boys. It was Elias' birthday party and she was feeding them an early dinner and then taking them to the movies. She set out the potato chips and made a salad. Todd started the barbecue. In the midst of all the frenetic activity, even switching a load from the washer to the dryer, there was a smile in the back of Julia's mind as she eagerly anticipated opening the letters. The party would be over by eight-thirty and then she could send the kids to their rooms.

The party proceeded fairly well. One kid, Tommy Schulz, fell in the theater and broke off a piece of his front tooth. He assured Julia that his parents wouldn't care, adding support to his statement by saying his brother broke off both his front teeth and they didn't care. Julia wasn't sure that was the case but at least it was a demonstration of how much the kid wanted to see the end of the movie or maybe how much he didn't want to go to the dentist, or both. She was somewhat bothered by her uncertainty about whether there was a new technique whereby if pieces of newly broken teeth were quickly put back in the mouth and fastened there, they would bond again. Perhaps that was severed limbs, she wasn't sure, but after briefly crawling around on the floor and feeling for tooth shards, she concluded that the pieces of tooth were not to be found.

The house finally quieted by 9:30. Julia methodically set up the scene. She started a fire in the woodstove and then made herself a cup of tea and smoked a modest joint. She chose to open the thick, light-blue envelope first. Across the top of the paper, on both sheets, were embossed initials, ALF. The writing was definitely a man's. The pages were filled with small, sharp angled printing.

__Dear Julia,__
__Your ad has....__

She stopped reading, wanting to save it a little longer. The other was a cream envelope with the handwriting style some girls perfect in the sixth grade and execute for the rest of their lives. She tore it open and as she lifted the flap, the envelope let loose with a perfumy vapor, probably expensive but not very pleasant. The smell was reminiscent of decaying fruit. The single page was covered with an endless sea of evenly spaced rounded letters. This letter excited her less than the other so she decided to read it first.

Dear Julia,
Your service sounds like just what we need! My son Gerald still lives with me. I know he needs someone to care for him but frankly, after 51 years, I've had enough....

Julia quickly scanned the rest of the letter and found herself disheartened by the prospect of dealing with Gerald and his mother. She put it down and took up the other letter.

Dear Julia,
Your ad has piqued my imagination. I find myself an old man, just today diagnosed with liver cancer. A few months to live, six at most. I have spent the day staring at the ocean from my porch, thinking about whether my life is in order.
A new freedom I feel as a result of today's news, is the freedom from embarrassment. A fear of embarrassment has compelled me to work extremely hard these last 50 years and kept most of my thoughts on matters other than work unexpressed.
As I survey my life, I see a wife who shares this beautiful home by the sea. She is the Mrs. but has not been with the Mr. for years. It's not entirely her fault, but rather a combination of her limited inclinations and my relentless work. We have shared the making of four children but actually little other than the act of love or lust that created them.
As the words flow out of this pen, some signal me more than others. A red flag is LUST. I realize now that I'm consumed by lust. What an ironic situation for one who truly,

physically, at this point, has nothing to offer. Last week while driving me to a doctor's appointment, my wife said, 'Lex, you must be ill, you radiate sickness. She opened the car window. Perhaps that is why I sit outside on the porch. The elements don't complain about my presence.

I have done extremely well in business so I cannot fault my financial production but I see the fruits of my personality's containment in my youngest child, Michelle, called Meesy since childhood. She is now a woman of 36 and looks to be permanently without prospects for love and marriage. She has expressed the wish for a husband but makes no effort to improve herself or mix socially. I think her development was thwarted by her beautiful and outgoing older sister who is four years her senior. By some fluke of nature, my first three children emerged blond, strong and able while Meesy was hard of hearing until an operation at age 13 and has always been small, short that is. My wife routinely passed over her in her race to promote the older three. Meesy is also quite stubborn and early on chose not to compete but to carve out an alternative path for herself. She currently works as a ward clerk on the Oncology ward at Beverly Hospital. She seems to love her work and I'm sure she will be my only solace. I would like to give her love and lust. That is my last wish. I hope you will call and can come here to meet with me and discuss your service.
    Sincerely,
    Alexander Lewis Fosdick (Lex)

Please note:
No one knows of my diagnosis as yet. Please respect my decision to keep this privileged information.

Julia called Alexander Lewis Fosdick the next day. A woman answered the phone. *May I inform Mr. Fosdick about the purpose of your call?* Julia replied that it was a business matter and gave her name. That seemed to suffice. A weary but melodic voice came on the line.

Lex Fosdick, here.

They had a brief pleasant conversation and arranged to meet on Thursday afternoon at 2:30.

8

Thursday dawned bright and beautiful. The directions were good and the drive was pleasant. FOSDICK, a white rectangular sign edged in black was nailed to a stately tree next to a driveway gated by pillars on top of which reclined stone lions. The driveway was deep gravel. It shifted beneath Julia's tires as she drove up to the big white Victorian mansion. The tennis court and pool were off to the right and beyond that, the blue sea. Geraniums bloomed profusely in large containers beside the front steps.

An older, gray-haired woman wearing a tea-time dress opened the door. *Oh yes, you are expected*, she said pleasantly and with her hand extended she welcomed Julia into the house and guided her through a series of well furnished living rooms and out sliding glass doors onto a porch. A tall, somewhat stoop-shouldered man rose out of his deck chair to greet her. His gray hair was mussed by the wind. He extended his hand, *a drink, coffee, tea, a snack?* A charming diffidence hovered about him.

Yes, that would be nice, tea, please.
Mrs. McCarthy, tea and cakes, please.

They settled into parallel deck chairs, facing the sea. It was a beautiful day, white clouds raced across the bright blue sky and white crested waves raced to shore from the dark blue sea.

Not too windy out here for you, is it?

Julia assured him that she was comfortable and remarked upon the beautiful location. He briefly told her the history of the place. It had been in the family for four generations, was built in 1894 by a sea captain great-grandfather. Then he took a deep breath, clearly not having gone to silence, and turned to the topic of his daughter. *Meesy has the makings of a great lover and mother*, he blurted out, his pride and concern evident. *She does her job at the hospital with commendable compassion and has always been the one to nurture our pets and other stray animals.* He stopped and looked at Julia for comment. She responded enthusiastically, *Meesy sounds like a wonderful person!*

He smiled and continued. *So how do you propose to help us, or her, become, so to speak, marketable? Excuse my business usage of language but it is my most familiar frame of reference… ah, in terms of references, perhaps you have someone I could speak with, about your service?*

Each case is unique and of course highly confidential, she paused there to add emphasis. *I find that the best example I can give is myself. Let me demonstrate.* She pulled her briefcase up onto her lap and took out a photograph. It was a glossy 8 by 10 photo of a very homely woman. She had thick glasses and a mustache, and her body bulged with excess flesh inadequately covered by a dark blue dress. Even her feet appeared chubby, stuffed into low black patent leather heels that matched her oversized bag. It was her cousin Louise. The picture was from Julia's wedding album. Louise was now at least fifty years old as she was in her thirties then, but there was nothing about the picture to date it. Louise's coloring was like Julia's and beyond that there was a definite family resemblance.

This was me, two years ago.

Lex looked astounded. He took the picture from her hand and stared at it and then stared at Julia. He peered intently at her upper lip. *With Meesy you don't have to worry about the mustache. Really? This was you two years ago?*

Pinkening a little, Julia lifted her cup and took a swallow of tea. She was astonished by how well it was going. It seemed like destiny unfolding and that belief silenced the little voice that chided, *you're lying*. She snapped back into the moment, *yes, but it didn't take two years. After three months I looked pretty much like I do now, and I got married six months later.* Julia was amazed that she spoke the lies so smoothly. Everything was proceeding just the way she had fantasized it would when she made up the ad. It was like déjà vu.

Lex continued to stare at her.

Julia took another picture out of her briefcase. *This is from when I got married.* She showed him a picture of herself at her wedding, flashed it by him, although she still looked fundamentally the same and wedding dresses never change.

This is impressive. I find you an extremely charming and attractive woman, and you say you have succeeded similarly with others?

Yes, a number of others. It takes about three months. Two of them are now married and another is getting married in three weeks, on the Cape.... She stopped talking in an obvious show of protecting the identity of her client.

Yes, strictest confidentiality is most important to me also. I don't want Meesy to be embarrassed. What does one say one is doing while being helped by you?

Oh... on a cruise, a trip to Europe, University Program in Spain, whatever would be believable in each case.

I see, and where do you go to work this transformation?

I usually start with a few days orientation to really get to know how the person ticks. I find Bar Harbor a good location for the initial period. After that we go wherever the individual's needs define, wherever change would be promoted most rapidly.

It sounds thought out and you certainly demonstrate the product well! He winked at her.

Julia, who was usually so caustic with idly flirting men, tolerated his attentions. What harm to let a sick old man play like a gentle fox, almost free of his embarrassments? Clearing her throat, she spoke firmly. *Of course, Meesy would have to make a commitment to the process. To a large degree it is simply a question of following orders until the underlying states of mind become reinforcing by themselves.*

Yes, a commitment on her part. I think she will do it. Let me talk to her, or let us both talk to her. He glanced at his watch. *It's 3:06. She should be home in about fifteen minutes. She works the seven to three shift. She usually comes straight home and gets into her gardening clothes and tends the flowers. You probably thought we employed a professional gardener but no, all this…* he gestured in the direction of more geraniums in long planter boxes fastened to the porch railings, *is Meesy's doing. She specializes in geraniums.*

Lovely! Definitely an attractive talent! Julia gushed.

Lex then asked if she would like to take a short walk along the beach and Julia was delighted by the idea. The winds had picked up and the surf was crashing so heartily that speech was impossible. They both seemed content with the situation. After ten minutes, Lex pointed at his watch and turned back towards the house. They walked up the gentle incline on the velvet green lawn. The slight upward climb winded Lex momentarily and he stopped to catch his breath and look back at the sea.

When they had nearly reached the porch, Julia heard the sound of a car approaching. It had a classy European car sound. An old purple BMW was creeping up the driveway at an infinitesimal pace, scarcely disturbing the gravel.

Classy car! Julia said, feeling a flash of hope that after all, the job might not prove to be that difficult.

It's an old one of mine. I hate to think what she would have gotten for herself. She would probably still be riding that Vespa I gave her when she was in high school. Meesy engages in almost no commerce. By that I mean she seems to avoid buying anything except supplies for her flowers and stuff for the animals.

Mrs. McCarthy provides her with clothes and her gardening clothes are my old sailing duds.

The flash of hope departed from Julia. She and Lex settled into the deck chairs again. The car slowly disappeared into the garages. A car door slammed and a short, sturdy figure appeared in the garage door for a moment and waved and then disappeared into the darkness of the garages.

Meesy! Lex called out in a voice still strong.

Be over in a minute, Dad. Just let me change my clothes.

Lex got up and moved another deck chair next to his. Soon, heavy footsteps came up the porch steps behind them.

Hi Dad, Mrs. Garber died today. Oh! Meesy stopped talking when she saw Julia's legs and feet on the chair next to Lex's.

Meesy, come here. Sit next to me. This is Julia, a new friend. We have a business proposition for you.

Oh? She said in a neutral tone as she settled into the empty chair. Julia sat up straight and smiled. She reached out her hand to Meesy. *I'm Julia. I've heard a lot of nice things about you from your father.* Her smile radiated a convincing warmth. Meesy shook Julia's hand but then pulled her hand back quickly. Julia noted that she didn't look 36 but then she didn't really look younger either. She seemed to be in the 'ageless' category.

You know I speak forthrightly, Meesy, Lex began, *Julia is experienced at helping people realize their potential. I'd like you to spend some time with her.*

A stubborn expression settled on Meesy's face. Her eyes narrowed, which caused the sides of her cheeks to pudge. She looked like a nervous woodchuck. She was wearing a large sweatshirt of a dirt-like color and baggy pants rolled up at the bottom. Her figure was hard to discern but definitely fleshy.

Dad, I got some fertilizer for the geraniums and I want to put it down today and besides my potential doesn't feel unrealized. She started to get up. Both Lex and Julia put out a hand to restrain her. Julia sensed that the job was slipping away so she pulled out the photo of Louise and handed it to Meesy who took it and sat down again. She studied it. Lex put his hand on her thigh. *That's Julia, two years ago, at the point when she decided to change her life.*

Meesy glanced down at the picture and then at Julia. *So?'*

She woke up on her 35th birthday and realized she wanted a husband and family, so she worked on her problems, her looks and her outlook and wrought the changes you see here today.

Meesy settled back in the chair and began to look childishly hopeful but then said, *I don't have any problems.*

Now, Meesy… Lex continued in a fatherly tone, *it would make me so happy to see you married with children. Please, you need to give it a try with Julia. I know it will make you happy. I've made all the arrangements,* he added with finality, winking almost imperceptibly at Julia.

Meesy made an attempt to protest. She asked why he wasn't satisfied that her brothers and sister were happily married and had given him seven grandchildren. He quickly replied that it did make him happy but Meesy was his favorite and her marriage and subsequent children would make him most happy. He ended his appeal in a low voice, saying he would not live forever, and then he coughed. Meesy's eyes filled with tears. She leaned over and put her head on his chest and said, *OK, dad. I know you haven't been feeling good lately. I think you need to see your doctor and I'll go with you.*

Lex patted Meesy's knee and moved his arm to encircle her top half which now straddled his chair. After a few minutes he said, *you'll have to arrange a leave of absence from work. Julia will be taking you out of town for a while, to Bar Harbor to start.*

It's a beautiful place! Julia added.

Meesy murmured with some excitement, *I love it there!*

So, Meesy, arrange for a three month leave of absence. Say your father is suffering from ill health and needs your attention. There won't be any problem will there?

Meesy stroked her father's forehead, pushing his hair out of his eyes. *No, I guess not, Dad.* She kissed his cheek and seemed to take in his gray pallor. Lex sat up straight and moved her back into her chair. *My dear, why don't you go and get your fertilizer while Julia and I work out the details.*

The details were spinning in Julia's mind. She'd made up the job as she went along and was now trying to figure out how she could pull it off. She decided to pressure Harvey into having the kids live with him for three months. She figured he would do it if she told him she had a well paying job that required a lot of travel for the first three months. For a moment she wondered if she could leave the kids for that long. For years her primary function had been being a mother. She quickly reassured herself that they weren't little children any longer and that Harvey was basically competent.

I can start with Meesy in three weeks. My policy is to not begin a new case until after the wedding of the last client, undivided attention up to the finish line.

Lex nodded approvingly.

My fee is twenty-five thousand a month plus expenses. The work requires 24 hour a day, 7 day a week attention to your daughter.

He didn't even blink. *That's fine. I'll give you a check for the first month when you start and I will set up an account for you with American Express. I would like to receive a weekly accounting of expenses and a weekly phone call from Meesy.* He smiled wanly, he looked exhausted. They shook hands and Julia said, *in three weeks....*

Julia accomplished the task of arranging a leave of absence from her life with remarkably little difficulty. Harvey and the kids were very excited that she had a job even though it required her to be gone for the rest of the summer and most of September. Surprisingly, no one asked exactly what she would be doing except Laramie. The others were stopped cold in their inquiries when they heard the salary. Todd raved, *you could get a new Volvo after six weeks, Ma!*

It was hard for Laramie to contemplate giving up her mother for three months but she accepted the explanation that Julia had been hired by a rich family to help their daughter feel better about herself, and she was comforted by the fact that Julia promised to call her every night.

About a week before the agreed upon date, Julia could finally turn her attention to her new job. The kids' affairs: dentist appointments, new sneakers, camp emergency cards, had all been taken care of or altered to fit the new arrangements.

Julia called Lex and arranged to pick up Meesy the following Monday at noon. She asked for an advance in order to procure a few supplies and to make the reservations in Bar Harbor. Lex was completely cooperative.

Julia then organized her affairs. She found a quiet student to live in the house and take care of the plants and the cat and said good-bye to her friends. She bought a few tools for her new trade: an exercise mat, a vibrator, some hairstyle magazines and other sundries.

Late in the afternoon on Sunday, the kids moved uneventfully to their dad's house. Julia spent the evening packing. She began to get excited and also a little worried about the task before her. She set the alarm for ten to give herself one more minor sleep-in. She figured it would only take an hour to drive to the North Shore to get Meesy. Even thinking that name gave her the willies. She decided she'd have to do something about that right away.

9

Monday dawned raw and rainy. To Julia it seemed an ominous sign but after about twenty minutes of driving north the sun broke through and the clouds dispersed, leaving a clear blue sky.

At Fosdick's, Julia rang the bell and in a moment Mrs. McCarthy opened the door. In the dim light in the front hall Julia could see Meesy sitting on an overstuffed chair. Her father was standing beside her. It looked like a Victorian portrait except that a misshapen duffel bag lay at her feet and a cute beagle was perched on top of it. He barked and wagged his tail as Julia approached. She took off her sunglasses and said cheerfully, *Hi! Looks like you're ready to go!*

Meesy nodded solemnly and Lex smiled warmly. His hand was resting on Meesy's shoulder.

How about some lunch before you go? Do you plan to drive all the way to Bar Harbor today? He asked.

Sensing that perhaps Meesy would never again be so ready to leave, Julia replied, *if it's OK with you, I think we should get going now, Meesy.* (God, she stumbled over that name, always almost saying Messy.) *I do want to get to Bar Harbor today and I think it's always safer to drive in daylight, don't you?*

Meesy stumblingly answered, *yes, but I haven't gone on any trips lately.* The *lately*, faded out to a whisper.

Lex looked pleased by the decision. It had probably been a long morning for him already. Julia carried the duffel and Meesy lugged a large canvas bag full of books. They settled her stuff in the trunk. Meesy exclaimed over the box with a picture of a yellow inflatable two-man boat on the cover.

Yes Meesy, I believe in having fun and it's June! I'm sure we'll go swimming and boating. I bought you a couple of bathing suits in descending sizes. She pulled out three bathing suits, purple, lavender and light blue, a polyester bouquet.

For me? Meesy seemed happy and horrified at the same time. Her gaze moved over the rest of the contents of the trunk. *Oh, you even brought a scale!* She exclaimed, an edge of depression in her voice. Julia patted her on the shoulder. *Believe me, Meesy, it's not that hard and it feels really good to get in shape. I know!*

Yes, I guess so. Meesy responded in a tone conveying resignation but also some hope. She ran back to the front steps and quickly hugged her father and then ran back to the car and got in.

Too late Julia realized that her speedy take-off caused the gravel on the driveway to spray onto the grass. Meesy winced.

The drive to Maine was long and uneventful. Mrs. McCarthy had made them an ample picnic: roast beef sandwiches, potato chips, cucumber sticks, peaches, a least a half dozen large brownies and some boxes of cran-raspberry juice. Meesy ate most of it before they got out of Massachusetts. At first she would ask Julia if she wanted anything but after a few refusals she would just reach into the basket and take something. She said a couple of times, *every time I go on a picnic I eat most of it before we even get there.* Julia just said *hmmm* but in her mind she mused, *eat it up, honey. After this you're gonna starve.*

On the way to Bar Harbor, Julia always stopped at Moody's Diner. They made an unbelievably good chocolate cream pie. She decided to incorporate this into her plan. *I haven't eaten all day, except fruit and tea for breakfast. I can't eat a lot or I will get fat again, so I've been saving myself for a piece of this fantastic chocolate cream pie they have at a great diner a few miles up the road. Would you like to stop?*

Oh, yes!

Fine, but think of it as your last dessert. If we are going to change your life, you will have to change your eating habits, as I'm sure you realize. Meesy nodded compliantly. They pulled in at Moody's. There was no crowd yet. They got a booth immediately. Meesy scanned the menu. *Oh my goodness! Pot roast, meat loaf, all of my favorites! Are we having dinner here? It's almost suppertime!*

No, just the pie. That has enough calories for three days. Listen, Meesy, someone in a state of good health, who is trying to lose weight, she lingered on the word 'trying' for an extra moment, *doesn't need to eat three meals a day. I know people may have told you that it is necessary to eat three balanced meals a day, but it's not.*

Meesy opened her mouth like a hungry baby bird and started to stutter out a complaint but Julia cut her off. *Would you rather look the way I did in that picture or the way I do now?*

They arrived at Bar Harbor at six. The motel was a mile out of town on a small cove down a hill from the road. The room was nice and spacious. There were two double beds and sliding glass doors that opened onto a balcony with a view of the water. Julia asked Meesy which bed she wanted. Meesy said she was sure that her father wouldn't mind paying for them to each have their own room but Julia had already considered that option and concluded that the process would be slower. Julia realized she had to be a 24 hour a day coach if she had a prayer of succeeding at the job. Besides, she saw the longing glance Meesy sent in the direction of the vending machines in the motel office.

No, we are going to be working at odd hours all around the clock, so to speak. We need to share a room.

Oh, all right. I guess I'll take a bath and go to bed and read, but I'm hungry! Meesy declared in a plaintive tone.

Well, tell your stomach there's a new regime, nothing but water until tomorrow.

There was a knock on the door. It was the young boy from the motel office. He was carrying a bike-like contraption. *You ordered this? Bar Harbor Bikes delivered it to the office this morning with your name on it.* He pointed to a slip of paper attached to the handlebars.

Yes, put it over there, please. Julia shoved aside an armchair and directed him to place it in front of the window facing the sea.

What's that for? Meesy asked.

Julia explained that it was a stationary bike. She said she used one at home. It was a good way to exercise. She took a metal clip-on stand out of her briefcase and attached it to the bike. *A bookstand, you can read and exercise at the same time. We'll take turns. You do it now for thirty minutes before you take a bath. It'll get your metabolism going.* Julia picked up a small tote bag and took out some colorful clothes. *I bought you some things. Nothing fancy, just some stuff you can be comfortable in while you are shrinking.* She smiled brightly and piled the clothes on Meesy's bed. *We'll pick up some good sneakers tomorrow.*

Meesy started complaining immediately. *I'm tired… I'm sore.…*

Julia was seated at the desk making ledgers to document their expenses and other statistics. She got up and went over to Meesy who had already stopped pedaling. Julia had a formidable presence. She wasn't aware of it but she had a powerful force field because she had so much unchanneled energy. Meesy cowered but Julia just checked the setting on the bike and switched it from 3 to 2 and then set the timer for thirty minutes. *There, that'll be a lot easier. Get a good book and read and pedal until the bell rings.* She used the firm tone she employed when approaching the point of exasperation with the kids.

    The whine of the bike started up again. When the bell rang Meesy slid off the bike and tottered to the nearest bed and collapsed on it. *7.6 miles! I can't believe I did it!*

    Julia congratulated her and went over to the bed and grabbed Meesy's arm and pulled her upright. *You've gotta walk around and cool down for a few minutes. It's bad for your body to just stop. You know, like how they cool horses after a run.* Messy nodded. The reference to a horse engaged her. Julia led her to the other side of the room and then stumbling over each other they turned and headed back towards the windows. Meesy was huffing and puffing. The room suddenly seemed very small. As they passed by the bed, Julia grabbed the new sweatshirt and steered Meesy out the door.

    They walked down a long gentle downhill stretch of lawn to the cove and out onto the dock. It was a beautiful night. Little panels of white clouds positioned themselves across the sky. A quarter moon shone against the dark indigo. There was a slight hint of warmth in the gusts of wind, foretelling the hot summer days to come. Meesy plunked herself down on the dock and stared up at the night sky. The sweat dried on her face and the redness receded. She said she felt good, strong, like after she had carried some thirty pound bags of fertilizer.

    Julia sighed deeply. It was such a beautiful night, a perfect night to be in love and here she was, stuck with mission impossible. But she also saw that it could be done, like contemplating a huge pile of dirty laundry, you had to work at it but it could be done. *Come on Mees, let's go in. I've got to soak in the tub for an hour for my back. Why don't you take a shower first.*

    Meesy emerged from the bathroom. She had on a matching nightgown/robe set in gray-blue. The robe was a lovely velvet material.

    Very nice, Meesy! Did Mrs. McCarthy get that for you?

    No, the only clothes I like to buy are nightgowns and robes.

Well, you have good taste! Julia exclaimed while thinking hopefully, *this could be a plus…* and then she decided that the time was right to start waking Meesy up. She took a box out of her large canvas bag. *Meesy, this is a vibrator. While I soak in the tub why don't you try it out. It helps you relax and get in touch with your sexual self.*

How? Meesy looked confused.

You turn it on, low at first, and put it on any sore muscles and also try rubbing it against your crotch, you know, against your body there. You will learn how it feels to have an orgasm. You don't know about that do you, Meesy?

Well no, not really. Meesy looked horrified.

Come on, Mees, give it a whirl. It's great. It's just for you, a private thing. I'll be in the bathtub with the water running. I won't be listening or anything. It's not pornography. It's just getting comfortable with your body and your sexuality. It's essential if you want to fulfill yourself as a woman. On this note Julia handed her the vibrator and quickly stepped into the bathroom but before shutting the door she called out, *while you are playing with that, think of names, names that you have always wanted. You don't have to be called Meesy.*

I d-don't? Meesy stuttered.

Julia soaked happily. After a long time she checked her watch and noted that she had been in the tub for almost an hour. She turned off the water. She had been letting it run very slowly but steadily. She flossed her teeth and moved bottles and jars around for a few minutes and then putting on her somewhat ragged old bathrobe, she announced, *I'm finished, Meesy!*

Julia opened the bathroom door and heard the TV and then saw Meesy sitting up in bed with a shocked but delighted expression on her face. *It felt great, Julia.* She giggled in embarrassment. *And I think I want the name Mimi.*

The next few days passed quickly. Meesy, who again, the morning after, asked to be called Mimi, was weighed every day and after three days had already lost six pounds.

They walked and jogged and in between lay on the big granite rocks and listened to the crashing surf. They ate fruit, they swam and they climbed little mountains. Occasionally, Julia went on short walks by herself and smoked a joint. She didn't want to introduce Mimi to pot as in some people it produced a voracious appetite. Mimi seemed to be enjoying herself although she also complained about being tired and hungry.

Julia decided to enhance the atmosphere with music and bought a small CD player and some inspirational selections. Mimi loved the music, even the hard rock. Julia gratefully acknowledged to herself that the woman had some class, some definite potential, an eagerness for life.

One cloudy afternoon a few days later, they went jogging along Ocean Drive. They kept it up for three miles. The temperature was perfect for running. They were warm creatures running through cool air. They walked almost a mile more and then stopped to sit on the rocks for a while. The sun had come out and the surf was pounding with the energy of high tide. Mimi flopped down. She looked like a beached whale, her body a silent mound. There was no detectable movement at all. She could have been dead. Julia stared at her, aghast. *Are you all right, Meesmi?* In her panic she combined the names.

A voice rose from Mimi, *Ya, I'm fine. Just a little tired.*

Julia was horrified. Fear clutched her insides. She had never even asked Mimi if she had any health problems. She should have gotten a doctor's certificate stating she was in good health and could withstand rigorous exercise. What if she had a heart attack? *You feeling all right, Mimi?* She asked again. *We've been working out a lot. Are you feeling any strain?*

No, actually I feel great… hungry though.

Julia was somewhat reassured but still suggested that they quit for the day and go to a bookstore and then have tea at Jordan Pond. It was a pleasant afternoon and evening but Julia scrutinized Mimi, monitoring her breathing and color. The fear of her collapse had reached a deep place in Julia and was not soon forgotten. But Mimi looked good and had no complaints.

Julia woke up every few hours during the night. On her way to the bathroom she stopped by Mimi's bed and peered down at her, listening to her breathe.

The next morning Mimi said she had never felt better in her life. She weighed in at 152, a ten pound loss in five days. She looked healthy and robust now, no longer just fat.

After some discussion of alternative sites, Europe among them as Julia really wanted to go to Amsterdam, they decided to stay in Bar Harbor. Mimi ended the considerations by saying she thought there was some special quality in the air in Bar Harbor that somehow allowed her to feel good even though she was hardly eating anything at all. That did it for Julia. *Whoa, not bringing myself any extra trouble!* She muttered to herself.

Over the next two weeks Mimi's stamina increased. She was a Taurus and once hooked, her determination was unmatchable. Julia found herself flagging as the daily runs increased to six miles in response to Mimi's mounting enthusiasm. Early on, Julia had suggested that Mimi chew gum to keep her teeth engaged in action without food and also to strengthen her jaw muscles to counteract the sagging chin effect that often occurred with substantial weight loss. Mimi chewed gum constantly.

By the middle of their fourth week Mimi had lost 26 pounds and looked to be in the peak of health, although still 20 pounds overweight. Her skin was pink with a healthy glow. Her hair had thickened and now had a luster. The streaks of gray shone like highlights. Men had begun to take slight notice of her. The comments were now, *Hey ladies*, instead of just comments to Julia. After six weeks a man in a gallery asked, *Are you two sisters?* Mimi was obviously pleased by the question. Julia was at first perturbed but then took the comment as an affirmation of her efforts with Mimi and said, *No, but maybe in spirit.* Mimi looked even more pleased.

Mimi invited Lex to visit them for the weekend. Seeking to maximize her weight loss, she ate only fruit and salads without dressing and on Thursday told Julia she wanted to buy some new clothes and get a new hairstyle for her father's visit. They bought a couple of nice outfits and she got her hair bobbed and she looked good, thirty-three and a half pounds gone from her.

They picked up Lex at the airport. His skin had a yellowish tinge but his face creased in happy smiles when he saw Mimi. *Meesy, you look wonderful! Your haircut is so pretty and you are a mere shadow of your former self.* He kissed her and shook Julia's hand and thanked her. They went out for a lobster dinner at a restaurant on the end of a pier. The sun set and the pink and lavender clouds faded slowly into a deep indigo night sky.

Lex stayed through the next day. Mimi suspended the rigorous work-out schedule and they spent the day on a deep sea fishing boat. None of them caught anything, an outcome the captain had declared was impossible, but they had a great day anyway. Lex was so happy with the changes wrought on Mimi that he couldn't stop exclaiming, *you look so strong and attractive and healthy and I love your new name!* Mimi kept repeating, *I'm not done yet.*

After Lex's departure Mimi renewed the exercise regime with a vengeance. Julia began to wonder if she had created a monster. Mimi had surpassed her in zeal and now took an array of vitamins every day and consumed a prodigious amount of fresh carrot juice, the fine properties of which she had read about in a book. Every morning Mimi waited eagerly for Julia to record her weight. She chastised Julia for her resistance to getting up early in the morning. She called it, "Your Hesitancy in Rising Syndrome."

After two months Julia was actually quite tired of Mimi. She had become a total jock. The slight excess of weight was no longer very apparent but the benefits of the nearly sylph-like figure and healthy glow were offset by her extremes of zeal. Mimi was now being approached by men but she had no grace or sensitivity and regaled them immediately with tales of great health gains and digestive improvements. Those who were attracted to her healthy glow were repelled by her fiendish devotion to 'The Healthy Body'.

Julia muttered despairingly to herself, *the progress to date, after eight and a half weeks, is only superficial. The end goal of marriage for Meesmi, oh dear, I made that mistake again, is still unattainable.*

10

ABOVE

Meanwhile, Jimmy worried that he wasn't performing his duties as a Primary Guide adequately. *This can't be right,* he thought. *Trying to turn this Mimi character into a marriageable property can't be a good enough use of Julia's time and talents to earn either of us points!*

He thought about getting a consultation with the Destiny Committee but then decided he would just keep a low profile. The Frenns finally seemed to trust him and he didn't want to do anything that would cause them to scrutinize him constantly as they had for his first few weeks on the job. He resolved that he would just keep muddling along.

In fact, Jimmy got totally enthralled watching Julia. He loved to just sit back and see what she would do next as if she were a character in a TV series. However, when he stopped to think about it, he worried that she wasn't making enough progress and thus he wasn't making enough progress. He decided that one way he could help her was to create a channel for her energy by making her irresistible to disabled children. He got this idea one day when he noticed that an autistic child seemed to come out of his trance when he stood by Julia. Her bountiful energy seemed to push him over the barrier of isolation. He said, *Hi*, to her and she smiled and said, *Hello*, to him and kept walking and that was the end of it as far as Julia knew. But the child's parents knelt beside him, stroking him and hugging him. Apparently it was the first word he'd ever spoken. Jimmy figured that enhancing her appeal to children would give Julia the opportunity to earn some credit and that would give him credit too.

BELOW
Suddenly Julia was besieged by disabled children. Wherever she went, they came to her and clung to her legs until she knelt down and talked with them. Kids even climbed up onto her lap in restaurants and hugged her for dear life. The parents were always dumbfounded and weepily grateful as the contact with Julia seemed to unfreeze previously inaccessible places in their children and allowed them to talk and even move more freely.

Everybody loves you! Mimi exclaimed. Julia just smiled and shook her head. She loved hugging the kids but couldn't explain to the parents why she was having such an effect on their children. But it did make her feel good, both because she loved children, and because it actually made her feel physically better. As Jimmy had theorized, it siphoned off some of her intense energy and made her feel less hyper. But she was still worried about getting Mimi to the altar.

One evening, after Mimi, at Julia's urging, had consumed a glass of wine, Julia asked her about her hopes for marriage.

Oh, I guess I want to. But really, I'm having the best time I ever had in my life. I love it here! I love my new body and the way I feel. I felt like a turd for so long. Can't we just keep going this way for a year?

Remember I have a patient but new husband. I promised him I'd be home in three months... and remember, your job is waiting for you.

Oh, God, I can't go back to that right now. I feel so alive! That job was like working on the corridor outside death's door. Maybe I could get a job up here, like an aerobics instructor or something.

What about your father? He's looking forward to your return and a marriage for you.

I know, I know. But it's my life. I feel like I finally took possession of it and the freedom will only last another month. She pouted, reminiscent of an eight year old, but as with most eight year olds, the pout faded quickly. It was replaced by the query. *Do you think I could borrow that rowboat? Rowing would be great for my arms and shoulders.* There was a rowboat tied to the dock next to the restaurant.

Mimi!

Mimi was gazing longingly at the rowboat.

Have you been thinking about men at all? Have you been enjoying the vibrator? This last word Julia spoke in a whisper.

Yes, I use it every night while you're in the tub.

Julia suddenly had a brainstorm, hopefully a solution to help Mimi complete her journey. With her weight down forty pounds and the development of unbelievable self control, the introduction of pot for the sake of insight development seemed safe. She also resolved to take away the vibrator while extolling the virtues of the real thing.

Julia felt hopeful about her new strategy. She suggested that they walk along Ocean Drive to see the sunset and watch the clouds change color as they faded into darkness.

ABOVE

Jimmy rushed over to Sunset Productions to request a spectacular sunset over the northeast United States.

BELOW

Julia selected a big flat rock with a fabulous view of the water. They were far from any parking lot so they didn't have to share the space with tourists. She took a joint out of her pocket.

Is that pot? Mimi asked.

Yes, have you ever smoked any?

Oh no, but my brother Gary used to smoke it all the time. He always was a jerk. Her expression soured.

Ah, like anything else, Mimi, the effect is influenced by the personality. I have found it to be an effective tool for insight development. I want you to try it. Julia adopted her strict teacher persona to insure Mimi's cooperation. Mimi compliantly took on her student posture and after Julia took a drag Mimi held the joint to her lips and sucked in. Julia instructed her, *OK, now take an additional drag and hold your breath, resist the desire to cough.* Mimi sputtered and after a few moments released the smoke in a paroxysm of coughing. After her turn, Julia handed the joint back to Mimi and this time she inhaled and held her breath without coughing. Julia instructed, *OK, now look at the waves coming in. Watch the light. Look at all the colors of the sunset.* They were quiet for a while.

Oh, it's soooo beautiful, Mimi raved.

Julia was feeling the effects also. *Blessed dope,* she murmured to herself. Mimi's face was aglow but with a softer light than that brought on by jogging.

Mimi, have you ever made love?

No.

They sat in silence again.

Do you want to?

I don't know.

It's really nice.

Ya?

If we run across a good man who is available, would you be willing to try it?

Ah, ya. I guess so. But I don't want to get pregnant or catch anything.

Of course not! Julia agreed, thinking, *Jesus, how am I gonna pull this off?* She brought the conversation to a close by saying, *I'll see what I can do… and I'm taking your vibrator away so you can build up some desire.*

Do you have to? Mimi asked miserably.

Yes, it's time.

Mimi sighed and said she wanted to go back to the motel and watch TV. *And I'm starving,* she complained. Julia gritted her teeth in frustration. *No, no food and no TV. I want you to think about being hugged by a man who loves you and whom you love. Think that he wants you to feel very close to him, then think about the feelings you get from the vibrator, those are the feelings you get from making love. Oh God! DO YOU HAVE ANY IDEA OF WHAT I'M TALKING ABOUT?*

Mimi, who had never heard Julia shout before, was somewhat taken aback. *Yes, I've got some idea what you mean*, she meekly answered.

Julia was suddenly depressed. It had been an extremely long eight and a half weeks. It was nearly the end of August. Reducing this blimp to marriageable proportions and then finding someone to marry her had become a tiresome pursuit. *I've got a lot of gall.* Julia muttered to herself, *I can't even find a guy for me and I'm tryin to get rid of a virgin here. Where the hell did this chick grow up that she's 36 and knows nothing!*

The next morning Julia regarded Mimi with a critical eye. Her yearning to go home and find out what would happen next in her own life made her consider, with renewed intensity, the goal of a speedy finish to this project. *The woman is looking physically good. The hair has thickened and developed a luster and the cheek bones have emerged to define the face. The face needs experience to give it sensitivity. The quickest thing would be to find someone to screw her. A stud who would like to perform a service just to get her started. I better buy some condoms.*

Throughout their daily routine, Julia scanned the surrounding men. She chose to go places where they would encounter crowds, situations she had stringently avoided before. Mimi objected. She had liked the exclusiveness of their lifestyle. Julia quelled her objections by purchasing a camera and telling Mimi that in this phase she was to study people. Julia wanted to give Mimi experience in observing and in keeping her mouth shut, thus giving Julia a chance to engage prospective men before Mimi turned them off with her tales of the glories of health foods and exercise. She told Mimi to take 40 pictures a day. Mimi slavishly followed her instructions, having by now developed faith in Julia that bordered on the religious. Julia did not share her confidence and muttered quietly, *if there is a God, I could use some help with this.*

ABOVE

As an ever faithful Guide, Jimmy had already been hard at work setting up a solution for this problem. He found the whole re-make of Mimi project somewhat shameful. He had expected to guide Julia to the discovery of a water filter that would save the world by making contaminated water potable. Instead he had to watch Julia spend her intelligence and sensitivity on making this not very interesting person into a candidate for marriage. The Frenn family, particularly Dinah, urged him to let Julia complete the Mimi project successfully. They convinced Jimmy that a substantial bank account would make Julia ultimately much more amenable to exploring new pathways. Jimmy's only solace was that his job required that he constantly gaze upon Julia and that had become a pleasure in itself. Hearing her entreaty he answered, *Yes, yes,* and neglected to block the transmission so she received it and had no doubt that it was the voice of God.

BELOW

Hearing, *Yes, yes,* in response to her plea which was actually just an utterance of frustration, put Julia into a state of awe followed by a surge of gratitude. At that moment, having for an instant abandoned her awareness, she was nearly knocked down. Hands pulled her upright and voices apologized.

She was surrounded by a group of Hasidim. An old man with a long, white beard, wearing the traditional black suit and an enormous hat, was accompanied by a younger man and woman and a bunch of little children. The little boys wore yarmulkes and had side curls and the little girls wore long dresses. Julia was shocked. It seemed an unlikely sight in Bar Harbor in August. She could only conclude that she was being shown that Judaism was the religion for her and she vowed to pursue a Jewish course in her life after completing her work with Mimi. She knew nothing about Judaism but the message seemed so clear that she was sure she would find her way.

Four days of searching for an experimental man yielded nothing. Mimi was thrilled with her mediocre pictures. She decided she might want to become a photographer. Julia had to admit that the woman was admirably open to new experiences and re-training.

Julia was about to conclude that they should fly to a large city, Dallas perhaps, and stay in the best hotel and work through a dating service, when they met Jens. He was a doctor. An internist with a love for research. His forte was the absorption of amino acids and he was doing some collaborative work at the Jackson Labs. He was staying in Bar Harbor for three weeks and his room was next to theirs. They had dinner together on his first night in town. He had asked them for restaurant recommendations and Julia had grabbed him thinking that at least he could give Mimi some experience in making small talk.

At dinner Julia mentioned that Mimi worked in a hospital and that got the conversation rolling. Julia was impressed by Mimi's knowledge of medical procedures. It was the first time she had heard about her work. She regarded Mimi with new respect and noted that she was actually quite charming, presenting herself as an intelligent, compassionate woman. When the after dinner coffee arrived, Julia decided to leave the two of them alone. She announced that she had to call her husband, thereby taking herself out of the running, and slipped Mimi the American Express card. *Jens, let us invite you for dinner tonight as a welcome to Bar Harbor. Mimi, I want some air. I'll walk back to the motel. Here are the car keys. I'll see you later.* She glanced at them through the window as she walked past. They seemed happily engaged in conversation. She wondered if Jens was married. Her curiosity kept her awake. It was 10:45 when she heard the key in the door. Mimi looked happy and a little loopy. She dropped her purse on the bed. *We ordered a bottle of wine after the coffee. My poor body is getting conflicting messages.* However, she said this in a lilting tone.

Julia felt hopeful. *Perhaps the total jock phase is over....* She interrogated Mimi. *So, what's he like? Is he eligible?*

Oh, Julia, you have a one track mind. Mimi sat down on the bed and began to file her nails.

Well, we haven't got forever you know. We do have a goal to accomplish. Don't forget Mimi, this is a job for me, with a time-line, a set of expectations, and you might say I have miles to go before I sleep.

Oh, that's Robert Frost isn't it? I love him. But Julia, don't be in such a rush. I'm making up for years of lost time. How fast can I go? Anyway, my dad won't care if it takes longer. He always said you have to wait for really good things and we're friends, aren't we Julia? It's not just a job, is it?

Julia gritted her teeth to keep herself from blurting, *It is just a goddamn job!* She repressed that thought and replied, *No, it's not just a job. But I do have a life that needs my attention. A new husband, a house, a cat, friends....* Every time Julia mentioned her new husband who was patiently waiting, a stab of pain went through her. Not only did she have no husband, but because of her lies she couldn't even mention her kids and that made her feel really bad. When she went for a walk every night to call Laramie, she told Mimi she needed the privacy so she could talk freely with her loving husband. The truth was she didn't even have a lousy boyfriend because she had decided not to see Mac anymore. How could she get Mimi married if she had so little success with herself? *But of course,* she reminded herself, *I am not average and I don't even aspire to marriage... do I?*

Mimi was apologetic. *I see what you mean, Julia. I forgot about your husband. I'm sorry. I'll concentrate.* She dropped her nail file and went over to the stationary bike. *I'll do ten miles.*

No, no, get ready for bed. We'll run in the morning. But tell me, what is the situation with Jens? Is he married?

No, actually, his wife left him two months ago. He says he's just beginning to accept it. She left because he was never home. She fell in love with her dentist.

Any kids?

No, the wife had a hysterectomy at twenty-five.

How old is he?

Forty-two.

Hmmm, sounds like a prospect. Did he give you any longing glances? Did you catch him checking out your body?

Oh, Julia, where is your sense of romance? I've just discovered men and you're making me feel bad with your cold-blooded assessments.

Humph... well, good for you. I'm glad you've discovered romance.

They had dinner with Jens the next night too, and Julia observed that Mimi and Jens were quite engrossed in their conversations. The following night Jens knocked on their door at suppertime and said some people at the Lab had recommended a seafood place about ten miles up the coast and could he invite them there tonight? Julia feigned illness and fatigue and asked that they go without her.

By the next evening Julia had invented a more permanent excuse. She said she was working on a novel and her most productive time was in the evening. She alluded to the lack of workspace and they picked up her cue and made plans to eat dinner together for the duration of Jens' visit so as to leave Julia an empty room to work in.

Jens was now a daytime discussion topic for Mimi and Julia. He was confiding the horrors of his marriage to Mimi who it appeared was listening with a sympathetic ear. The recently departed wife was a drinker who during the fifteen year marriage had gone from social drinking to flat-out alcoholism. Jens attributed it to her lack of children but the wife apparently thought that Jens' workaholism was the cause. Julia commented that it sounded like he was lucky that his wife had fallen in love with her dentist and was no longer his problem. *But has he filed?* Mimi didn't know what she meant. Her areas of naivete were unpredictable.

Filed for divorce. Alcoholics are notoriously unstable. He should get out officially while she still wants out. God knows how long this relationship with the dentist will last and then she might want to come back!

Oh no, Jens doesn't want her back. She even had blackouts. Once he came home late from work and found a charred stump of meat still cooking in the oven and the house filled with smoke.

Well, that's what I mean. Did he mention whether he has a lawyer yet?

No, he didn't say anything about that but he did say that he's gotten more enjoyment out of talking with me this last week than he did talking to his wife for the last fifteen years. You could detect a note of pride in her tone.

He did! That's great! Ah…how do you feel about him?

I like him a lot, Julia. Mimi blurted this out and then blushed.

Well, well, well, seems to have definite short-term possibilities. Long term is still unclear.

What do you mean?

Do you feel anything like desire for him, Mimi?

She blushed a deeper red. *Yes, I'm having some thoughts. I know what you mean now, Julia.*

Good, good. Listen, if the opportunity arises, she giggled, *feel free to go to his room after dinner some night and watch TV, or whatever. You know I can always use the time to write.*

Oh, OK. But if anything should happen, Julia, I don't want to get pregnant or get Aids or anything.

Of course not! Tell him you don't have any birth control and ask him to use a rubber.

A rubber? Oh ya. I always wondered what they looked like on.... Mimi stopped talking and turned scarlet and then added, *my brother Gary used to fill them with water and drop them out the window onto my head.*

The next day Mimi reported that Jens' wife had filed for divorce. Apparently she and the dentist wanted to marry as soon as possible. The divorce would be final in six months. Mimi continued to be faithful and avid about her exercise and her diet but she had an additional glow about her.

Julia decided to help the situation along. On Thursday she announced that she was having a very successful writing spell and if she could just find an unbroken stretch of evening hours she might be able to complete the section she was working on. Could Mimi and Jens possibly watch TV in his room tonight and give her until midnight to work? Mimi said, *certainly, if it's OK with Jens.*

In fact Julia fell asleep at ten. She woke up with a start at three-thirty and noticed that Mimi's bed was empty. She snapped awake and tiptoed to the wall connecting their room with Jens'. Pressing her ear against the wall, she strained to hear any sound. She heard nothing. She tiptoed to the bathroom and held a glass to the wall, putting her ear against it. She vaguely remembered this trick, but she still heard nothing. *God forbid they had an accident!* She went to the door to see if Jens' car was in the parking lot. It was there, a green VW beetle. Then she noticed a slip of paper on the floor. It was a note from Mimi. *Julia, I'm staying with Jens so you can work undisturbed. See you in the morning.*

Julia sighed contentedly and smiled. She smoked a joint and after a period of reflection asked, *what about me?*

You would think that it could only happen in a storybook, but no, Jens asked Mimi to marry him as soon as his divorce was final. He was leaving Bar Harbor in three days and Mimi suggested that they leave too as she was eager to get home and begin making the arrangements for her wedding.

During their runs over the next few days, Mimi confided that she loved sex. *You were right, Julia, right about everything!* She gushed. Julia congratulated her. Mimi didn't notice the slight edge of bitterness in Julia's voice.

It was really astounding. The formerly pudgy Meesy of indeterminate age and sex had become a siren. She was a firm and generously proportioned woman with obvious intelligence, spirit, a laugh in her eye and determination in her stance. Even her hair had become glorious. The birth of Mimi, three months and seventy-five thousand dollars plus expenses.

11

They drove back to Marblehead on Sunday. It was the third week of September and the air was quite crisp in Maine and more than the occasional leaf had already turned red and orange.

Mimi and Jens set their wedding date for March 24. The wedding was to be held at a small Unitarian chapel in Marblehead. Julia doubted that Lex would still be alive if the doctor's prognosis held true, but no matter, she knew that he was thrilled by the outcome. The delay was simply a legal issue to allow the necessary time to elapse for Jens' divorce to become final.

Julia delivered Mimi home and accepted Lex's invitation to stay for dinner. Lex was noticeably diminished. His skin had gone from gray to yellow and he was very thin. However, he radiated happiness about Mimi's plans. As he escorted Julia to the door he pressed an envelope into her hand and uttered a last thank you. Mimi was teary but reassured when Julia promised to stay in close touch.

Julia stopped for coffee at a diner down the road. She was very tired from the all day drive as well as from the three month project and she wanted a small space before re-entry into her life, a proverbial coffee break. She opened the envelope from Lex. It was a check for ten thousand dollars. An accompanying note said:

> *Dear Julia,*
> *Allow me to thank you with this bonus check. You have succeeded beyond my wildest dreams. All the best to you!*
> *P.S. Could you please assist Mimi with her wedding plans if she asks for help. Her mother has been less than supportive to her in the past and will probably remain so. I doubt that I will be at the ceremony as my health is failing fast now, but I'm not afraid and am extremely grateful to you. You have fulfilled my fondest and last wish.*
> *Love,*
> *Lex*

A few tears ran down Julia's face, *such a sweet man!*

Back to reality, she had made eighty-five thousand dollars in three months and had spent virtually nothing on living expenses. At least she felt financially secure for a while.

ABOVE

For Jimmy, time had passed very slowly. Watching Julia was a job, babysitting at a spiritual level. He had studied her intently for the first couple of weeks until he could assess and even somewhat predict her behavior, and he had learned to control his thoughts while he worked on the monitor.

While Julia and Mimi were in Bar Harbor he had dutifully watched the incoming tides, scanned the roads for drunk drivers, and generally done all the routine maintenance guidance tasks but he couldn't figure out how to influence Julia on a spiritual level. Amesbury, who had become his mentor, advised him that it was a difficult time to intervene on that plane as her mind was focused on the "Mimi Reformation" and considering Julia's basically flighty and distractible nature, it was wise to let her finish that task without interference.

Jimmy had languished somewhat although he did what he could. He influenced the motel clerk to put Jens in the room next to theirs and he aided Jens' attraction to Mimi and visa versa, especially at the beginning, by sending down thoughts to enhance both of their fantasies. However, these interventions were small potatoes and only added to his deep Earthly ache for self-fulfillment. During Julia's night times he often left her on the beeper and went to visit Florabelle. She always amused him with her lewd speech and genteel flowered appearance but all in all, Jimmy felt that he wasn't making much progress and yearned for life.

After Julia finished the Mimi project, Amesbury suggested that it was time to begin the real work, as she was available, *fair game*, he said. Jimmy had no idea how to begin. He asked the Frenns for advice but they replied that he was more competent than they were as the last three months had been the quietest in Julia's life to date and besides, as a Primary Guide, he was supposed to know what to do. The Frenns were relieved, thrilled, and grateful that they didn't have to worry about Julia any more. They thanked Jimmy often for taking care of her and left well enough alone.

Amesbury was more helpful. He suggested that Jimmy analyze her strengths and weaknesses in order to figure out what circumstances he could create to enhance her growth and ultimately his. He and Amesbury had long discussions. Amesbury's theory was that the past failures to bring Julia to fruition were caused by the family's softness. He explained that every time Julia hit an obstacle in her life, whether it was running out of money, or pot, or a low spot in the vagaries of love, the family ABOVE would rush in to make things better. If she was depressed because she had no money, they would manipulate the family finances so she would be sent a check. If the problem was loneliness, they would send her a boyfriend. But the men they were able to dredge up on such short notice were often of questionable character and the short-term pleasure usually led to long term problems.

Dinah had been Julia's mother in this life and had died young leaving Julia motherless at the age of twelve, so she particularly tried to bolster Julia's spirits in times of trouble. The Frenns were a sensitive bunch. They couldn't stand the sight of tears.

Amesbury suggested that Jimmy toughen up. *Let her suffer circumstance,* he said. *After all, desperation is the mother of invention.*

Money was not an issue at the moment but Jimmy did interfere in a pot delivery and when Julia weakened and wrote a letter to her old boyfriend, Mac, Jimmy made sure that she wrote the address incorrectly and it was returned, 'Addressee Unknown.' Jimmy discovered that he had no difficulty throwing a mist around her whenever an interested man approached. Observing him shield her from a professor of psychology, Amesbury gently questioned his motives. *Jimmy, my man, that fellow seems a good candidate to foster her progress. He runs a school for handicapped children and you know how good she is with kids. It could be a real opportunity for her!*

No, no, Amesbury, remember she's supposed to invent a water filter, you know, made out of the white of egg. A psychologist couldn't help her with that so I'm just protecting her from her Achilles heel, the vagaries of love.

Amesbury was surprised. *A water filter? But she has no scientific training or even inclination?*

Jimmy replied huffily, *Forabelle said that Julia was supposed to invent the water filter that I didn't get to invent while I was Harry Miles.* But then Jimmy admitted that those decisions came out of the Destiny Committee and Florabelle had nothing to do with it. He sighed and slumped.

Amesbury mused that perhaps Jimmy was himself attracted to Julia and that was why he so effectively prevented her from having any contact with men.

Jimmy would have flushed and squirmed had the spirit state allowed, but he just vibrated irregularly indicating maladjustment. Amesbury had witnessed his faulty adjustment many times before and now commented that as Jimmy did not seem to be able to fully integrate his spirit state it would be very difficult for him to progress. Jimmy sadly agreed but added that he had certainly been trying to the best of his ability. Amesbury patiently inquired again about Jimmy's feelings for Julia. Jimmy finally admitted that after watching her for the past three and a half months he had fallen in love with her. After a quiet moment he murmured desperately, *how can I be her Primary Guide if I have these feelings? Oh, I'm such a failure! I'll never get back to Earth!*

Amesbury sent him soothing vibrations and suggested that he take a break, perhaps go over to Sunset Productions and volunteer.

No, I can't. I'm too depressed....

You do understand, don't you, Jimmy, such an emotional state as 'being in love' is an Earthly phenomenon. You're letting Earth feelings linger and that's blocking your progress.

I know... I know....

They hovered in silence for a while and then Amesbury declared that he would talk to the Destiny Committee on Jimmy's behalf. Perhaps with his excellent reference and the Frenn's high praise for Jimmy's guidance work thus far, they would consider an early return. Certainly the opportunity to become Julia's life partner existed, and Jimmy's recent spiritual growth and stability would perhaps further influence them. Amesbury concluded that it could be theorized that an intelligent, able, and motivated life partner for Julia would create circumstances to allow her to finally use her extensive gifts. He murmured that he had some friends in high places. *After all, I've been here a long time.*

Jimmy was thrilled by the idea.

It was nighttime on Julia's part of Earth so Jimmy felt free to put her on the beeper. As a kind of plea and also a demonstration of his worthiness, he went to a seminar to keep himself occupied while Amesbury appealed to the Destiny Committee.

The seminars were another new feature introduced by the SuperArch. He proclaimed that no opportunity for further development should be wasted either on Earth or at Home. He set aside a formerly unused portion of the periphery for Sensitivity Seminars. In fact they were lectures on tape. There was no interactive feature as the name seminar implied but when challenged about this the SuperArch aptly responded that the term seminar applied to one's spiritual integration of the materials, a seminar of one.

Jimmy sat down just as the introductory music started, signaling the beginning of a new tape. The musical interludes were performed by a trio of harp, saxophone and guitar called the Theocratic Trio. The music was soothing yet stimulating. It faded out and the lecture title was announced, *UNCOMMON DECENCY.*

> *We all know the phrase 'common decency,' It means to act in an expected pattern conforming to accepted manners of behavior, treating others with courtesy. We, here, on the spiritual plane, who are seeking to develop our souls to their utmost, need to aspire to a state of UNCOMMON DECENCY. This means behaving in ways that exceed the expectations, rising to new levels of goodness and selflessness. History contains many examples of UNCOMMON DECENCY. Most are unrecorded in the official annals....*

Jimmy began to drift off. The image of Julia sunning herself on the rocks in Bar Harbor came to mind and then another image of her curled up in bed with that angelic innocent look that her beautiful face took on when she was asleep.

Jimmy went back to the Frenn site and waited for Amesbury. He returned in due time and told Jimmy that the Destiny Committee was considering his request and would communicate their decision when it was made.

Did they give you any idea when that would be?

Amesbury indicted no but Jimmy pestered him anyway, asking for his impressions. *Did it feel like a favorable response?*

Amesbury replied that the Committee had simply listened to his proposal and gave no indication as to their impressions.

Jimmy continued to diligently watch over Julia. Occasionally, when he was alone, he would whisper, *I love you.* When he thought about it he excused himself saying he was building up her sense of self worth but the next time he would whisper, *you are loved.* It had a more universal ring to it.

BELOW

Although Julia was relieved to be back with her little darlings, finally able to let go of the fear she had felt while away from them, she was quite depressed for her first few days at home. It wasn't as though being with Mimi had been a vacation but it had been a task away from her life and allowed her to leave her problems behind.

The kids were full of stories about living with their dad including accounts of a new girlfriend-in-residence. Laramie said she was very pretty and very nice and asked to spend one evening a week with her as they were building a dollhouse together. The girlfriend, Nancy, was an architect. Julia found herself growling that Laramie might not have time for that because she had to concentrate on her homework. *After all, you are now in fourth grade!* Laramie insisted that she could get her work done right after school. Julia caught herself before she argued further realizing that it was a nice opportunity for Laramie and the problem was simply that she, Julia, was momentarily jealous. Her baby had gotten close to someone else while she was gone.

Things fell into a routine quickly. Happily, all three kids seemed to have made a good start in school and none of them tried to stay home with feigned illnesses, a situation that had plagued Julia in prior years. Yet, she reminded herself, *they have only been in school for two weeks.*

Julia spent her first week at home putting her house in order and investigating the offerings of nearby banks to determine the best place to store her money. She bought a few new plants and rearranged the furniture and even washed the floors. On the Sunday before the Monday of her second week home, she vowed to use the upcoming week to formulate her new project. This plan allowed her to spend a leisurely day reading the papers, sure that a brainstorm would strike her soon.

On Monday she sat at her desk and drank one cup of coffee after another and worked her way through half a box of donuts. The weather was prematurely cold, blustery and gray. The winds blew the dying leaves and they made a rasping sound. The thought of the coming of winter was depressing and inspired her first idea. *I'll open a flower shop. All winter I'll be surrounded by flowers!* She mused on this fantasy until she heard Laramie clumping up the stairs to the kitchen door. Serving her the usual after-school milk and cookies, Julia tried out her idea. She knew she could count on the child's enthusiasm.

What do you think about the idea of me opening a flower store?

Sweet Laramie responded predictably. *Oh, Ma, that would be great! You mean like Stewart's?*

Stewart's was a florist shop in Centerville, about ten miles down the road.

Yes, like Stewart's but maybe a little smaller to start.

But, Ma, the only trouble is you always kill plants. Janey's mother has the same plants for years and years. We throw ours away every few months.

Oh, Laramie, I could learn. I think it would be nice to spend the winter in a florist stop.

Ya, I guess so, Ma. You can do anything, Ma. I believe in you!!

The kids announced that they wanted to spend every weekend at their dad's. They said they had gotten used to spending time with him. In the past Julia would have rejoiced at this turn of events because it would give her more time to conduct her love life in private, but now she had no love life. Still, she welcomed the free time although she had no pot to transport her mind to visions.

Julia vowed to get started on freshening up the paint in the kitchen and dining-room. The kids' fingerprints had turned the white paint to light gray with smudges and the smoke from the wood stove had also contributed to the less than gleaming effect. She wanted to get the painting done while she could still keep the windows open. But she couldn't make herself do it. Instead, she went to the library and got a stack of books. Unfortunately, none of the books engaged her. By three o'clock on Saturday afternoon she knew she had to think of something to do. She felt the pinch of loneliness and wished for a lover or a mother or a friend. She drank another cup of coffee and gazed morosely out the window, contemplating the leaves gathering on the lawn. *Goddam, another thing I gotta do, rake the leaves.* That voice came into her mind again, *I love you, Julia.* She felt a warmth come over her and a feeling of hope. *But why?* She exclaimed. *Maybe I'm going crazy?*

Julia had good friends but they had adapted to her being away and reallocated the little spaces of time they used to save for her. She knew that they cared but just hadn't adjusted to her return. All she had to do was make a few phone calls to get the system back on track, but she didn't want to just yet. She liked the freedom of uncommitted time.

12

ABOVE

Jimmy continued to watch Julia diligently, loving her from afar. She was his connection to Earth and his love for her was the expression of his desire to be alive again. He no longer worried about how to guide her to full bloom. Everything, at least the grand schemes, were on hold until he got an answer from the Destiny Committee. He was in a state of spiritually suspended animation. He performed all his duties well and adopted a rigorous schedule of attending seminars during Julia's nighttimes. For recreation he usually assisted at one sunset a day and gained the reputation for casting down beautiful rivulets of lavender. The Feedback Representative reported that the sunsets at which Jimmy assisted were commanding unusually high levels of contemplation thus allowing for greater spiritual intervention. Jimmy preened at the compliments and hoped this good notice would not be lost on the Destiny Committee.

Time passed very slowly for Jimmy but finally Amesbury appeared at the Frenn site with news. He exuded excitement. Little pearly pink waves of energy rose off of him. He held a scroll in his hands. He opened it with a ceremonial flourish worthy of trumpets and read aloud.

> IT IS HEREWITH DECLARED THAT THE DESTINY COMMITTEE HAS DECIDED FAVORABLY ON THE PROPOSAL MADE BY THE SOUL CURRENTLY KNOWN AS JIMMY CARTER.
> HE IS ORDERED TO RETURN TO EARTH AND EXECUTE HIS FURTHER DEVELOPMENT IN TANDEM WITH HIS CURRENT CHARGE, THE SOUL NOW KNOWN AS JULIA MONTAGE, **IF** THE FOLLOWING CONDITIONS ARE SATISFACTORILY MET:
> 1. JIMMY MUST SUBMIT LETTERS OF REFERENCE FROM:
>   HOST FAMILY FRENN
>   MENTOR AMESBURY
>   SUNSET PRODUCTIONS
>   SEMINAR SUPERVISOR
> 2. JIMMY MUST PASS A TEST TO PROVE THAT HIS HISTORIC SUSCEPTIBILITIES RESULTING IN PREMATURE DEMISES HAVE BEEN EFFECTIVELY CURBED. **WE D0 NOT WANT TO SEE A REPEAT PERFORMANCE, CLUE: NO TRUCKS**

Jimmy was elated. He knew he would get glowing references. He beamed. But then he began to wonder about the test and whether he would pass it. He still loved trucks and had even found his attention sometimes straying if he spied a wonderful car or truck while guiding Julia through traffic.

Do you think I can pass the test?

Amesbury shrugged indicating that he had no idea but he said, *if you don't pass, it would be futile to go back to Earth. Another tiny lifetime wouldn't be beneficial for you or for Julia.*

No, I guess not… but I wish I knew what questions they will ask. I'll try to study for it, try to prepare. Some self-examination might be productive… I guess.

Jimmy felt a growing sense of panic but he hid his feelings. Only Amesbury knew about the Destiny Committee decision but Dinah noticed Jimmy's anxiety. She saw his low level flashings even though he had figured out how to keep them nearly unseen. Jimmy was clever and went to great lengths to hide his maladjustment.

Dinah kindly asked Jimmy if she could help him. He told her there was no problem but her intense scrutiny overwhelmed him and he finally confessed the difficulty. She was surprised and then pleased that her recent daughter Julia would have a fine soul like Jimmy to be her companion in life but Dinah had no idea how he would be tested. They wafted around the periphery together and considered the matter.

After some discussion they concluded that the test would measure his ability to use good judgement to temper his wild enthusiasm. In his prior lifetimes he was always obliterated by allowing his curiosity to overwhelm his good judgement. Jimmy recalled his death by his own hand when he invented the domino technique of felling trees. A great idea but he lacked the judgment to notice that he was positioned as the last tree in line. He then mused on his love of trucks, recalling the times he had been squashed beneath their wheels.

Dinah had made fine progress through numerous difficult lifetimes. She had advanced to almost a grade 9 but was still hampered by an inability to protect herself, an excess of selflessness. Her current assignment was to be the first violinist in the Celestial Symphony and to create a lecture series on self preservation. She shyly confessed to Jimmy that she wanted to go down for another Earth term because there was so much trouble BELOW but she hadn't completed the lecture series so she wasn't eligible to apply for a Descent Pass. In his spare time Jimmy listened to her presentations and made helpful comments. It gave him insights as he too had suffered from a lack of the sense of self preservation in his short lifetimes.

Jimmy and Dinah concluded that although the feelings that overwhelmed them were different, his problem was blind curiosity and her problem was an over-commitment to the welfare of others, their problem was basically the same, a critical lack of the sense of self preservation. Realizing this, they both felt heartened. Perhaps they could help each other.

From then on, whenever they had time, they would meet and make up games to practice their judgement. Jimmy would tell Dinah stories. One such story was that she was married to a demanding man who asked that she iron everything including his underpants. Then her aging father came to visit and got sick, needing bedside service. Then the school called and said her son would flunk third grade unless she tutored him daily in math and English. What should she do? At first Dinah would answer, *Well, I'll just have to find a way to handle it all. I'll just keep going even if I get sick. I'll still keep going.*

Jimmy tutored her until she could respond to such a scenario by saying, *I'll send my husband's shirts to the cleaners and tell him that I don't have time to iron the rest of the stuff and it doesn't need it anyway. I'll hire a nurse to come in at least during the day to take care of my father. And I'll meet with the teacher and principal and ask them to recommend a tutoring service for my son. Then I'll take a nap or a walk by the sea.*

Jimmy cheered.

Dinah would then engage his fantasies and try to stump him. *Jimmy, you are driving on a highway on a rainy night and a truck passes you going very fast, say 90 miles an hour. You realized as it flashed by that this was the truck you'd been dreaming about. You'd read about it in magazines but you'd never actually seen one. What would you do?*

Jimmy's immediate response was to say he would step on the accelerator and try to catch up to it to get a better look.

No, no, Dinah would say and soon he was responding by declaring that sighting such a truck would make him realize that they were out of the development phase and on the market so he could call dealers to locate one. Dinah congratulated him on his good judgement.

They had a good time trying to trick each other into responding with bad judgement but after some practice both of them seemed to have learned the lesson well.

When Jimmy received the summons to go before the Destiny Committee he was nervous but felt as prepared as possible. He had been cautioned in their first epistle to not discuss his proposal with anyone until a final determination was made so only Dinah sent him off with wishes for good luck.

The Destiny Committee chambers were located above the Admissions Department. The entryway was a long inclined corridor. In his nervous state Jimmy almost didn't notice the new décor. The walls were lined with portraits. Actually, upon closer inspection, he noticed that they were just black and white snapshots but there were hundreds of them. A banner across the top read,

CITIZENS OF THE WORLD WHO HAVE FULFILLED THEIR DESTINY WITH GLORY.

Under each picture was the name of the primary guide and family. Jimmy recognized some of the faces, but he didn't really take time to stop and look. His nervousness compelled him to hurry on.

The doors to the Destiny Committee chambers were open. It was a large round room, extremely bright because there was no ceiling, just sky. The Committee seemed to be at full attendance as every seat was taken at the table which curved around the perimeter of the room. Jimmy hovered at the entrance, waiting to be acknowledged and instructed. The white robed figures all appeared to be intent on whatever was before them on the table. After what seemed like a very long time, long enough for Jimmy to contemplate fleeing the scene, words came to him in a friendly tone.

Come in, come in. Lone, how nice to see you again.

Jimmy felt that same pull, the way he always reacted when confronted with his past. Because of his Earthly yearnings his mind wasn't clear. The mind of an Earthling is almost entirely closed to the spiritual. With death and the acceptance of the return to spirit, the limitations of the mind disappear and all is known of the evolution of one's soul. However, Jimmy, in his resistance, had been savoring the impulses of the sensual and blocking access to the vastness of his mind. He didn't recognize who had addressed him but remembered that his last spiritual incarnation was as the Lone Ranger, so he bluffed. *Hello, hello, nice to see you again!*

Words expressed with less emotion came to him. *No matter, we can see that you have not allowed yourself to become entirely integrated, so no point in referring to any past contacts. I suppose it's not such a bad thing as long as you successfully pass the test, otherwise....*

Jimmy nodded. He was asked to come into the center area. The brightness was even more concentrated there. He hovered, waiting for further instructions. He picked up mutterings. *What a mess he is. Look at those flashings. What resistance and he's been here for quite a span.*

Jimmy put the voices out of his head. It was a critical moment. He tried to ready himself. The questions began.

Jimmy, what is time?

After a moment's thought he answered, *it is a measure.*

Apparently this answer was acceptable. Another question was asked.

What is life?

An energy, he said and then added, *an experience in time. A chance to be savored and spent thoughtfully.* Jimmy began to relax. He could feel that he had made progress. The boring spans of time guiding Julia, the enforced inaction and scrutiny of thought had paid off. He was aware of having the ability to contemplate. It was reassuring to realize that he had made progress. He only hoped it was enough.

The next question, *what is a lifetime?*

An opportunity, Jimmy said.

Jimmy, that's a little too glib. We would like to hear more.

Ah… a lifetime is a time of unconscious evolution for the soul. Here at Home evolution is conscious. In a lifetime one must struggle with constant decisions that are clothed in mundane matters that would appear to have no further ramifications. But there is a consequence for every act. It's like a game of chess. The implications of every move must be considered very carefully. So, a lifetime is a series of self chosen paths, each path leading to others…. Phew, he was glad to have come to the end of that one.

What is love?

To love someone is to want to be with them. Jimmy could certainly stand behind that answer.

Could you say more about love, please?

Ah, to love is to care what happens to someone. Ah, I don't really know what else to say, that's why I want to go back to Earth, to learn about love. I've never really had any experience with it. In all my lifetimes it was always about ideas for me. I can't remember any people, just ideas and places. Jimmy started to feel upset. *Wait a minute, haven't I ever had people who loved me? Didn't I ever have a family?* He was getting more upset. *Where is my family group? How come I got assigned to Frenns and nobody even told me about my own family group? I've had plenty of time to visit them. What am I, some kind of servant type? I've got no rights to family of my own?*

Jimmy, Jimmy, Lone, slow down. There have been plenty of people who loved you in your various lives. Of course you had mothers, fathers, sisters and brothers, uncles, cousins and all that. You were loved, but you did not love back. You were always thinking and doing. You were never interested in going back to the same family. You never even mentioned them!

Oh….

There was silence. The feelings of anger and hurt drained out of Jimmy. He looked up at the huge sky. The brightness did not quite obliterate the millions of brighter points that were stars. Noting that Jimmy was calmed, the judges again directed words to him.

Jimmy, you have passed the test. We feel confident that you now have the sensibilities necessary to insure your basic survival. This will be an essential lifetime for your development. We support your plan to join with Earth person Julia. We think that you can benefit each other. You can help her move into the active sphere of doing as she has been mired in love and conversely she can guide you to experiencing a love relationship. It seems a perfect meeting of inclinations which is why we assigned you to be her Guide but your progress and yearning make the possibilities of an Earth partnership seem a more productive union. Because of the increasingly perilous situation on Earth, we will allow you to keep a consciousness of the spirit world so you can be swift in your personal development and simultaneously work to improve the Earth world. We wish you Godspeed!

Jimmy muttered thanks and made his way out of the chamber. He stopped at the door and asked, *when will I go down?*

He was instructed to meet with the Frenn family and tell them the plan and to then ask Mick at the Assignment desk for descent details.

13

Jimmy returned to the Frenn encampment. The whole family was there, an unusual occurrence. Dinah pulled the only empty chair over next to hers and signaled to Jimmy to sit down. They all stopped what they were doing and stared at him. He had hoped to talk to Dinah privately about how to make his announcement to the family but the scene appeared to be set.

How is everybody? He asked jovially. *Is anything happening? It's a rare day when everyone is here!*

James communed, *a little while ago the green light started flashing on our monitor. That means that one of ours is having his/her destiny altered as a result of a decision from the Destiny Committee. We are confused because we haven't put in any requests and as far as we know, none of our Earth people has been so outrageous as to provoke a response without our even knowing about it. The only person we are unsure of is Julia as we have left her guidance entirely to you. Is something going on with her?*

Jimmy was startled. He jumped up and dashed over to the monitor, gasping. *Not that I know of. I've only been gone, ah, a little while and last I knew she was sound asleep.* He peered down into the monitor. *No, she's fine, still asleep.*

They all stared at the flashing green light. Dinah murmured, *could it be a mistake? I've never heard of a mistake like this. Could it be that Honeywell crossed some wires!*

Jimmy suddenly understood that the flashing light was signaling his imminent change of destiny. He took a moment to concentrate on enforcing integration of his image before explaining the situation. *Ah… I think I know why the light is flashing.* He felt the pressure of all of the Frenns staring at him. He noticed Amesbury approaching. That would complete the group. *I met with the Destiny Committee today. I submitted a proposal to them some time ago and while they considered it they asked me not to talk about it.* As he spoke he could feel that the primary reactions being emitted by the group were either suspicion or cold scrutiny, except for warmth coming from both Dinah and Amesbury.

The Destiny Committee decided that I will descend to Earth to become Julia's partner in life. The Committee says we are an ideal match and can further each other's growth.

Sonny began making disparaging clucks and sighs and could be heard muttering, *Jesus, I'll never get out of here! That guy just arrived and he's on his way down again! Now we'll have to guide Julia and him as well.* He spoke up. *Is this decision final? Do we have a say in it?*

Jimmy tried to radiate reassurance because he didn't want the Frenns to protest the decision. Perhaps that might even change his fate. He quickly communed, *it won't mean more work for you. Julia and I won't need your active guidance. I'm being sent down as a new version of a Walk-In. I will retain the knowledge of the spirit world while in an Earthly manifestation so I will have the consciousness of both worlds. As a matter of fact, you will be able to communicate directly with me and I would be happy to aid you in any way I can. My descent should make things easier for you!*

James summed up the situation. *In essence we will have an agent on Earth. That should certainly be convenient!* He looked around to see if the family was in harmony on the matter. Only Sonny still seemed unhappy. He muttered to Hugo, *how do we know she will like him? I guess he's a handsome dude but she seems to go for the look in a man's eye, the rest of what he looks like doesn't matter to her. Remember that guy she went out with a couple of years ago? He looked exactly like a toad, I mean exactly! But it made no difference to her.*

James interrupted, *Sonny, I think it's time for you to request a review with the Destiny Committee. Perhaps your day has come too.*

This comment quieted Sonny. James then stood up and as the patriach, spoke for them all. *Jimmy, thank you for your fine work. We truly appreciate your efforts here and look forward to viewing your successes on Earth. I hope you will consider yourself a member of the Frenn family and call on us if we can assist you in any way. And one last thing, I would like an opportunity to meet with you briefly before you descend.*

In turn, Jimmy thanked them for their support. The whole exchange was quite formal. The green light stopped flashing.

Dinah and Amesbury drifted over to Jimmy to congratulate him. Sonny hovered close by. *Can you help me, Jimmy. I don't know how to get in touch with the Destiny Committee.*

Amesbury interceded. He told Sonny he would instruct him and then carry his proposal to the Committee as he had done for Jimmy.

Dinah, for the first time, was radiating little flashes. She admitted, with a shudder of extreme emotion, that she wished she could go with Jimmy. He declared fervently that he wished she could go with him too. They were both flashing brightly, indicating major maladjustment. Jimmy suggested that they go over to Sunset Productions to try to calm themselves. They worked together to prepare a sunset for Australia. It relieved them both. Afterwards they took a waft on the periphery. Dinah shyly asked Jimmy if he thought it might be possible for her to go BELOW as Julia's baby. Jimmy was taken aback but after a moment's consideration he replied that it seemed like a wonderful idea. *But,* he reminded her, *Julia had her tubes tied after Laramie's birth.* Dinah reminded Jimmy that spiritual forces can overpower limitations of the physical body.

After their waft, they stopped again at Sunset Productions and sat on a bench to watch the workers send down the cascades of colors. It was a peaceful moment but suddenly Jimmy was struck by a buzzing in his mind that demanded all of his attention. Words followed.

JIMMY, WHEN THE DESTINY COMMITTEE MAKES A DECISION, IT MUST BE IMPLEMENTED IMMEDIATELY. PLEASE PROCEED TO COMPLETE THE TRANSACTIONS WITH FRENNS AND THEN MEET WITH MICK TO FINALIZE YOUR DESCENT PLAN. THERE IS NO TIME FOR LOITERING!

A few phrases of trumpet music ended the transmission.

Jimmy panicked. He immediately returned to Frenns and sought out James. He found him sitting alone.

Ah, Jimmy, my, ah, son, sit down. What I wanted to speak to you about is actually to ask a favor.

Jimmy had admired James from the start and replied, *anything sir, I'd be happy to do anything I can for you.*

James nodded somberly. *What would make me very happy, Jimmy, is if you would consider being Jewish in this next life on Earth. I lost the practice of my religion in my last lifetime and that has caused confusion and uncertainty in my progeny but I think they are open to the regeneration of this faith in their lives. I have been sending down clues and setting up influential circumstances ever since my arrival here but these messages have not been strong enough to override the secular culture that dominates in America. I left a heritage of scientific inquiry and that has proven to be a far more influential model for the following generations than any signals I have sent from here. There's an unfortunate enmity between the scientific and the religious outlook and the preference for the former prevents reception of so much that we strive to do up here. I myself see no conflict in the two outlooks. I have come to the conclusion that Earthly survival is dependent on the development of an attitude of community as self, not individual as self. It is the only hope. Of course, I take no credit for this revelation. It is the impulse that guides us all here. This is a very critical era as man has developed the ability to obliterate the entire Earth with the flick of a switch, so to speak. We here are all working to promote religions and contemplation beyond self of any kind in the hopes of raising a unified consciousness to stave off disaster. It is truly a race for survival. As the patriarch of the Frenn family I am trying to raise the consciousness of my people on Earth. You may have noticed that I have succeeded in a few instances but the bulk of the family, although not grossly selfish or materialistic, is grounded solely in the tangible. Are you following me Jimmy?*

Yes, Sir, I think so.

Good. You see, Judaism is my historical faith. I was at Sinai and have come down through the ages as a Jew, but as I said, recently assimilated. It's amazing how quickly an outlook can disappear if the rituals are abandoned. Actually Jimmy, I hope this doesn't shock you but you too have some background in this faith. Way back, before Sinai, you were one of the Hebrews, a wandering shepherd boy with your flock, a nomad as we all were. However, when the marauding armies of the Canaanites came, you followed them. You fell in love with the chariots of iron. Do you remember, Jimmy?

Not really, but I know my mind isn't completely clear.

Well, the point is that you have similar roots but since the time of the conquest you have remained detached from any groups and followed the path of your curiosities. I am not saying you haven't been a valuable human being, you have performed many heroic acts! I am just saying you have not been part of a particular family or community.

I know, I know. That's what I hope to accomplish in this next lifetime.

Good. What I'm trying to tell you is that you too are from the twelve tribes of Israel but in experience you are one of the many scattered members of the ten lost tribes. You have always been with brethren. The South American Indians, the North American Indians, all the native peoples are part of the ten lost tribes, so you have practiced many rituals during your lifetimes that are similar to those of the Jewish faith. They have a common ancestry. Therefore, I don't think you will find the Jewish practices alien or difficult. If you are willing, Jimmy, I have a friend here who could educate you on the basics.

Yes, I guess that would be fine. I imagine that Julia would be open to my being Jewish?

Oh yes, I am sure she would. She has been receiving signs from me for many years. I think she would welcome it. A last detail, a simple change in your name would provide the external identity. Could you make your last name Cantor? How does that sound to you, Jimmy Cantor?

Fine, I guess.

Good, I will arrange for my friend Ephriam to meet with you. Why don't you waft over to Mick and get briefed on your descent plan and then come right back. We want to have a goodbye party for you.

Jimmy made his way through the busy throngs in Guidance. He wafted slowly, savoring the scene, suddenly a little nostalgic. Arriving at Guidance Reception, he realized that he hadn't seen Mick since his arrival and remembered that Mick was not impressed with his choice of image. He readied himself for a perhaps disagreeable interchange. He was surprised. As he approached the counter Mick looked up from the screen, he appeared to be watching cartoons, and greeted him with warmth.

Hey, Jimmy, how ya doin? I hear you been visitin' Florabele all the time. Why not me? You coulda watched cartoons with me!

Jimmy stuttered out a surprised, *N-nice to see you too!*

Mick continued. *Naw, naw, no problem. I know why you're here. I got a memo from the Destiny Committee. On your way again, huh?*

Jimmy nodded. Mick dragged a big log book up onto the counter and opened it. *United States, right?* He thumbed through the book to the proper page and ran his finger down the line of entries. He stopped at a blank line and held up a pen, poised to write. *You can keep the name but you can change it too. What da ya wanna do?*

Keep the first name as James but make the last name C-A-N-T-O-R. He spelled it out.

Mick wrote the name in the register. *So, you need help with the story? That's what I'm here for, details of descent. I like the Drop-ins. It's really creative! The ones who go back as babies, it's just paperwork. With the Walk-ins, it takes a lot of coaching and hours of observation. It's important that no one questions that Uncle Fred is still Uncle Fred. If a guy goofs up the only out is a mental breakdown or amnesia or some fool thing, a tremendous waste of time so I gotta be real careful. It takes hours of quizzing: what's you mother-in-law's name, what's the dog's name, all that stuff. It's a drag but with you guys it's fun.* He gestured to Jimmy, *sit down, sit down.*

Yes, I sort of remember going through all that when I went down as Harry Miles.

Oh ya, I remember that Miles Guy. Wife was Sabrina, mother-in-law named Gretchen, car a Toyota Corolla, what a bore! Can you believe I remember this stuff! Mick sighed deeply. *So, Jimmy, any ideas? What do ya wanna say you been doin' for the last thirty-five or so years of your life? First, how old are you gonna be? If you stay in that image you could be thirty-two to forty or so.*

Jimmy vaguely remembered that Julia was thirty-seven so he decided to be forty.

That means your birthday was in 1960. What date you want? You know anything about astrology?

No, not much.

This broad you're joinin' up with, what sign is she?

I really don't know. Lemme think. I think her birthday was in the spring.

Mick pulled up a keyboard from a shelf below the counter and typed in the name Julia Montage. In a moment the screen was filled with lines of writing. On the top line was the date 5/26/63. *She's a Gemini. Why don't you be a Scorpio, very sexy, that could help you. Memorize this date, October 24,*

1960. Scorpios can be devious but the sexual attraction between Geminis and Scorpios is intense and from the record it looks like she loves sex and you're totally inexperienced so being sexy would help you out.

Jimmy repeated the date to himself. *October 24, 1960. October 24, 1960. October 24, 1960… could you write it down for me Mick, or just hand me that pencil. This is the first time I've seen a pencil up here.*

Mick laughed, *ya, I like pencils. I picked em up when we all got into décor. Actually, everything's on disc, I just like pencils and paper. I rigged it up so that whatever I write goes automatically on the disc so I get to play old fashioned. At first the Super Arch thought I was resisting progress but then he concluded that it was probably good for Reception to have an old fashioned homey look. It soothes people to watch me write their names in the register. This machine age may be efficient but it's not comforting. Hey, don't worry, they'll give you a printout of the whole thing at the Reception Center down there.*

Reception Center?

Ya, I'll tell you about it but first let's make up the story for you. You're now almost forty. Let me see… he looked at his watch. *It's October 2 down there so you're gonna be forty in a couple a weeks. You gotta make up a story to cover the last forty years. Where you were born, brothers and sisters, summer vacations, broken arms, pet guinea pigs, the whole works.* He sat back and gazed expectantly at Jimmy.

Ah, I guess I should say I grew up far away, so I don't have to bring in any family. Maybe I could say they all died?

Ya, you could do that and it would get you sympathy at the start which could be helpful as I hear you're not too good at the relationship stuff.

Jimmy radiated embarrassment. Mick noticed and sent him calming vibes and said, *hey man, I'm a 10. We just know that stuff. Have to in order to run this place. Does this look like an easy place to run?* He and Jimmy gazed over the huge vista of Guidance. *So, Jimmy, no feelings please, just use me as a tool to ready yourself.*

Jimmy suggested that he could have been an orphan. *How about I was born in Kansas, very premature so I had to stay in the hospital and my mom and dad and brothers and sisters were all blown away in a tornado?*

Mick considered this for a moment and then declared that it sounded OK. He thought about it some more and seemed to get into the story. *Ya, that's fine. So you don't remember any of them and were raised by some old people, maybe grandparents, who died when you were ten and then you went from foster home to foster home and you haven't kept in touch with any of them because you were an angry, bad kid.* He stopped and stared at Jimmy.

Jimmy agreed that the story worked but asked, *What about my adult life. I'm nearly forty?*

Mick was busy writing in the ledger and encouraged Jimmy to go ahead and figure out what he'd been doing since high school. He reminded him, *this Julia broad is an educated type so you better think up something professional so you won't have to waste time convincing her that you're OK in spite of the fact that you're a ditch digger or whatever.*

Jimmy began to argue that point saying her favorite men seemed to be cowboy types, but Mick shut him up. *Trust me, Jimmy, I've seen a lot of these cases.*

Jimmy still didn't agree but decided to pick a safe, middle of the road type image. *I've been a consultant. I've worked in South American lumbering operations.*

Hey, that's nice, Mick commented. *Can you speak Spanish?*

I don't remember.

OK, no problem. We'll have them run you through it at the Reception Center. So, you just got back from South America?

Ya, I guess so. Let me be in Boston to do some research before I go out west to do a project with the Indians, like a feasibility study on how to create an industrial base owned and operated by the Indians.

Hey, you got a thing for Indians? Oh, ya, I remember, you've been one a couple of times. Does Julia like Indians too or just cowboys?

She likes Indians too.

That's good. We can set you up with a research grant. You'll be at Harvard for six months and then out to Arizona.

Jimmy started to get excited about the life he was about to enter. Mick finished writing and closed the ledger. *So that's it. I guess you'll be keeping the image?*

Jimmy felt uncertain. *Well, what do you think, Mick?*

Hey, you're lookin' good, tall, great eyes, go for it!

Jimmy relaxed. Mick pushed a button on the machine under the counter and after an insistent humming, the machine stopped and made a beeping noise.

Uh oh, we got a problem. Lemme see. It's the birthday you picked. 1960 seems to be the only year in recent history when there were no tornado fatalities in Kansas. Can you beat that? What are the odds? We need a new state of birth or a new birthday. You wanna be older, like born in 1959 or you wanna come from a different state, like say, Oklahoma or Nebraska.

Do they have tornados?

Well, let's put in Oklahoma and see what happens. He pulled up the ledger and erased something and wrote in something and then pushed a button on the machine again. It whirred and hummed and in a few moments printed out a report. Mick gathered up the papers and turned to Jimmy, *it's all done. Oklahoma musta had some tornado fatalities in 1960. You're finished here. You'll be given a copy of this in Reception.* Seeing Jimmy's quizzical look, Mick explained. *It's like a summer camp. We are sending down so many more Walk-Ins and Drop-Ins that we needed a place to have them embark from. A place for last minute priming and acclimatizing. We have you stay there for a couple of days until you get the hang of things and can proceed without support. You'll like it, everyone does. Well, all the best to you, Jimmy. Hope it's a real good one this time. Oh, I almost forgot, because you are keeping the abilities of spiritual perception, when we want you, the signal will be a buzzing like you heard earlier when the Destiny Committee contacted you asking that you proceed with your descent plans. So, go back to Frenn's. They are planning a Bon Voyage party and then go see Florabelle and she will put you on the elevator.*

Back at Frenn's, Jimmy found a distraught Sonny on the monitor. He sent hostile vibes to Jimmy, communing , *I thought I wasn't going to be stuck guiding Julia but what am I supposed to do, let her get mugged or killed!*

Why? What's going on? Jimmy grabbed a wand and dashed to the monitor.

When she woke up from an afternoon nap she decided she was going to get some pot so she went to Medford and she and a friend are on their way to some project to try to buy some. She never did this before but for some reason she couldn't get any from her friends.

Jimmy murmured, *oh shit!* He put on the earphones.

14

BELOW

How the hell do you open this door? Julia was in her friend Kate's car. They were parked on a dark city street.

That door always sticks, Kate muttered.

Julia whacked at it with her shoulder while pulling on the door handle. *You sure this is the right street?* The place looked eerie. Tall lights shone bluely down onto a cement courtyard between the brick walls of three story project buildings. A carcass of a car lay partway on the sidewalk, everything gone but the frame. Kate got out and went around the car to Julia's door and kicked it. *This is the place. It looks familiar*, she said.

Just then a police car pulled up next to them. The driver leaned out and asked if they had a problem.

No, no, the door's just stuck… Kate said gaily while walking back around to get in the car. The policeman gave them both a long look. *Do you live around here?* He asked. They both stuttered out a "n-no." Kate added that they were just visiting. It sounded lame but the policeman seemed to have lost his focus and was staring at Julia, attracted by her beauty. She was wearing black and it became her.

This neighborhood's not safe. If you want to visit you'd be best off comin' durin' the day. There was trouble here last night. You'd better leave.

Kate started the car and called out, *Thanks, we're leaving....* She murmured to Julia, *it's not gonna work out tonight.*

No shit, Julia whispered. The cop car followed them to the bottom of Haven Street. When the light changed they got on the expressway. Kate apologized that it hadn't worked out. Julia just sighed and shook her head and thanked her for trying and said at least they hadn't gotten into any trouble. She was tired and a little ashamed about the mess she could have gotten herself into. *A grown woman with three kids!* She exclaimed and then sighed again.

After having a cup of coffee at Kate's house, Julia pled exhaustion and went home.

ABOVE

Jimmy watched her until she was inside her house, then he put down the wand and wiped his spiritual brow. His cavalier attempt to toughen her up, per Amesbury's advice, had endangered her life. If he'd let her friend Sherry pass along a little pot from her home grown supply, Julia wouldn't have sought it out in such dangerous territory. *Who am I to judge?* He asked himself, realizing once again the power and influence he had as a Primary Guide. *I've gotta learn to play chess so I can focus on all the implications,* he declared somewhat desperately but then suddenly remembered he was on his way, didn't have to do this job this way any longer. He was glad he had sent a nearby police car to check out the project at that moment. But he also felt a surge of anger. That policeman had given Julia a long look with the power of a kiss. Jimmy saw the bright pink waves of lust he sent in her direction. *I better get down there quick*, he mumbled to himself.

Sonny stood by the monitor radiating frustration. A pennant with a huge F on it flew about ten feet above his head. Jimmy assured him that everything was under control and there wouldn't be any more problems. He told him that in three days he would be with Julia and during the interim period he would ask Dinah to watch over her. *Just to be safe I'll do something that I've never done before. I'll give her a three day case of the flu so she can't go anywhere and do anything stupid.*

James wafted over and took Jimmy by the arm and led him to a chair. He introduced him to Ephriam, an elderly man with a long white beard who was wearing white robes and a prayer shawl. For the next hour Jimmy was tutored on the basics of the Jewish religion. He concentrated, breaking away only for a moment to ask Dinah to watch over Julia.

With the Jewish holidays and practices all a jumble in his mind and words like kugel, challah and gefilte fish evoking slight memories of eating, he thanked Ephriam who had been a friend of James Frenn's in third grade in his last lifetime, and gone on to become a rabbi. Ephriam's final instruction to Jimmy was to find a synagogue immediately upon arrival BELOW. He also reminded him that it took the presence of at least ten men, a minyan, for prayers to be said.

What about women? Jimmy asked, but when he saw Ephriam's forbidding expression he just numbly acknowledged that he understood and would look for a synagogue right away.

Jimmy had been concentrating so intently that he hadn't noticed the party happening around him. Dinah was playing the violin and was accompanied by a few members of the Celestial Symphony. They were making lovely music and the site was crowded with souls. They all communed together, HE'S A JOLLY GOOD FELLOW… HE'S A JOLLY GOOD FELLOW… and then Jimmy made a short thank you speech and everyone wished him well. Even Florabelle was there and after Jimmy made the rounds she took him by the arm and said, *The time has come.*

Wait a minute! Jimmy pulled away. He frantically looked around for Dinah. She heard his call and came to his side. He murmured a hurried good bye and told her to finish her lecture series so she would be ready when he sent the message that she could come down to be Julia's baby. Jimmy tried to hold the image of Dinah in his mind as Florabelle led him away. She escorted him to a fancy gilt elevator cage and explained that, like everything else, it had been dolled up. She quoted the SuperArch, *Proprieties breed positive attitudes.*

Florabelle pushed Jimmy into the elevator and slammed the door shut. Jimmy felt a tremendous drop, a sickening, wretched, body-oriented feeling, and then there was a sudden jolt and he was aware of working hard to take a breath. He felt the incredibly heavy sensation of having a body and then he felt **there**, back on Earth.

He found himself sitting under a tree on a bench that was built around the tree's sturdy trunk. He heard the buzzing of bees and the tweeting of birds and focused his eyes on the intense colors, the red and orange, green and blue of the flowers, grass and sky. He felt a breeze mussing his hair. He stood up and stretched, already nearly used to the bulk of a body with substance.

An attractive woman wearing a jumpsuit and red running shoes appeared next to him. *Welcome to Earth. I'm Minnie, your Reception Center Guide. This will be your adjustment site for the next few days.* She took his hand. *Come, we'll go to the dining hall and start you off eating. It's a good re-introduction to the workings of the body.*

After the first few steps, walking proved to be easy. Jimmy found that his body could do it automatically. The path wound through a corridor of shade trees and Jimmy shivered for a moment in the cooler air. They left the shady corridor and were out in the sun again. They crossed a field to get to the buildings. Jimmy enjoyed the sensation of temperature. He looked closely at Minnie, wondering if she was a spirit or a person. He decided to ask. After all, these few days were his opportunity to gather the information he needed. *Are you like a real person or what?*

Minnie laughed and explained that she was a grade 10 but because of the job description and the locale, she had to have an Earth body. *Let me tell you though, I'd just as soon not be bothered.*

Minnie led Jimmy into the dining hall. Most of the tables were taken and a jumble of voices filled the room. Many people were dressed in casual clothes, one man looked quite odd in a tuxedo. There were windows on all sides of the room through which could be seen lovely vistas, rolling meadows and beyond that a forest of tall trees.

After staring about for a few minutes Jimmy figured out how to pick out the new arrivals. They were the pale ones. He shared his observation with Minne and she confirmed it, telling him it took a few days to gain color. They sat down at an empty table and a waitress brought them menus. Jimmy ordered a tunafish sandwich. Ephraim had told him it would be easier to come to an understanding of Judaism if he followed a kosher diet. Jimmy didn't remember all the particulars but he did recall that tunafish was OK as it had no hooves and did have fins and scales, something like that.

At first, putting food in his mouth seemed very strange. Minnie had to tell him to chew and not to stop breathing while he did it. Swallowing was nearly impossible until he realized that it was not thought that commanded these actions but just blind permission to the body to function. After a cup of tea Minnie asked him how he was feeling. He said, *fine*, but added that he was a little tired. She told him that was normal. Re-entry was exhausting and the spirit initially found the body a heavy load. She suggested that he sleep until the next morning when his classes would begin. She led him to his room. It was a typical motel room. She explained that the TV was a regular TV and also a monitor like they had ABOVE. He could use it to check on Julia and also to receive any last minute transmissions from the spirit world before he was launched into the Earth zone. She left him a schedule of classes, explaining that the ones printed in dark type were mandatory but the others were electives and he should let her know at breakfast which of those he would like to attend. He listened to her parting words with his eyes closed, weariness had so overcome him. Immediately after she left, he collapsed onto the bed and fell into a deep sleep.

Jimmy woke up at 4:32. The numbers glowed in green on the clock next to his bed. Despite his exhaustion he dragged himself over to the TV and turned it on. After a moment of fuzziness, the picture cleared and he could see Julia curled up in her bed, a half smile on her beautiful face. He breathed a sigh of relief, turned off the TV, and went back to bed.

The phone rang. The clock said 8:00. It was Minnie. She told him that breakfast was being served in the dining room and he would find clean clothes in the closet. Jimmy was still tired and found the process of showering, brushing his teeth and getting dressed annoying. As he left the room an uncomfortably full sensation reminded him of the need to pee.

He found his way back to the dining room and was greeted by the smell of eggs, toast, and coffee. He felt a twinge of hunger and eating breakfast was enjoyable. Minnie congratulated him on his appetite. She then explained that for most of the morning he was required to attend a workshop called Earth Orientation. It was a review of Earthly procedures: crossing streets, using public transportation, operating lawnmowers and snow blowers, all the familiar little asides that needed to be learned to insure that he would come to no harm.

In the time slots from 12 to 1 and 4:30 to 6, you can choose from a series of seminars like, Dating Behaviors, Men's Fashions, Civic Responsibility, Chinese Cooking, Handyman Skills.... There's a long list. Did you look it over last night?

No, but I guess I'd like to take Men's Fashions or Dating Behaviors.

All right, that's fine. Let me fill in your schedule for you. She typed his selections on some empty lines in the grid that was his schedule.

You've got Men's Fashions at noon and Dating Behaviors from 4:30 to 6 after School Review which is mandatory.

OK. Jimmy sighed. He remembered how much work it was to have a life.

The Earth Orientation Course was a hands-on experience. After a review of traffic rules, they were asked to cross streets. Then they were required to mow a small patch of grass and push a snow blower back and forth a few times. They were taken to a bus stop and had to ride downtown and back. While downtown they went to a department store where they had to figure out what size clothes they wore and select and purchase a complete outfit. No details were omitted. They were taught how to knot a tie, polish shoes, put up an umbrella, write a letter, make a phone call, run a vacuum cleaner and a dishwasher, and manage all the other mundane routines of life in American in the year 2000.

One Arab guy in the group only figured out he was in the wrong class half way through so an Arab trainer was brought in to coach him on Arab customs. The rest of Jimmy's group was comprised of two older women who were being assigned to the child abuse investigation unit of the Massachusetts Department of Social Services and four other men, three youngish guys like himself and one older fellow. The older man was going to be a judge and the three young guys had jobs in Massachusetts prisons. They all did quite well in the course except for one of the young guys. He said he was distracted by the sensation of having a penis and balls as he'd never lived a life as a man.

The morning went quickly. Everything the Earth Orientation teacher told them to do was vaguely familiar and the practice brought it into the realm of the commonplace. At the end of the course Jimmy thanked the instructor, telling him it was helpful to have the practice. The instructor explained that it was a relatively new program. *At first the Drop-Ins had literally just been dropped into life on Earth and there were some problems. One guy tried to walk across a river and was drowned and a young woman got herself electrocuted trying to use a hair dryer in the bathtub so this Reception Center was set up to orient people to Earth life. The results have been very good.*

Billy, the awkward young guy who was having trouble adjusting to his penis and balls, attended the Dating Behaviors Course with Jimmy. They got to practice on a woman instructor. She led them through making small talk, asking someone out on a date, ordering at a restaurant, inviting oneself up for coffee, talking of world events and so on. Both Jimmy and Billy found it a very helpful course but on their way to lunch Billy admitted that he was scared because he had no idea how to work his penis in a sexual way. *I've figured out how to pee but that's it!*

Jimmy admitted he didn't feel very confident about sex either and suggested that they ask Minnie if there was a course on Sexual Practice for Men. Billy was pretty upset. *What do I do if there isn't?*

Jimmy assured him they could probably get someone to give them some independent study. He stared at Billy. *Why did you decide to come back as a man?* Billy explained that he needed a lifetime of service in order to be considered for a promotion that would allow him to join his family group the next time he came to ABOVE and the only thing available was for a man so he took it. It seemed a touchy subject so Jimmy didn't inquire further.

The Men's Fashions Course was helpful. After trying on many different styles of clothing, Jimmy got a sense of what he liked.

Dinner was a festive affair. The trainees were given the opportunity to order lavish meals and wines and liquors of all types. Most of them got drunk and a little disorderly and had to be led to their rooms. At breakfast the next morning, there were many requests for aspirin and the breakfast speech was on the topic of moderation in the use of drugs and alcohol.

As he was leaving the dining hall, Minnie caught up with Jimmy and told him that everything had been arranged. He had an apartment and was scheduled to have an interview the next day with the people at Harvard who would be giving him the grant for the project with the Indians in Arizona. Noticing that Jimmy adopted a nervous posture, Minne assured him that it was just a formality. They were already unalterably influenced to the positive about him from his references and resume. She told him he would receive his complete dossier later and it would contain all the information he needed. Jimmy relaxed and found himself staring at Minnie as she talked. She was beautiful. Her skin had lovely tones, her hair shone and her eyes were a deep blue. Being a grade 10, Minnie was aware of his reveries and cut them short by perfunctorily explaining that he was marveling at the intensely sensual element of life. It made everything ABOVE seem pale in comparison. *It is simply a feature of organic matter.* She further explained that sexual sensations were currently uppermost in his mind as they too were not experienced in the spiritual state. Jimmy couldn't keep himself from muttering, *you better believe it!!!!* Minnie laughed and brought him to an even higher plane of delight by telling him he needed to choose a car. A helpful police officer who was also a Drop-In, spirited away unclaimed stolen cars for use by new arrivals. Jimmy eagerly asked when he could review the possibilities. Minnie told him she would pick him up after his session on Saving the World. Jimmy was so excited that he actually jumped for joy. Images of trucks raced through his mind.

Jimmy spent the morning being individually coached in various subject areas. By lunchtime he had total knowledge of Spanish and the Indian languages, Indian culture, geology, principles of economics and accounting, and a list of the synagogues in the Boston area.

Lunch was burgers and fries, delicious. He sat with Billy who seemed a lot more adjusted than he had the day before. Jimmy asked if he had gotten any help with his sexual concerns. Billy said it was no longer a problem. His Reception Center Guide had told him not to worry because sex was a body directed occurrence and the mind only got in the way. Jimmy considered this for a few minutes and then forgot about it, preferring to think about getting a car or maybe a truck. Billy hadn't heard about this option and called his Guide over to discuss it. Her name was Cherry and she had glossy black hair and shiny red lips. She was gorgeous. After she left, Jimmy asked Billy if looking at her didn't give him some clues about his body's sexual

e. Billy said, *No, I think I'm going to be gay because you look a lot more appealing to me than she does.*

This admission startled Jimmy, but after a moment he replied that it probably didn't matter. *Whatever turns you on, Bill....*

The Saving the World Workshop was excellent. The first hour was a video of news clips describing world events throughout recent history. The soundtrack was an insistent repetition of commandments for good behavior. A background of muted but still clearly recognizable rock music completed the package. Then there was a session on Values Clarification. Jimmy and about fifteen others role-played many little skits to reinforce the essential values they were being sent to Earth to model. It was fun and acting out the different roles reminded them all of the dimension of humor in life. The last hour was a series of readings. Each trainee was asked to read a selection aloud. The entire workshop was an intense dose of vitamins to the soul and afterwards Jimmy felt boundless in the strength of his spirit, and grounded in his body.

Late that afternoon on their way to the garages, Minnie and Jimmy stopped at a café and had coffee and pastries. Minnie handed him a briefcase. In it he found all his vital papers: birth certificate, driver's license, apartment lease, passport, five hundred dollars in cash, a bank book showing a balance of twenty thousand dollars, charge cards, a resume, a couple of journal articles he had apparently authored, health records and a membership card for an HMO. She then told him that one of his future colleagues at Harvard would invite him to a party on Friday night and he would meet Julia there.

The garages were huge outbuildings behind a lovely house in the country. Minnie said it was once an apple farm. She pointed to a hill covered with old apple trees. She parked next to the barns and with Jimmy's help, opened the large doors.

It was quite dark inside but Jimmy could see enough. He left Minnie by the doors and dashed around looking at all the vehicles. The majority seemed to be rather inglorious models of your standard older American car.

Perfect for the low profile person, he shouted to Minnie.

Yes, that's what we're about. Think of yourself as driving onto the planet from outer space and wanting to fit right in. And by the way, your apartment is in Cambridge and you have to park on the street so you'll want something that will still be there the next morning, or something you won't mind if it's gone.

Jimmy went from car to car but he had lost some of his initial glow. After an hour of this Minne got impatient. *Hey, Jimmy, what does it matter? All of these vehicles drive perfectly and your level of spiritual understanding will keep a car running well indefinitely. You can buy something grand when you get out west.*

Jimmy was unwilling to rush. He was now a little figure at the other end of the huge barns.

Minnie yelled, *the keys are in them. Just pick one out and drive it over here!*

There were no trucks. Jimmy finally picked a dark blue Dodge van. The back had built-in shelves and seemed to be stocked with electrician's supplies. He drove it over to Minnie. She stepped up to a screen set into the wall and punched the license plate numbers in on a keyboard below the screen. After reading the information that came up on the screen she told Jimmy that the vehicle he'd picked was reserved for a Drop-In who was going to be an electrician at a nuclear power plant. Jimmy was impressed. *Very smart to have our guys working in there!*

Oh yes, we're trying.... Minnie commented.

This interchange seemed to elevate Jimmy to a more serious plane. He drove the van back and momentarily returned driving an older blue van with a built-in bed in back. Minnie checked it out and it was available. They drove tandem back to the Reception Center.

Jimmy loved driving. He was a little scared though, so much was happening. He wondered if he was supposed to check out that night or the next day. He hoped it was the next day. Minnie parked her car in the Reception Center lot and jumped out and ran back to Jimmy's van. He rolled down the window and she handed him the title and registration for the van and a map and written directions on how to get to his apartment. He stuffed the papers into his briefcase and began to roll up the window in preparation for getting out of the van. She put her hand on the edge of the window, preventing him from rolling it further. She stretched her hand in to shake his. *Time for you to be on your way. You know everything you need to know. Best of luck to you!*

Jimmy protested, *I'd rather go in the morning!*

Minnie shook her head and Jimmy nearly broke down in tears. *At least let me pick up some stuff from my room!* He pleaded.

Minnie assured him that he'd left nothing behind. She reminded him that he had nothing with him when he arrived and told him that he would find plenty of clothes at his apartment because the Men's Fashion Workshop staff had purchased a wardrobe for him in the colors and styles that he liked.

Jimmy was amazed. It seemed that they had thought of everything. He stopped resisting and reached out to give Minnie an awkward hug and a kiss on the cheek. She stood next to the window while he reviewed the directions to Cambridge. Then, without further protestations, he drove off. For a moment he stared at Minnie in the rear view mirror before concentrating on the road ahead.

15

Jimmy's apartment was nice. It had four rooms: a spacious bedroom, a cozy study with a fireplace, a big living room, a good functional kitchen, and an adequate bathroom. It was comfortably furnished, even had plants hanging in the windows and a vase of cut flowers on the table. Jimmy spent the evening looking at the clothes and books and playing CDs. At one o'clock in the morning he finally went to bed. The next day was Thursday. His interview at Harvard was scheduled for eleven and then he was going to find Julia. The idea of waiting until the party on Friday night was intolerable.

Thursday dawned a bright, cold and blustery day. Jimmy dressed nattily in gray flannels and a dark blue cashmere sports jacket. Running down the street swinging his briefcase he got some admiring looks from passing women. It was fun. The interview went well and he was given free range of all the Harvard libraries and assigned an office and a secretary. He talked briefly with his colleagues but then left, as his excitement about seeing Julia was building to an almost unbearable peak.

On Wednesday night, Julia's last thought before going to sleep was that tomorrow she would do something of consequence towards the goal of defining her life. For the past three days she had been out flat with a flu. When she woke up on Thursday she unfortunately felt no better, no more able to go out and set the world on fire than she had the day before. She resolved again that it was just a matter of will, but first she needed a good idea. That's what she was waiting for.

As it happened, she was almost off the hook for the day because Laramie climbed into bed with her complaining that she felt sick. Julia resigned herself to the fact that the kid had caught her flu and decided that they would both just sleep all day. Julia usually determined the status of an illness by taking the child's temperature but unfortunately the thermometer was once again broken. Laramie's forehead didn't feel hot and she looked good. Julia inquired about the date of her next spelling test and lo and behold it was that very day. She told Laramie that she should go to school and the child sighed deeply but then ate a good breakfast and left for the bus stop with her brothers.

The quiet of the house settled heavily on Julia. She had another cup of coffee and then moved on to a piece of the raspberry danish she had promised herself she would not touch. Finally, to prevent a totally slothful descent, she conceded to herself that a great idea could arrive just as easily, or perhaps more easily, while she raked leaves. Once she got out to the yard with the rake and the bags she realized that it was a little too blustery to make good progress but the idea of confronting the other half of the raspberry danish inspired her to conclude that she could rake small piles and immediately bag them to keep the flying-leaves-factor under control.

She actually got into it, a simple but blessedly consuming task. She had worked a couple of hours and stuffed twelve bags when hunger began to drive her towards the house but she resisted the impulse. Finishing the back yard, she went around to the front to survey the leaf situation. Just then a blue van pulled up to the curb. Julia hoped the van had a mission at the house across the street because she hated being bothered while she was thinking.

No such luck. A duded-up guy got out of the van and started walking across the lawn towards her. He looked like a stockbroker. Actually, he looked like some movie star, Julia couldn't remember which one. *What a nice smile... but he's grinning at me like I'm some long lost relative!*

Jimmy felt the blood rushing to his head. It was Julia! She was wearing her usual sweat clothes rags that he'd seen her in so often. *Finally, I'm with Julia!* He began to run towards her but then saw the panicked look on her face and remembered that she had no idea who he was. He was just some guy running across her lawn looking ecstatic. He stopped and then Julia, who had turned to run away from him, stopped also. They stared at each other.

Can I help you? Julia spoke firmly and had the rake propped in front of her.

I'm a friend of... Jimmy stopped, *ah, your name is Julia, right?*

She nodded.

Ah, I met Mimi....

Julia smiled and said, *oh, yes, Mimi.*

I couldn't believe what you did for Mimi.

She told you about me?

Yes, well, ah... I have a friend like Mimi was, and I'd be so happy if you could help her. Jimmy wasn't quite sure if he liked the story he'd conjured up and was concerned about the future problems it might make for him but he'd jumped into it and there was no going back.

Now that she understood the man's mission, Julia transformed herself into her professional counselor mode. She thought perhaps it was a signal that she should take on another matrimony case. *Well, I'd be happy to discuss it although I'm not quite ready for another client but I might be soon. Of course I would need to hear the particulars.*

Could I take you out to lunch and tell you about her? Jimmy's only goal was to spend some time with Julia. She was so beautiful in the flesh. Jimmy was one hundred percent in love with her.

Not right now, I have things to do but how about next week? Um, maybe Thursday?

Oh well, I see, well, fine but… my car won't start. I have to call a gas station to come and give me a jump.

Why don't you try it again. Maybe it will start. Although this man was earnest and likeable, somewhere, way below the surface, Julia smelled a rat. *This guy is trying to get close to me*, she muttered to herself. *He might be a Jesus freak or a psycho. I'll meet him in a public place next week.* She told him, *my husband is sick today and the house is one big germ. He's sleeping. He's a real light sleeper so I don't want to bother him and don't you have a cellphone? Why don't you try the car again. Maybe it will start.*

Jimmy felt out-maneuvered but he couldn't bear the idea of leaving her now that he was finally with her. Feeling desperate, he sent her the old message. He turned to walk back to the van and said inaudibly, *Julia, I love you.*

The effect on Julia was amazing. She immediately recognized the voice and was nearly deafened by the message. It sounded so loud in her head. *It must be a message from God*, she thought, *and this man is the messenger.* She ran towards him calling, *Mister, stop!*

Jimmy stopped and turned around. Julia came up to him and stared intensely into his eyes. He was nearly overwhelmed by the desire to kiss her but instead he sent his forces of passion. Then she was overwhelmed and looked down at the ground but in a minute she stared at him again. Jimmy sensed that he was more in control than she was and making the most of the moment he asked, *is there a nice place to walk nearby?*

She nodded dumbly and pointed to the van. They both got in and she instructed him to drive across town. *Next left, second right…* her directions filled the air between them. Jimmy cautioned himself to back off a little.

He didn't want to fall into the category of one of Julia's weird men episodes. He remembered all the guys that he had made trip and fall down the stairs when they followed her out of restaurants after glancing at her and having her return their glances. She had a smoldering look. He decided it would be better if they were introduced legitimately before they got in too deep. He started a conversation to normalize things. *I hope you don't find me too intense. You remind me of a close friend, really like a sister. Someone I knew in South America. I lived there for ten years. Just got back here three days ago, so you can imagine, I'm not really all here yet, and I do miss Deena.* At the last moment he decided not to say Dinah, as she would undoubtedly rave about how that was her mother's name and the seeming coincidence would start off another set of supernatural wonderings in her mind.

My friend Deena looks a lot like you. It will be good for me to go to a party at a colleague's house tomorrow night, a guy named Howard Morlin. He lives in a town called Newton. I think I need some good old American socializing to get acclimatized. South America is very different from here!

Julia was sorting out all this new information. First of all, she too was invited to Howard Morlin's party. *What a small world!* Then she thought about the part about South America and concluded that he must be an interesting guy, and she was going to meet him anyway. She began to feel less weird about the goings on.

They went for a walk in the woods, both moving at a jaunty pace. They talked about the cold weather and then about the fact that Jimmy would start a new job on Monday. She asked his last name and then asked if Cantor was a Jewish name. He said it was. By the end of the walk they were acting like pals.

Julia told him she had to get home for the kids. Jimmy accepted that they would have to part. He pulled up in front of her house just as Laramie got off the school bus. Julia got out of the van and waved goodbye to Jimmy. Laramie yelled, *wait a minute!* and ran over to the van. *Who's that, Ma?*

Jimmy rolled down his window and said, *Hi*. Julia introduced him and after a long look, Laramie said, *Hi*, and then turned to her mother. *Is there any raspberry danish left?*

By early afternoon on Friday Jimmy ran out of patience. He wanted to be with Julia. Even though it was only 2 in the afternoon he got dressed for the party. But after looking at himself in the mirror and not finding the reflection up to par, he undressed and tried on his other new clothes seeking the perfect outfit. He wanted to look good but not too formal as being with Julia had reminded him of her hippie style of dress. He finally chose a turtleneck and cords and a sweater. Then he had nothing to do.

He turned on the TV and tried to concentrate on an old Betty Davis movie. The plot moved too slowly for his racing mind so he switched to the news. He watched the Early News and then the Six o'clock News and then the Nightly News. By 7 o'clock he was about to jump out of his skin. He paced around his apartment and by 7:30 he couldn't stand it any longer and left for the party. The invitation said that it started at 8 and he remembered from his Dating Behaviors Course that it was proper to arrive at a party a half hour or so after the appointed time but he excused himself this faux pas by the greater justification that he didn't want to give any other guy the edge on getting close to Julia.

He arrived at Howard's house at 8. Howard remarked upon his promptness. *I find it especially shocking as you have just come from ten years in South America where people are never on time!* Jimmy helped Howard put out the cheese and cracker plates and cut up raw vegetables to go with the dips.

At 8:30 the guests began to arrive. Jimmy enjoyed making small talk, especially with the women. They all looked gorgeous to him but he kept glancing at the door, waiting for Julia. She arrived at 9. Howard greeted her warmly. Jimmy positioned himself next to Howard and as he had hoped, Howard introduced him to her. *This is a new member of our department. He will be doing research for six months and then heading out to a field assignment in Arizona. James Cantor, Julia Montage.* Howard was then called away by his wife.

Julia seemed nervous. She tapped her fingers on the front hall table and with her other hand she twisted her hair. She rarely went to parties but she had promised Janey, Howard's wife, that she would come to this one. Jimmy sent her soothing vibes and offered to get her some punch. She accepted. When Jimmy returned she was engaged in conversation with a tall, grey-haired man and two other men hovered nearby. He started to get angry but then calmed himself and handed her the punch and stood next to her. As soon as there was a break in the conversation, he suggested to the attentive men that they should go and get some of the delicious punch for themselves. Under his words could be heard a demand that they clear out. The three men muttered remarks about how hard it was to make a truly good punch and moved away. Jimmy realized it was only a temporary victory and began to scheme. He asked Julia where her kids were. She told him that they were with their father for the weekend. Jimmy immediately made his move. He asked her if she would take a quick trip back to his apartment with him. *I had a pizza for lunch and can't remember turning off the oven. It's only a twenty minute ride. We'll come right back. I'm sorry, I'm not usually so forgetful. I'm still adjusting to being back in the states and to my new apartment.*

Julia assured him that she understood and she didn't mind going along to keep him company. Jimmy knew she would respond that way as he had watched her run back to her house many times, convinced that she'd left the stove on.

Julia offered to drive and he accepted, figuring she would feel more in control in her car and, if things developed as he hoped, she wouldn't feel compelled to leave in order to go get her car. He sent a silent thank you to Minnie as he had no worries about his old van and didn't even care if it was there when he went back to get it.

Julia drove a little too fast and had the radio on a little too loud but none of it mattered to Jimmy. He adored her and marveled at her Earthly reality. Julia felt his intense scrutiny and it both flattered her and scared her. She was used to having men flirt with her but his focused attention was overwhelming. She glanced at him. *God, he's attractive!* She thought and she gave up worrying. *What the hell, maybe it will be the beginning of a new and wonderful relationship or maybe just a fling, or maybe nothing. We'll turn off the oven and be back at the party inside of an hour. Let it be*, she decided. Way back, when mired in a draining and desperate affair while still married to Harvey, she had been stoned one night and really listened to the Beatles song, "Let it Be." It had soothed her frazzled mind then and ever since.

They climbed the two flights to his apartment and her curiosity grew. A wise friend had once told her that you don't really know a person until you have been in his home. Jimmy unlocked the door and welcomed her in.

This is a really nice place, she thought. *Everything seems new though, there's no overlay of minor disorder.* She commented on what a neat man he was. He replied that he needed some time to make it messy and homey. *Gimme a break! I've only been living here for three days!*

Julia admired the furniture and asked him if he bought it all new or had it shipped from South America. Thinking fast, Jimmy replied that a friend had found the apartment and furnished it for him. He'd sent her money a couple of months ago. Julia heard the "her" and got slightly lit up with her old problem of jealousy but then forced herself to drop the thought. Her pride in accomplishing that overwhelmed her desire to know more about his friend which was a happy turn of events for Jimmy because he hadn't thought up any further details about his non-existent friend.

Remembering the mission, Jimmy went over to the stove and remarked happily, *oh good, it's off. I always worry about leaving the stove on. I don't know why*. Julia found it comforting. He was a like-minded lunatic.

Jimmy looked around frantically for a way to detain them. *My friend stocked the apartment with some CDs. The music is amazing. I guess I've missed a lot being in South America for the past ten years.*

Julia's interest was caught. She checked out the CDs and picked one by John Lennon. *You remember him, don't you?* He nodded yes and she slid the disc out of the case and put it in the player. She turned up the volume, she liked loud music. The song, "Nobody told me there'd be days like this," set them both to dancing, first alone and then facing each other. They were breathless by the end of the song.

Jimmy got them some bubbly water and asked if Julia was hungry. She said, *sure, if you want something. I'm always hungry. This is a nice place. I'm not much of a party person, too many people.*

Jimmy agreed but he was surprised that it was so easy. In his Dating Behaviors Course, the instructor had said that women usually resist being alone with a man in his apartment unless they know him well. But then he remembered, *this is Julia. She's always game for a great love experience.* He had been actively engaged in preventing just such happenings as this for months.

Jimmy prepared a lovely plate of snacks and brought it into the study where they had settled. Julia built a fire in the fireplace, mentioning that she had a wood stove at her house. Jimmy barely kept himself from saying, *I know, I know.* He realized in time that he could not possibly explain how he knew. He trained himself to say, *really,* whenever she told him some fact about herself.

The evening proceeded gloriously. Early on Julia asked him if he had any pot. He said he didn't think so but about five minutes later she took a jar off a shelf and said, *this looks suspiciously like pot*, and then opened the jar and smelled it and said, *ummm, it's pot!* She looked at him questioningly. All he could think to say was that his friend had thought to even furnish him with that. She was so happy to find it that she didn't stop to be jealous. He watched her expertly roll a joint as he had watched her so many times before. They smoked it and he felt no effect but she definitely seemed happier and exuded a new intense sexuality.

Billy's Reception Center Director was right about sex. The body leads the way. They spent most of the night happily romping in bed. Whenever he had a chance to stop and think, he was grateful that he had shielded Julia from the other men who had pursued her and saved her for himself. Also, he figured that her recent months of deprivation had made her that much more eager for him. *Not a bad deal...* he muttered to himself. He found a moment to wonder how he could have ignored this part of life in his other lifetimes. It seemed quite incomprehensible.

16

In the morning Jimmy woke up first. He slipped out of Julia's embrace and tiptoed into the living room. He worried about what to do next. *We have come this far, should I ask her to marry me when she wakes up?* He wished he could have one more session of the Dating Behaviors Workshop. He felt like he hadn't quite learned enough. He concluded his thinking spell by deciding to just hope that she would spend the rest of the weekend with him and by Sunday night he would have figured out what to do.

It was 10 o'clock and he missed Julia. Now that he was awake he didn't even like the idea of losing her to sleep. He crept back into the bedroom and slowly opened the curtains, hoping the light would wake her and they could make plans for a lovely day. Julia opened her eyes. She squinted and groaned and turned towards the wall to escape the brightness. He jumped onto the bed and gave her a big hug. She muttered groggily, *what time is it? Do we have to get up already?*

Jimmy sensed her despair and suddenly remembered that she was not a morning person. He didn't know what to do so he kissed her all over her face, big, sloppy kisses. Finally she laughed and said, *all right, all right…* and sat up and stretched and smiled.

What do you think we should do today? Do you want to show me around Boston? Or we could visit some of your friends?

She looked aghast. He wondered what he'd said that was so wrong. She got up and modestly wrapped a big towel around herself. This woman whose body he had ravished all night long suddenly seemed modest! She went into the bathroom and in a moment he heard the shower. Jimmy made tea and toast and soon Julia appeared in the kitchen, dressed and with a somber expression on her face. The apartment was bright and she seemed to shrink from the light. Jimmy was becoming more and more confused because she seemed to be a different person from the woman who had shared his bed.

He questioned her about the best sights in Boston and she replied that there were many worthwhile sights but she wasn't a good guide. Perhaps he had another friend to take him around the city? She said she had to get home. She had things to do. Jimmy was horrified at this turn of events and mystified. He wondered, *do I have bad breath?*

She went on to say she had plans with a friend for the afternoon. Jimmy could tell it was a lie. His spiritual awareness allowed him to see through people. He always knew the truth. At this moment his special perceptions were somewhat of a curse as his feelings were hurt because she obviously wanted to get away from him. *What did I do?* He asked himself. Suddenly there was a buzzing and then Dinah's voice. *It's not you. She's shy in the light of day. I hate to suggest this as it is certainly not a good idea in the long run but why don't you ask if she wants to smoke another joint?*

Julia was staring at Jimmy. He must have looked distracted during the transmission. She asked, *are you feeling all right?*

Ya, it's just my stomach. I feel a little nauseous. I ate some herring at the party before you got there and I don't think it agreed with me.

Oh…. She was no longer so distant, caught up in concern for him. *Why don't you smoke some. Normally I never would in the morning,* she explained demurely, *but it's great for settling your stomach. It has well known medicinal properties. You want me to roll you one?*

He nodded and sent up a silent *Thank you*, to Dinah.

Once she was stoned, Julia relaxed. She put on a new Bob Dylan CD and sat in the darkest corner of the living room. Jimmy made tea and snacks and they got into long raps about the governments in South America, Arizona, Indians in Arizona, possible oil deposits in Arizona, the weather in Arizona, Julia's desire to write a book, book publishing, and so on. At noon he made them grilled cheese sandwiches and they shared a big chocolate bar. Jimmy was completely happy.

As the pot wore off, Julia started to worry about what he would want to do now. The last thing she felt like doing was going out into the hordes and trying to park. She gauged her options. She wanted to make love again but only if she could get the shades down in the bedroom. She had recently decided that her flesh didn't hold up to the image she projected but she could keep it under control in the dark. However, her desire to make love was not sufficient to keep her there as a tourguide for the afternoon. *In any event, I'd like to find a way to get him to give me some of that pot*, she thought.

Jimmy, of course, knew what she was thinking. It would have been amusing if he didn't have to strategize all the time to counteract her impulse to flee. Except while stoned and making love in a dark room, Julia was pretty uptight. But then he realized that she didn't know him very well yet. It seemed odd though, that she would have sex with him and then feel uncomfortable about going out to be with him in the world.

He decided to pursue the love-making. His first act was to pull down the shades in the bedroom. They had a great time and then took a nap and woke up at four. Julia was satiated and wanted to go home and be alone. Jimmy decided not to interfere. Her need for space was apparent. He now wished that he had allowed her to get involved with one of the boyfriend prospects while he was guiding her from ABOVE so he would have seen how she conducted a love relationship and would know more about what to expect from her.

He couldn't bear to let her go without a plan to see her again so he asked if he could drop by when he went to pick up his car. Not wanting to offer to drive him to his car, Julia felt she had to agree to his request. He said he would call first. At the door she made a rather formal thank you and goodbye speech.

Julia was very relieved to be on her way home alone. She wasn't used to company. The last person she had shared so much concentrated time with was Mimi and she'd never paid any attention to Julia. With Jimmy, on the other hand, she felt devoured. Every time she looked at him he was staring at her.

She stopped at a 7-11 Store to buy a lottery ticket. The six numbers just popped into her mind. When she got home she took the phone off the hook and made herself some soup and turned on the TV. Jimmy rang her doorbell at 9:30. Julia was sleepy and annoyed when she opened the door and found him standing there.

You said you'd call....
I couldn't because you have the phone off the hook.
She felt guilty for a moment but then realized that the cat could have knocked the phone off the hook. She didn't have to take the blame.
Oh, no wonder it's been so blissfully quiet. The phone is off the hook!
Jimmy edged in and quietly closed the front door. Julia noticed he had pushed himself into her house but she didn't feel like fighting him off.

Earlier in the evening, Dinah had communicated to Jimmy that she had won the lottery and wanted to bestow the win on him and Julia. Jimmy had sent heartfelt thanks up to Dinah and raced to Julia's house to convince her that they should buy a lottery ticket. But as soon as he mentioned the idea she laughed and said, *no problem! I've already got one.* Jimmy asked if there was a store close by where he could buy a ticket. She looked at the clock and told him that they probably couldn't get there by 9:45 which was the time of the lottery drawing. Jimmy could tell she just didn't feel like going out. He insisted because he didn't want her to win without him. He asked her to give him directions to the store. Since he seemed so intent on getting a ticket, Julia offered, *if you give me fifty cents, we can go halfsies on the winnings. And you know we're not gonna win anyway. It's just a tax on the poor.*

It's a deal, Jimmy said. He pulled fifty cents out of his pocket and handed it to her. She made him a cup of cocoa and showed him around the house and then they turned on the TV and sat on the couch waiting for the lottery drawing.

Do they have lotteries in South America?

Oh, ya, I used to win all the time. I guess I'm lucky.

Did you win a lot of money?

Some money, also some chickens, a goat, and a rug once.

Julia laughed. She let him hold the ticket. It worked like a charm. The numbers came down and they were the numbers on the ticket. Julia nearly fainted. She got very pale.

How much did they say the prize was? She whispered, taking the ticket from his hand.

I think they said twelve million, but our share depends on how many winners there were.

How can we find out?

I guess we can go to the lottery office on Monday.

I wish I could get stoned. This is just too much!

Jimmy took the cue. He suggested that they go back to his place. Julia agreed but before they left she carefully put the ticket in the fireproof box her father had given her for storing important papers. She covered the box with a towel saying, *one must be ever vigilant against burglars.*

They spent another glorious, passionate night and Jimmy made them breakfast at noon on Sunday. He didn't put up the shades and Julia didn't get nervous and make her departure until 3:30. They arranged to meet in the morning and go to the lottery office together.

Julia listened to the local news at eleven and found out that there were three winners and the pot was twelve million, thus she and Jimmy would each get two million dollars. *Not bad,* she mumbled to herself. She decided not to tell the kids. She didn't want them going crazy. It was a school night.

On Monday morning, before heading out to pick up Julia, Jimmy stopped at his office to tell them he would be in by early afternoon. His boss, Stanley Owens, collared him and brought him into his office. Apparently Jimmy's proposal to assist the Native peoples in planning an industrialization strategy had been accepted by the Indian Council but they weren't interested in having him come out in May. They wanted him now as winter was their best planning time. Jimmy silently cursed the mishaps that occur in life's planning when there is no guide ABOVE to coordinate things. Being his own guide had its limitations, especially in terms of the perspective that was sacrificed when one had no over-view of the situation.

Jimmy felt that he had no choice so he agreed to use the week to get organized and then move to Arizona over the weekend. He realized he would have to think fast to try to get Julia to accompany him.

They each picked up a check for $50,000. Julia was in seventh heaven. *I'm not gonna get a job, she declared. I'm gonna write a book. I need to buy a new computer. Is there anything you need Jimmy? We could go shopping on the way home.*

Jimmy explained the unfortunate circumstances that had arisen at work and that it meant he had to move to Arizona at the end of the week. He blurted out his plea. *Will you come to Arizona with me?*

Julia didn't answer immediately but Jimmy could see beautiful images of the West rising in her mind. She loved the West and had been heard to vow many times that one day she was going to live out there. But the voice of reason intervened. *It wouldn't be good to rip the kids out of school and anyway, I would have to arrange some deal with Harvey or he'll take me to court and try to get custody of the kids.* Harvey, who had never had the time of day for the kids when he and Julia were married, had suddenly become a devoted parent. She explained her concerns to Jimmy and he had to accept her reasoning. He couldn't expect her to jeopardize her children.

That buzzing in Jimmy's head happened again and was followed by a message from Dinah. *I PASSED!!! CAN I COME BELOW AS JULIA'S BABY?*

He sent back the message, *PROBABLY, BUT I HAVEN'T WORKED IT OUT YET. I'VE ONLY BEEN DOWN HERE FOR FIVE DAYS!*

A message came back, *OH, I'M SORRY. I GUESS I'M JUMPING THE GUN. LET ME KNOW AS SOON AS YOU KNOW.*

Jimmy communed agreement and found himself asking Julia, *do you want another child?*

She looked astounded by the question.

He rephrased it. *I was just wondering because you're such a good mother.*

Julia was flattered but told him she'd had her tubes tied after Laramie's birth. Once again Jimmy had to refrain from saying, *I know, I know.*

Jimmy went to work. He had a lot to get done by Friday. He called Julia a couple of times a day and listened to her production of fantastic ideas. One recurring idea was that she would start an orphanage and also an amusement park to keep the orphans employed and to generate funds for orphan higher education. When afire with an idea she was very convincing and Jimmy found himself agreeing but suggesting that Arizona might be a good place for the orphanage.

Jimmy called Julia every evening asking to get together but she kept him at bay always saying that one of the kids was sick or the cat just threw up, some reason why he could not come over and why she had to get off the phone right away. The problem was that she loved the idea of their relationship so much that she didn't want to ruin it by seeing him. During her long years of marriage to Harvey she had gotten into the habit of day-dreaming about a fine life and creating her good times in her mind.

By Thursday Jimmy had put in sixteen hour days at the office for four days straight and was determined not to be put off again by Julia. He didn't call but just arrived at her house at 8 in the evening. He figured it was early enough to spend some time with the kids but late enough so that they would have to go to bed soon.

Laramie answered the door. She yelled to her mother, *it's that Jimmy guy*. He smiled at her and asked if he could come in. She looked him over uncertainly but then he tempted her by reaching into his pocket and pulling out a string of blue beads. He handed them to her saying he'd bought them in Peru and had been waiting to find a beautiful lady to give them to. She breathed out a grateful, *thanks*, and ran off to show them to her mother. He followed her.

He found Julia in the kitchen leaning over Elias who was sitting at the table looking totally miserable.

He doesn't know how to do his math homework and I'm terrible at teaching math. I mastered teaching second grade math, but this is sixth grade math and it's that new kind, not like when we were in school.

Jimmy offered to help and both Julia and Elias immediately accepted his offer. After helping Elias, Jimmy spent some time with Laramie listening to her description of the doll house she and Nancy were building, and then Todd invited him into his room to see his swimming trophies. Finally, the kids went to be bed and he and Julia quietly made love. At 2 in the morning he tiptoed away. She promised to come to his apartment after she dropped the kids at their dad's for the weekend. She said she would help him pack and would take him to the airport on Sunday.

The weekend was blissful and bountiful. Julia gave it her all as she was reassured that the end was in sight. She loved to leave a great impression.

Julia decided that during the next eight months, until the kids were out of school, she would concentrate on writing a book and then she would move out to Arizona and join Jimmy. Jimmy was happy about her decision but knew only too well how often Julia changed her mind. He invited her and the kids out to Arizona for the kids' Christmas vacation and at the airport on Sunday he gave Julia a sapphire ring and asked her to marry him. She was amazed. He laughed and demanded an answer. She said, *I guess so.*

When Julia got home on Sunday night she finally told the kids that she had won the lottery. They whooped and hollered and imagined all the great stuff they could buy. On Monday Julia bought a new computer and started to work on her book. She called it "The Flying Trapeze" because it was about a circus family.

Of course Harvey found out right away that Julia had won the lottery. He called to congratulate her and said he always knew she was special. He was stupid and transparent enough to suggest that now might be the time they should go to a counselor because he thought he was finally ready to work on the issues that had caused them to divorce. Julia had to suppress a giggle and her desire to ask, *what about Nancy? She goes out with the trash?* But she did take the opportunity to mention that she might want to move out west in the summer and she would be willing to pay for the kids' flights to Boston for holidays and vacations. Harvey wanted to get mad, she could feel it, but he held himself in check in worship of her money. He asked, *how much did you win, anyway?*

A lot, a whole lot, she answered.

17

After a month of buying anything that struck her fancy, Julia got bored with the whole thing. She had never gotten much pleasure out of consumption. She spent her days working on her book and wearing her old comfortable sweat clothes. The kids complained that she was no different now that she was rich. They bugged her to buy a new house but she told them that she wanted to wait until they had visited Arizona because they might want to buy a house out there. She also explained that she didn't have two million dollars in the bank because the winnings were doled out over twenty years.

On December 21, just before the start of a blizzard that threatened to paralyze Boston, Julia and the kids boarded a plane for Arizona. Jimmy picked them up at the airport in his new Toyota Landcruiser. He drove them to a big log cabin he had rented near the reservation. From his front windows you could see the sun disappear behind the mountains, turning the sky a rosy red. Julia loved the cabin and she loved Arizona and she even loved Jimmy. It was so easy to be with him and he made her feel so happy. She sometimes asked him if he was an angel sent down from above.

Jimmy was reassured that Julia hadn't commenced any passionate affairs in Boston thus far, but he wasn't happy to send her back there on New Year's Day. As for his work, Jimmy had quickly become good friends with the members of the Indian Council and spent his days going from house to house to talk with people about the tribe's options. A core group of seven people emerged as the prime movers behind the incorporation of the tribal holdings and the creation of a business plan.

Soon the Indians saw beyond Jimmy's green-eyed Anglo appearance recognizing him as a kindred spirit, a brother. They accepted his Anglo looks as the Earthly cover for his spirit, which it was. At a community meeting held just after Julia and the kids left, the chief, a wise old man named Fred, impressed his beliefs on Jimmy. He had a fatalistic vision that the larger American culture would never cease trying to assimilate them and ultimately would obliterate them unless they created an economically vital endeavor to define and protect themselves. Despite Jimmy's fervent entreaties that he consider the oil option, Chief Fred had no interest in digging up his Mother Earth to suck her dry. Jimmy then tried to sell them on the idea of a casino, regaling the Council with tales of the spectacular wealth a casino called Foxwoods, owned by the Mashantucket Pequot Indians in Connecticut, was generating. Chief Fred disdained this idea also. Finally Chief Fred and the Council and Jimmy agreed to do a feasibility study on starting a business to grow medicinal herbs and flowers and trees. They gave Jimmy a list of the medicines they obtained from the wild and his job was to look into possibilities for mass production.

At a Council Meeting in late February Jimmy announced that he now understood the resources and desires of the Native peoples and their land and what they envisioned for their future in terms of economic independence. He said his next step was to go back east to do the research and he would come out to Arizona once a month to report on his progress.

Actually, Jimmy could have stayed and done the research right there on his computer. All the data he could find at the Harvard libraries he could also access on-line. The Indians knew that too but they also saw his predicament with Julia. They liked Jimmy and they liked Julia. The Council members agreed to Jimmy's plan and even offered to care for his house while he was gone. When Jimmy called Julia to tell her he was coming back, she was thrilled.

After a stop at his apartment to pick up some clothes, Jimmy went directly to Julia's house and to the kid's surprise and eventual consternation he never left except to take his monthly trips to Arizona for a few days.

The boys' polite behavior wore off quickly. When Jimmy was at work they begged Julia to make him leave, asking her why she let him live there.

Does he help you with your homework? She asked them.

Yes....

Does he say nice things about you that make you feel good?

Ya....

Does he take you places and take care of you when you're sick?

Ya....

Sounds like a pretty good guy to me. What's the problem?

Oh Ma, it was good with just us. I took care of things... Todd said in a tired tone.

I know you wish we were a happy family with your dad here but it didn't work. Remember how miserable we all were?

I wasn't miserable, Ma....

Neither was I... piped up Laramie.

I'm sorry, I'm so sorry I couldn't have done it better for you guys, Julia cried a little, softly, her elbows on the table, her hands covering her eyes.

It's all right Mom... really Mom, we know you try to make everything good.... Oh, Mom, sighed Laramie.

That was the end of the conversation about when Jimmy would leave. They all lurched a bit and then settled into a pattern of co-existing and sometimes having a good time together.

As he had promised, Jimmy took Julia and the kids to different synagogues on the Jewish high holidays and dragged them off to other Jewish celebrations he read about in the newspaper or saw on the internet. The kids complained. Julia tried to appreciate each new experience with a joyful attitude. She wanted to find a Jewish place where she felt comfortable.

Julia was a lousy cook. She could throw together yummy, gooey, cheesy, beany, ricey messes with spinach added at the last minute, but when confronted with a recipe she freaked. Nothing came out right. She tried to cook Jewish dinners on Friday nights but they weren't very good.

Jimmy often found himself telling them about Indian festivals and customs. Julia teased him. *You must have been an Indian in another life.*

Jimmy never referred to ABOVE, although it was difficult for him not to share his knowledge with Julia. They had become so close.

In May they decided to get married and Julia said she was open to the idea of having Jimmy's baby but she didn't know if it was possible. Jimmy sent the message up to Dinah, *come on down*. It made him very happy to think of having her company again. He realized that he already loved two souls. *I'm making progress!* He congratulated himself.

ABOVE

The Destiny Committee had told Dinah that as soon as she received the go ahead signal from Jimmy, she should ask Mick for descent instructions. She nearly flew to Reception and could barely contain her eagerness while waiting for the soul in line in front of her to finish talking with Mick.

Mick made the proper notations in his log book and told Dinah to inform her family group and then to proceed directly to the Infant Re-entry Information Site in corridor 7, next door to the Long Range Planning Department.

Dinah's joy was diminished slightly by her anticipation of the protests that her announcement would engender. She decided to tell the family members individually rather than make a group announcement.

James was happy for Dinah, although, of course sad because he would miss her company but he understood that this was a good opportunity for her. Iris was overwhelmed by the news. She radiated great waves of despair. Dinah assured her that her love for her was eternal and it was only a question of time before they would be reunited. She didn't suggest that Iris herself might want to return to Earth because she knew that Iris would never consider leaving James. Hugo was sad to hear of Dinah's imminent departure but supported her decision. Sonny got mad. He complained that he would be the only soul left on the site who had sufficient energy to oversee the family matters. He said it wasn't fair and that he hadn't even gotten a response from the Destiny Committee about his proposal. Dinah assured him that he would hear from them soon and that he shouldn't worry about having increased responsibility when she was gone. *After all, James ran the show singlehandedly for years and even though he is an old soul, you shouldn't confuse elderly souls with elderly Earthlings. James has immense storages of energy. And, if there does prove to be too much to do after I leave, you can always call a family member back from Surplus.*

Sonny was silenced but not cheered as his unhappiness lay chiefly in the fact that he wanted to return to Earth and was frustrated by the delay.

Amesbury was delighted to hear Dinah's news and wished her bon voyage. Dinah asked him if it was necessary for her to locate all the family members scattered throughout ABOVE and inform them of her imminent departure. He assured her that the news would be included in the General Announcements. Dinah was relieved, although she felt slightly guilty that she wasn't going to personally say goodbye to the family members ABOVE and to the many souls she had befriended. She was grateful that she wouldn't have to hear their inevitable responses. She had been a one-soul counseling agency and many in ABOVE had come to depend on her good advice.

After a final good-bye to James and Iris, Dinah made her way to the Infant Re-entry Office. She went up to the counter and identified herself and was given a card with a number on it. The reception area was large but almost every seat was taken. After a short wait, Dinah's number was called. She was led to a small cubicle by a soul wearing a tuxedo. He asked her a few questions that seemed designed to elicit any ambivalent feelings. Dinah's responses about her desire to return to Earth and in particular as a child of Julia and Jimmy were overwhelmingly positive. The soul, who introduced himself as Jeeves, acknowledged her positive attitude and explained that they now asked all potential returnees these questions to eliminate those who were less than sincere. Dinah was a bit confused about the process but he assured her that the video program she was about to see would explain all the details. She was instructed to go back to the waiting room.

A short while later a soul dressed in a nurse's uniform came into the room and announced that all those waiting to see the program should accompany her. Most of the souls got up and followed her into a small auditorium. The lights dimmed and the movie began. The narrator stated that in accordance with the new policy all candidates were now fully informed about the technology of being born again as it was hoped that to be informed was to take responsibility. He then described reproduction in the mature male and female and explained that a soul could take possession of the fetus anytime during the gestation period. However, it was recommended that the entry take place before the sixth month as it was important that the soul have an opportunity to view its future environment and become accustomed to the mother's personality. Also, there was a much higher incidence of pirating, fetuses being inhabited by pirates, when occupation was not accomplished by the last trimester. The most desirable time for habitation was right after conception. A full term residency by the soul gave the fetus increased protection and almost always insured a healthy body which was obviously a great advantage. Up to that point in the movie the illustrations were all cartoons. The next segment was a short film of real people. The voice-over described the actual process of a soul entering the fetus. The scene was a dark room with a close-up shot of a double bed in which lay a sleeping mother-to-be. The soul was sent down and after hovering above the sleeping woman for a moment it was projected into the fetus. The film showed a barely discernable fluttering over the woman's belly and then she heaved slightly and groaned and the narrator explained that the installation was complete. The narrator continued, *the recipient often feels a sharp momentary pain at the time of the occupation but it is usually not even enough to fully awaken her.*

The film went on to describe the do's and don'ts's of the re-entry process. It was stressed that after the installation the soul cannot leave for any reason unless total abandonment was desired. *There is no such thing as going out for lunch and returning later!* Any leave taking would result in miscarriage and obviously that was a serious step and upon return to ABOVE the soul would be required to make a satisfactory explanation as to why such a course of action had been taken. As to the sex of the fetus, the soul was given the choice if occupation was taken by the third month. After that a sex assignment would have been made by the Demographics Committee which advertised the empty fetuses on The Bodies Available Bulletin Board. Dinah recalled that she used to scan the board frequently to see if any of the situations piqued her interest. She remembered an ad that she had almost applied for, *FEMALE, FIRST CHILD OF HUNGARIAN REFUGEES NOW LIVING IN SWEDEN. BOTH PARENTS ARE CONCERT PIANISTS, CHILD WILL BE EXPECTED TO LOVE MUSIC AND PURSUE IT AS A CAREER.*

A change in the narrator's tone cut short Dinah's musings. He spoke very sternly. *We believe that proper prior surveillance of the life situation of your potential body should eliminate all last minute changes of heart. We do not condone miscarriages and we greatly frown upon Sudden Infant Deaths. Please souls, do your research!* There was a short musical interlude and then the narrator continued. *We would like to stress the advisability of early occupation.* There was a picture of what appeared to be a peacefully sleeping fetus in utero. *The pre-natal period is the only rest period a soul ever has and it is very beneficial just before the start of a new lifetime.*

In the last segment of the film the prospective Earthlings were instructed to remain in the auditorium after the presentation ended in order to contemplate their decision until they reached a state of certitude.

After a period of contemplation Dinah was even more eager to go BELOW to be Julia and Jimmy's child. When she got up to leave the auditorium she was stopped and briefly interviewed by a soul who identified herself as Camille. After the interview Julia was asked to sign a statement of intent. She was then put on a kind of subway car and transported to a place that was called the Garden of Eden. It was a site high in the Himalayas, a kind of mid point between ABOVE and BELOW, where souls took on most of the properties of life as a practice for fetal existence. It was a short stop as conception had already occurred in their chosen mothers and after a very brief stay they were sent on.

According to the regulations, Dinah should not have been sent to the Garden of Eden before Julia had conceived but her statement about having been given the go ahead signal was misinterpreted. When she arrived at the Garden the receptionist realized the error but it was decided that she should stay as all her good-byes had been said ABOVE and it was an unnecessary strain on the soul to flit back and forth between the different states.

Dinah enjoyed The Garden of Eden. It was a beautiful place as the name implied. There were lush flowers and blossoming trees, birds and chirping insects and perfume in the air. She thought each day there would be her last but every time she tuned in on Julia she found no host embryo.

In July Dinah sent down a message telling Jimmy that she had been standing by for three months and there was still no fertilized egg available. She concluded that the physical alteration caused by Julia's tied tubes must have to be physically fixed.

Jimmy, who by now had told Julia that he sometimes heard voices telling him what to do, relayed the message that she would have to have a surgical reversal of the tube tying before they could have a child. Julia had the surgery and although the surgeon said he could not guarantee the results, she got pregnant in late August.

They were going to services every week now and kept a kosher home. Julia had chosen to join an orthodox congregation. She said it had the most spirit and she had also started reading about Hasidim. She re-read an old New Yorker article that described daily life for Hasidim in Brooklyn. When she had first read it, years earlier, she thought the lifestyle was totally weird. Now she thought that the lifestyle made sense and it even appealed to her. When she found out that she was pregnant she became more zealous in her observances.

Of the children, only Laramie kept the pace. She and Julia attended Hebrew classes and complied with the rules of no talking on the phone, light switching, carrying an umbrella, or driving on the Sabbath. The boys thought their mother had gone insane and in early September they asked to move in with their father. Julia reluctantly agreed.

Jimmy went along with it all. He received a message from James thanking him and marveling at his accomplishment in terms of Julia's new piousness. Jimmy didn't take the whole thing too seriously as he believed that having a good life just required having a decent outlook.

Jimmy was so happy in his discovery of love that he was barely attending to his research or keeping up his contacts with the Indians. Their sex life became a little less vibrant once Julia was pregnant but he still reveled in their everyday closeness and especially loved the way they cuddled all night long while they slept. During his days in the Harvard libraries or at meetings with experts he yearned to be at home. Being with Julia became his total focus.

Jimmy received a couple of warnings from ABOVE. The first message was, *REMEMBER YOUR TASK, JIMMY. YOU ARE ONLY ATTENDING TO YOUR PERSONAL DEVELOPMENT!*

A couple of weeks later he was contacted again. *YOU MUST BRING SOME ENLIGHTENMENT TO THE GOAL OF PEACE IN THE WORLD. AFFILIATE!!!!*

To this message Jimmy responded, *I go to the synagogue every week!*

After a few weeks as members of Beth El Congregation, social contacts began to develop for them. However, besides announcements asking for donations for Israel, there seemed to be no organizing to help needy people locally. This puzzled Jimmy because he knew there were Jewish charitable organizations that helped people. He did get some advice about investments, but basically he concluded that the practice of Judaism at Beth El was highly personal, affecting one's own life and a shared ritual with those in one's chosen religious community.

The more Julia learned about Judaism the better she liked it. She enjoyed the rituals and the practice and especially loved that the world could be brought to a halt by the Sabbath. She found that she felt almost as good on the Sabbath as she had when she smoked pot. All day on Saturdays she would fantasize about her life and other people's lives. As she learned more about Hasidism she began to lobby Jimmy that they should become Hasidim. It struck her that Hasidic life was like a week full of Sabbaths. Every aspect of behavior was prescribed and one's life was entirely conducted in a small enclave.

Jimmy didn't mind anything Julia proposed but he did point out to her that he couldn't do his Indian project if they moved to Brooklyn. He would have to get a job in the diamond business and it didn't really interest him. Julia replied that the point was to live in the community and support the family. A job was just a means to the end of financing the family. She also said that they should try to have as many children as possible.

Soon after, Jimmy received his third warning. *YOU ARE ALLOWING YOURSELF TO FLOUNDER AND YOU ARE SUPPORTING JULIA'S ESCAPE INTO JUDAISM. REMEMBER WHY YOU WERE SENT DOWN!!!*

Jimmy tried to turn the tide. He ordered home delivery of the New York Times declaring with fervor that they should be informed of world affairs and find a way to influence things for the better. Julia calmly threw the papers away without reading them. She declared that success moved from the micro to the macro and if they could have a good family life it would follow that the world would be a better place. Jimmy countered, *I think we have to reach out to create change. It's not enough to be personally satiated.*

Julia argued, *it is more than enough to live a controlled religious life. After all, the Jews are the Chosen People and that means that by living as Jews we are fulfilling our role.*

I don't think so… Jimmy replied. He tried to explain that he felt that a chosen people would have a greater responsibility to try to change the world to improve conditions for all mankind. Julia appeared to be listening but at the end of his speech she pulled him down and pressed his ear against her belly. *Listen to your baby, Jimmy. Feel him move!*

Jimmy abandoned his thesis and with his ear propped against Julia's side he fell into a dreamless sleep.

18

The baby was born in an uneventful birth in mid May. It was a girl. They named her Deirdre. She was a beautiful and strong baby and when he looked into her eyes Jimmy could tell that it was Dinah. Now he not only wanted to be home as much as possible to be with Julia, he wanted to hold his baby. He had to drag himself away to go to his office and stayed at work for shorter and shorter days.

The Chief called to ask what was causing the delay. He and the other council members were eager to implement the plan. Jimmy's grant sponsor at Harvard was also calling to inquire about his progress. He commented that no one had seen Jimmy lately and his secretary said she wasn't getting any work from him. Jimmy made up some excuse to keep them all at bay but he told Julia that they had to make plans to move to Arizona immediately if she wanted to have a husband with a job. Otherwise, he was sure he would be replaced on the project. Julia said it was the will of God that he should get out of that work. She told him she had been in touch with a Rabbi Nachman in New York City and he wanted to talk to Jimmy about giving him a job in his family's diamond business. The rabbi would also help them get settled in Boro Park. Julia ended her speech with the eager statement, *we wouldn't have to worry about anything, Jimmy. There's a rule for the right way to do everything and we could stay in that tiny community safe for the rest of our lives!*

Although he didn't feel particularly drawn to the religious aspects, Jimmy gloried in the idea that he could spend most of his energy on loving Julia and Deirdre. He agreed to meet with Rabbi Nachman. At that moment Jimmy got a very loud message from ABOVE.

JIMMY CANTOR, THIS IS JAMES. YOU ARE NOT FULFILLING YOUR ASSIGNMENT! DROP THE JUDAISM. IT'S ONLY IMPEDING YOUR PROGRESS BECAUSE YOU ARE USING IT AS A SHELTER. JOIN THE CATHOLIC CHURCH IF YOU WANT A RELIGIOUS AFFILIATION. I NEVER THOUGHT I WOULD SAY THAT BUT THE CATHOLICS ARE MAKING GREAT PROGRESS IMPROVING CONDITIONS FOR THE POOR IN MANY COUNTRIES. OR BE AN AGNOSTIC BUT GET OUT THERE, I'M WARNING YOU!, THEY ARE CONSIDERING PUTTING YOU ON THE RECALL LIST!

Jimmy was horrified. He jumped when the loud voice came into his mind and throughout the transmission he stood at attention staring straight ahead. When he seemed to come out of it Julia asked him if he had gotten a message. She now accepted his claims that he heard voices telling him what to do. Jimmy nodded and said he was told that they should not be Jewish but should consider becoming Catholic as the Catholics were trying to improve conditions for all people. Julia was not pleased and told Jimmy that a message like that had to be from the underworld, from some kind of evil spirit. *It's just that we're so close to living the good life. This is a last attempt to throw us off.* Julia looked so beautiful sitting in the rocking chair nursing Deirdre that Jimmy was again drawn in and meekly murmured, *yes, dear.*

Later that evening Jimmy dropped off Laramie at her father's house and gassed up the car for their trip to New York the following day. They were going there to meet Rabbi Nachman and look at a house in the Boro Park section of Brooklyn. Around 10 o'clock another message from ABOVE came to Jimmy.

> ***YOU HAVE BEEN WARNED!***

He turned up the radio.

In the middle of the night there was a terrible thunder storm. Howling winds and waves of rain deluged the neighborhood. Jimmy and Julia and Deirdre snuggled in bed together. A lightning bolt struck the house. It traveled down the electric cable and started a fire. In a flash the bedroom was consumed and in that instant the three of them were killed.

ABOVE

The incredible pull, the pain, the blinding light, no breath…. Then, dropped in the field again.

Immediately upon opening his eyes Jimmy knew what had happened. He heard the tinny notes of the Star Spangled Banner and stared about in a panic. Behind him, about five feet away, he saw Julia, and Dinah was lying prone a little ways beyond her. She again had the middle-aged woman image she'd had when he met her in ABOVE. Jimmy lay back for a moment, relieved that they were all together and beyond that not wanting to be conscious. The others were not yet stirring.

Jimmy heard a tinkling of bells and then Florabelle's words. *You can cut the damn music, it's just Jimmy and Dinah and their ward.* She sounded disgusted. The music stopped mid phrase. Jimmy kept his eyes closed even though he knew it was a feeble defense. Florabelle wafted over to him and gave him a spiritual kick. *Come on, asshole. You really blew your fuses down there. The sex went right to your brain. Another conquest for that worthless wench.* She glared at Julia. *And look where it got you. I can't believe you turned up the radio to try to block our messages. You really are an asshole. Stop playing dead and get up!*

Julia was whimpering and muttering, *what happened? Where am I?* Then she saw Jimmy and cried out, *Jimmy, what happened? Where's our baby?*

Dinah answered, *here I am!* Julia looked over at her and when she saw a middle-aged woman she got even more confused and began to sob.

Florabelle was all business. She instructed Jimmy to report to the Destiny Committee. She told Dinah that she could return to Frenn's and assured her that nothing would be held against her because she had no power as their infant daughter and therefore no responsibility. The Destiny Committee had decided not to leave her down there as they knew she had gone BELOW to be with Jimmy and Julia. *They brought you back up so you could choose a new situation for your return to Earth.*

Florabelle then turned to Julia and informed her that a Junior Guide from Admissions would take her through the regular entry procedures. She added in an aggrieved tone, *don't be surprised if you're up here for a long stay as spiritual development for you while on Earth seems to be impossible. Not only have you impeded your own progress but Jimmy's as well.* Julia was horrified and confused. She called out to Jimmy, *don't leave me!* He started to go to her but Florabelle put a hold on him and said, *leave the bitch alone!*

Florabelle transported Jimmy to the entry of the Destiny Committee Chambers. Jimmy communed with her, begging her not to be so hard on Julia. *After all, she has shown me the power of love!*

Right, look what the power of love has wrought. Such power may bring about the end of the world! However, sensing that Jimmy was very distraught, Florabelle gruffly assured him that Julia would be well taken care of in Admissions and he would be able to see her after she was processed.

As he stood outside the doors to the Destiny Committee Chambers, Jimmy was overwhelmed by an understanding of what had happened. He felt really stupid to have botched his assignment so badly. He contemplated slinking away and hanging out at Sunset Productions but immediately realized that in ABOVE there was nowhere to hide. He sensed a spirit at his side and realized that one of the members of the Destiny Committee had come out to escort him into the chamber.

Back again so soon, old boy?

Jimmy nodded ineffectually, his image blurring momentarily. He was led to the central arena. He awaited instructions.

Have no fear, Jimmy. We are not angry with you, just a little disappointed. But we have learned something from your mishap down BELOW. The evolution of the social structure of the world has become clear to us through your experience so in essence you have been very helpful to us. We consider America to be the scene of the future. We expect the peoples in the rest of the world to act much like Americans if their industrial and economic development allows them to rise above the stresses of sheer survival. Of course, the potential for nuclear disaster may curtail any future but despite this peril we must anticipate. We now understand that the power of intimate love and the consequent satisfaction of personal drives in combination with a lifestyle of ease, can blind mankind to communal development.

Jimmy felt called upon to make some kind of explanation. *I guess I was a little overwhelmed with my personal development but if only you could have given me a little more time I'm sure I could have come to terms with the power of love and fulfilled my other duties.*

Perhaps, Jimmy, but it appeared that you were about to embark upon a course from which it would have been very difficult to extricate yourself and we didn't have more time to give you. We needed to have you function here ABOVE if not down BELOW. We are all nearly out of time.

What do you mean by that? The usual sense of awe that an interview with the Destiny Committee inspired was diminished by Jimmy's anger and shock at having been so suddenly plucked out of his Earth existence.

One of the judges countered Jimmy's aggressive tone with a forceful voice. *We are all in big trouble, all of us ABOVE and BELOW. We received a message from GOD, and I mean THE GOD, about whom we had only surmised in the past. HE is considering giving up on our planet Earth and making a new beginning elsewhere. Apparently HE now feels that the sum of our progress is negative, despite all of our efforts up here. The changes wrought by the rapid technological advances on Earth, combined with a world-wide increase in selfishness and greed, have created a likelihood of total death of the planet. HE acknowledged the many pockets of good progress in both individuals and communities but said that on balance the negative forces are triumphing. We were told that if a nuclear calamity occurs HE will not support an attempt to rebuild. We will be cut loose from HIM. HE will consider this experiment finished!*

Jimmy was horrified. He had never imagined that at a point in time it could be over. A basic premise had always been that you can have another try at it, both ABOVE and BELOW.

The judge heard Jimmy's thoughts. *All of us, Jimmy, are shocked as you are. None of us had any idea that this could happen. We believed absolutely in the infinity of existence. But in HIS first and probably last message we were told that our assumptions are wrong. Hopefully we can get the balance back to the positive and be able to continue onwards to infinity but there is a threat. I am sure you now understand why you were recalled. We don't have the time to tolerate the machinations of idle free will. Perhaps there will be time for that at some future point.*

Jimmy got it. He asked what he could do.

We have assigned you to Surveillance. You will be a soldier in a new sentry corps we have established to guard against nuclear destruction. Others will continue their guidance efforts with new found determination. I'm sure you will feel the change in attitude up here. No more complaining or laziness and idle gossip. We have all mobilized against a common enemy, GOD, who is so disturbed by what HE sees as to contemplate total abandonment. Some have said we could go on without HIS support and try to rebuild Earth after the destruction but that is an ignorant viewpoint. The rest of us realize that it could not be successful.

He was interrupted by another judge. *Actually, Tom Brown there doesn't represent the majority view. The general consensus is that we would certainly try to carry on. I'm on a new committee that is formulating a survival plan.*

Judge Tom Brown spoke again. *Of course none of us can calmly contemplate the end of our existence as we know it. However, I doubt that we can survive without GOD. In any event, we hope such an eventuality will not occur but I have told you this to impress upon you the need for excellence in every quarter.*

I understand, Sir, Jimmy said solemnly. *Where do I report to get trained for my new assignment?*

A chap named Ludwig has taken on the training of the guards. He has many lifetimes of being a spy and will teach you all you need to know about surveillance. So, Jimmy, welcome Home. Don't dwell on being a failure down BELOW. We only recalled you because the critical state of existence didn't allow us to grant you the time to straighten your path. Forward march, Jimmy. Carry with you in your tasks the new maxim given to us by the SuperAch, DO OR DIE. Death now has a meaning to us here that it never had before.

Thank you, Sir. Jimmy backed out of the room.

Jimmy had neglected to ask where Ludwig and the Guard Corps were located so he zoomed over to see Mick in Guidance Reception. There was a long line in front of his desk. Jimmy got on line and as he moved up he heard fragments of conversations. Mick seemed to be running a counseling service. He was analyzing the problems of the Earth person and asking poignant questions to help the Guide sort out his feelings and decide what would be the most productive course of action. Jimmy looked back and saw that the line had grown to twice the length that it had been when he joined it.

When Jimmy finally reached the head of the line, he said to Mick, *I've never seen a line this long in front of your desk before.*

Mick explained that all souls in ABOVE were aware of the critical situation and were doing their max to influence their Earth people to positive action. *It's like a new place up here, all work and no play. I haven't watched cartoons in a long time!* Jimmy could tell that even Mick was worried. He asked him, *did GOD speak to you directly, or what?*

Mick glanced at the line behind Jimmy and said he didn't have much time to explain but basically what had happened was that things were normal. A lot of souls were returning from a lottery drawing. There was a soccer game going on and everyone was kibitzing as usual when suddenly it got totally dark. *You could not see a thing and a voice was heard. It was a voice that seemed to originate inside of each soul. It said that much of the Earth seemed to be going from bad to worse and if Earth people had a nuclear war it would be interpreted as the ultimate operation of free will to the end of total destruction. In that case there would be no point in continuing and other experiments in the universe would be supported.*

Jimmy couldn't help himself and asked, *how did you know it was GOD?*

Oh jeez, Jimmy, we knew! Who the hell else do you know who can pull the plug on everything including the sky? It was pitch black! You couldn't even see the halos on the little children! Look, all these people need to talk with me. Come back later.

Jimmy asked where he could find Ludwig and was told that a training camp had been set up behind the Admissions sector. Jimmy wafted off to Admissions and suddenly remembered Julia. Even though the DO OR DIE directive had taken over his consciousness and made him feel compelled to rush to his new assignment in order to do his bit to save the world, he decided to take a small detour to see how Julia was faring.

A huge white banner hung over the entrance to Admissions with the words DO OR DIE painted on it in very large purple block letters. Jimmy explained to the receptionist that he was looking for a recent arrival named Julia Montage. He was directed to the fifth cubicle on the left.

He found Julia alone. She was sitting in a rocking chair viewing an orientation video entitled, LIFE IN ABOVE. She looked to be barely integrated. Her image was a mass of vibrant flashes. When she saw Jimmy she rose unsteadily from her chair. She was still trying to send impulses to a non-existent body so she moved jerkily. She tried to talk, having not yet grasped that thinking was sufficient for communication. Her utterances were garbled but after a minute Jimmy understood the gist of it and could tell that she was very angry. He told her to just think what she wanted to communicate and he would receive it. She was a quick learner and it came through loud and clear.

YOU BASTARD!! Meeting you was the worst thing that ever happened to me! Now I'm dead! What are my children supposed to do without a mother? And where is my poor baby? Why did that idiot old woman say she was my baby Deirdre? What are you going to do about this, you bastard! You better get me out of here and back where I belong and then I never want to see you again!

Jimmy felt terrible. She was right. If she hadn't met him she would still be on Earth, probably not being very productive but at least alive. She was only brought up because she was with him. He felt an unbearable weight of pain and sorrow. He didn't know what to do.

Julia awkwardly moved around the little room trying to pick up things to throw at him. She tried to lift up the rocking chair but had no coordination or strength. She was in such a rage that she seemed to be beyond communication. She stumbled around the room emitting a low growl.

An Admissions Guide appeared in the doorway and asked if Julia had finished the video. He noticed her frazzled state and saw Jimmy sitting in the corner. Julia tried to get out the open door but the Guide stopped her. She collapsed on the floor and wailed. The Guide asked Jimmy, *what happened? A few minutes ago she was confused but compliant.* Suddenly the Guide recognized Jimmy as having been a Senior Guide in Admissions. He said it couldn't be more of a godsend as Julia obviously needed help. He then asked who had sent Jimmy to the room.

Jimmy could barely express himself and felt far from able to be helpful. He told the Guide that there was more help needed than he could give. The Guide began to question him, reminding Jimmy that he could handle anyone in his days of working in Admissions. Meanwhile, Julia was half talking, half communing, *you bastard, you bastard....*

After waiting a moment for some helpful response from Jimmy but getting none, the Guide slipped out the door saying he would bring a Supervisor. Julia was having a tantrum and trying to kick the wall. The flashes around her image had turned into whirls of light.

The Guide returned with another soul, a grandmotherly type wearing a long skirt and a shawl. Julia was still flailing around on the floor. The Supervisor sent out a flow of calming vibes that even crossed the room to Jimmy and he felt unburdened enough to lift his head. The lady introduced herself saying her name was Lillia and she had come to help. Julia was somewhat soothed by the vibes and began to tell her what had happened. The telling of it immediately got her upset and angry again and after a few moments Lillia stopped her, saying that she already knew all about it. She asked Julia to get up and sit in a chair so they could discuss the options. Hearing this, Julia complied, hopeful that her fate could be altered.

Lillia told Julia that she was brought up with Jimmy because she was a powerful and old soul. It was not a question of just being at the wrong place at the wrong time. *The world as we know it, Earth, is in a crisis. You are needed ABOVE to give guidance to those BELOW in order to avert the ultimate destruction, to make sure that your children do inherit the world, that there still is a world....*

What are you talking about? What about my children now? It is a crisis for them to lose their mother!

Lillia agreed but asked Julia to contemplate the situation on a less personal level. Hearing that, Julia blew her fuses again. She tried to yell that Lillia was obviously not a mother or she wouldn't make such a stupid statement. Lillia responded that she would like to demonstrate to Julia how she could greatly contribute to the survival of the world and make major progress in her personal growth. *But first we have to deal with your feelings about losing your children in this lifetime.* Julia interrupted again asking if one option was that she could go back down to BELOW. Lillia said, *perhaps, but I don't recommend it.* She gently communed that Julia seemed to be quite stuck in the excesses of the sensual and was not making any progress down there. Julia just looked furious and miserable. Lillia led her to the Viewing Center to see her last life scene. The operator punched in the appropriate code and Laramie, Todd, and Elias came into view on the screen. They were having dinner with Harvey and Nancy. The kids seemed sad, especially Laramie, but they also seemed to feel secure and to be well taken care of. Harvey happened to be discussing money, his favorite topic. *All the money that was coming to your mother from the lottery win will not be awarded because of her death but there is enough insurance money for you to attend colleges with no scrimping. After your mother's house is sold we will use the money to buy a large, comfortable house and Nancy and I are going to be married so you will have a stepmother and can feel that your lives have some stability. I'm not trying to replace your mother with Nancy, that would be impossible, but I just want you to know that both Nancy and I are here for you as parents.*

    Laramie went over to stand next to Nancy and after a moment accepted Nancy's offer to sit on her lap even though she was quite big for a lap. Nancy had a kind expression on her face. Harvey suggested that the boys do their homework. The boys said good night and left the room and Laramie asked Nancy to tuck her into bed. Nancy seemed happy to comply. Julia watched the scene and slowly stopped all her agitated quaking and sat in stunned silence. The scene on the screen was now Harvey sitting alone at the table, sipping his after-dinner coffee. The operator gently asked, *is there anything else you'd like to see?* After a moment Julia shook her head and communed, *I guess they will be fine. I guess I'm the one that needs to be with them.* She became agitated again and tried to talk to Lillia. *Why did you say that perhaps I could go back? They have accepted that I'm dead. Are you saying I could be raised from the dead?*

    Lillia continued to send her soothing vibes. *No, no, I only meant that if you truly could not adjust here because you felt you had to assist your current*

Earth children, we could consider sending you down as a Walk-In to be near them as a family friend or a teacher, something like that.

Julia was offended. *I don't want to be their teacher, or some family friend. I'm their MOTHER!!*

Lillia was gentle but clear. *I hope you have seen that they are in good hands and should grow and develop well. You certainly can be extremely helpful by guiding them from here and as I said before, be ultimately most helpful as one more soul working for the continuance of planet Earth.*

Julia had been feeling the ebb and flow of anger. It rose again and she snappishly communed, *what's this crap about the destruction of the planet? I don't get it. What's going on here?*

Lillia put an arm around her. Her clearly shimmering image touched Julia's flashing arm and her energies flowed into Julia. They wafted away together.

Jimmy felt released for the moment but then the ominous feeling returned so he headed off to find Ludwig and the Guardian Corps and told himself he would check on Julia later.

19

As he wafted through the corridor behind the Admissions Department, Jimmy heard loud commands. *LEFT, RIGHT, LEFT, RIGHT....* Coming out into the open he saw a strange scene. There was a drill exercise going on. All manner of souls were wafting about in an attempt at marching formation, souls arrayed in flowing dresses, ballet outfits, athletic uniforms, nurse's whites and even a man in a red velvet smoking jacket. *HUP TWO THREE FOUR....* Jimmy struggled to squelch a snicker.

A big guy in the image of a German First World War soldier, pointed helmet and all, was giving orders. He stood just below Jimmy at the bottom of a short flight of stairs. He apparently heard Jimmy's snicker because he suddenly stopped giving orders and turned to glare up at him. *I would appreciate it if you would not express negative opinions. Are you unaware of the state of peril?*

No, I have been told and I'm here to help... to enlist.

Fine, but you must clear your mind of that judgmental debris. We are engaged in a holy crusade and we can suffer no laggards. I have decided to give the

Corps some initial military training to achieve the optimal level of discipline. Top form is essential. A lot of detailed technical instructions will follow. Fall in!

Jimmy marched along with the rest and soon viewed himself as a cog in a large and efficient machine.

Ludwig divided the Earth into eight equal segments and organized the Corps into eight teams. Schedules were arranged to insure that no zone would ever be left unmonitored. Each team member was responsible for an eight hour shift of the Earth day. Jimmy was assigned the afternoon to midnight shift in Western Europe.

They were instructed on the safe operation of nuclear reactors and how to detect movement of nuclear armaments. In between classes they chanted a disarmament mantra. They directed it to the soldiers who handled the weapons.

> *No one can win a nuclear war. You will kill your parents and your children. Resist and disobey so that life on Earth can continue. You will be a hero to God.*

In a matter of days the impact of the Disarmament Mantra could be discerned. All over the world soldiers began to organize to prevent the use of nuclear weapons. The effect was particularly noticeable in the former Soviet Union. Even immoral businessmen trying to make a buck selling off missiles to rogue nations seemed slowed in their tracks. News stories from around the world reported tales of soldiers hearing voices. Many said it seemed to be the voice of God cautioning mankind to prevent annihilation.

Military leaders began to decry the signs of anarchy developing in the ranks. Ludwig called a meeting of the Corps and announced that the mantra had to be chanted more widely so it could be heard by generals and government leaders as well. The outcome of this phase was not universally positive. Some generals and world leaders immediately proclaimed that they had uncovered a conspiracy. Within a week, numerous bulletins announced that some peace terrorists inspired by the Communists, the Imperialists, the Nazis, the Muslims, the Jews, and so on, depending on which side was proclaiming, had sabotaged closely guarded military installations.

Ludwig concluded that they must be ever vigilant but could only depend on the rationality and good judgement of the common man. Jimmy suggested that they invent a deadly disease and infect all the top officials of governments thus giving the more sensitive and reasonable underlings the power. Ludwig pointed out that upon their promotion they too would fall under the spell of ego. History had demonstrated that power corrupts.

All of the souls in ABOVE worked tirelessly to try to influence their Earth persons to do good deeds. In recognition of the perilous state of existence the SuperArch lifted the formerly very restrictive rules on the use of guilt. The commandment making it a sin to overwhelm an Earth person's free will was eliminated. The SuperArch explained this change by saying that although it was still the ultimate goal that each soul evolve to the point where he or she made unselfish choices, the present situation required action.

There wasn't much fun in ABOVE anymore. Much of the Guidance work was now just sending down heavy doses of guilt. Passing by any group made the changes obvious, *make her feel bad about it*, or, *keep him up all night feeling guilty*, were representative comments. There were no more delicate assessments of values, careful considerations of alternative paths or gentle offerings of glimpses of opportunities to Earthlings. Instead, criticisms were heard constantly and punishments were righteously doled out. No guide wanted <u>his</u> Earth people to act badly and risk being blamed if GOD turned away from them all. An animosity was created between Guides and their Earth people.

However, there were some good results BELOW. The peace movement grew in every country. In some parts of the world, corporations and wealthy individuals began to use their excess assets to set up programs for the disadvantaged. Millionaires adopted whole classrooms of poor children and gave them counseling and the promise to finance their future educations. Billionaires gave money to improve health care for all poor people. And some countries instituted land redistribution programs so that even the poorest peasants could have a small piece of land to call their own.

People on Earth were generally acting better. After this regime had been in place for a while there was widespread consensus ABOVE that the Ultimate Disaster would be averted. It was assumed that since the sum of good deeds in the world had greatly increased, GOD would be impressed and consider Earth to still be an experiment worthy of HIS continued participation.

Under the auspices of Ludwig's exacting oversight and precise scheduling, the surveillance activities went well. Due to immediate detection of a problem and transmissions to those in charge to perform corrective actions, a disaster was averted about once a week. On one shift Jimmy detected increasing heat in a reactor in France and had to send down a violent nightmare to wake up the manager and make him check the system and bring it back to normal operation.

Every week, on Earth time Sundays, the Guardian Corps met to discuss the prior week's happenings on Earth in order to share information about disaster prevention. A weekly incident was always the case and sometimes two. It amazed them all that the world had survived thus far without more nuclear reactor accidents like Chernobyl. Most of the problems were with reactor malfunctions but the huge stockpiles of missiles were disasters just waiting to happen. The Pakistanis were going around the world trying to buy missiles and the Russians were discovered installing missile delivery systems in Cuba again and the Iranian's seemed to be involved in that caper also. This threat was escalated when due to mishandling, one of the weapons was activated and if not for very quick thinking on the part of the guard ABOVE, Washington, D.C., would have been obliterated.

That week, long discussions were held at the Sunday meeting debating whether the American government should be alerted to the recent missile installations in Cuba. Some argued that an intense dream should be sent to the Secretary of State. The SuperArch was called in for a consultation. It was decided that the Corps role was only to monitor and to perform corrective actions when faced with imminent emergencies. They would not become involved in politics. The frequent incidents filled the guards with a sense of foreboding and awe. There was no absenteeism or inattention while on duty. Jimmy had to acknowledge that GOD was right. Earth suicide was now a reality.

After long discussions and many waftings around the periphery with Julia, Lillia was able to convey to her the critical situation faced by the Earth people and those ABOVE. She then helped Julia review her past lives so she could put her last Earth life in perspective. Julia recalled that her children in this life had accompanied her on life journeys many times before and that they were not wholly dependent on her presence for their survival. This insight made her feel momentarily better. A further realization was that she had been destined to become a powerful personage in the public domain in her last lifetime but had spent her power strictly in the realm of the personal. When Julia recognized this she questioned Lillia. *How could one thwart one's destiny?*

Lillia explained that the power of free will, prior to the current emergency, had always been held in sacrosanct regard as true evolution of a soul was only accomplished through enlightenment gained from self chosen paths. Julia had been holding herself back for some reason. Perhaps the reason would become clear to her after further thought. *Now that you have understood the why of your return to ABOVE, you will be given a short period for a reunion with your family group and then you must report to the Religious Education Office.*

Although Julia was gradually regaining awareness of her prior existences, so much had been reorganized in ABOVE that she found herself quite disoriented. Lillia dropped her off at the gates to Guidance. After hovering there and surveying the scene for a few minutes, Julia decided to ask the guy at the desk for directions to her family group. She had always loved eavesdropping so she didn't mind her slow progress in line. It gave her a chance to listen in on many conversations. She murmured to herself, *that guy behind the counter looks like some kind of jerk! What's with the Mouseketeers hat?* However, after listening to him advise the soul in front of her, Julia concluded that he was weird but wise. Her turn came. She stood in front of him and waited for his attention. He looked up and when she did not immediately launch into a tale of woe about an Earth person in her charge, he inquired, *what can I do for you?*

Julia told him she was a new arrival and was assigned to the Religious Studies Department. Mick said she didn't need to register with him but should report directly to her department. He told her to go back out the gate and down the path on the right and she would see a sign directing her to the Religious Studies Department.

Julia remarked that she liked his mouse outfit. She didn't really mean it but she wanted to say something nice. Mick warmed up to her. It was rare for him to receive a personal comment as all his contacts with souls were as a functionary. This was especially true now that the DO OR DIE regime had begun. So even though she was insincere, he still enjoyed the attention and reciprocated by offering her the opportunity to change her image.

Julia contemplated the idea and decided to go for it. She asked for the image of a young woman, eighteen to twenty, and to be tall and blonde and blue-eyed and gorgeous and as an afterthought she asked him to throw in a hat with long, white, furry rabbit ears.

Mick muttered approvingly when he heard the request for rabbit ears. He made the proper notations and then flicked a switch and a fog descended around her. She emerged tall, blonde, and gorgeous. The rabbit ears hat added some humor to her image and endeared her permanently to Mick. If it hadn't been for the souls jostling in the ever increasing line behind her he would have loved to schmooze but he had to move on to his next supplicant. He gave her directions to the Frenn site.

Julia wafted along the grid to reach F-2. She noticed the hum of intense busyness in the air. But occasionally someone said hello to her and she got a few appreciative comments about her rabbit ears hat. At the intersection of F and 2 she stared at the groups of souls and at first they all looked like strangers but then she recognized James Frenn. He was wearing the same baggy gray suit and blue shirt she remembered him in as her grandfather when she was a little girl. Next to him was a man wearing flowing Grecian robes. Julia approached slowly, studying the other souls gathered at the site and suddenly she recognized Dinah. In the first flash of recognition she saw her as the soul who had said she was her baby Deirdre and that caused a stab of irritation but then she suddenly saw that it was Dinah, her beloved mother in this last Earth life whom she had missed so intensely since her death twenty-five Earth years earlier. Julia forgot her transposed condition and tried to run to Dinah but her legs wouldn't cooperate, forcing her to remember her newly altered state. She communed in a shout, *Dinah, Mama,* and wafted towards her with all the speed she could muster. Dinah turned to her and welcomed her with open arms. Their hug was not very satisfying as the image is vacuous and can't convey any feeling but the contact of the souls was still gratifying to them both. Julia communed how much she had missed Dinah and then suddenly it all made sense to her. Dinah had come back to Earth as Deirdre. Dinah indicated that it was true and Julia suddenly felt overwhelmed by the Earthly desire to cry about the opportunity that had been and was now gone. Dinah comforted her by reminding her that they were together now. She reintroduced Julia to the family members, all of whom she had known in her Earth lives as well as in her existences ABOVE.

After welcoming Julia, Sonny triumphantly announced that he was being sent down to do the task that neither she or Jimmy had been able to accomplish. He was going to be a Drop-In and would be given an assistant professorship at the Massachusetts Institute of Technology so he could invent and market the water filter made of the white of egg. Sonny was doubly excited about his assignment because his former brother Daniel was now living in Boston and would be about the same age. Sonny planned to become fast friends with him and through this friendship he hoped to be able to see his parents again. Julia and Dinah wished him Godspeed.

Julia was assigned the job of directing the Love and Compassion Curriculum. She was to design messages to inspire the Earth's clergy, all the priests, rabbis, and holy men of whatever denomination and persuasion. Lillia assured her that the job would tap her great know-how and interest in the machinations of love and would also challenge her to fulfill her karma and become effective in the public domain. Her task was to guide the religious in bringing their flocks to constructive action for the betterment of mankind. The assignment sounded a bit overwhelming to Julia but then the idea of the absolute end of the world also sounded overwhelming so she determined to do her best.

Julia's job turned out to be very time consuming and difficult. She had to intensely scrutinize every priest, rabbi and holy man of whatever sect and use her well developed sensitivities to analyze each individual ego and create a strategy to influence the person to develop leadership abilities. At the same time she had to fill him or her with genuine feelings of being intensely loved and with the overwhelming desire to love others. Her assignment was no less than personally introducing the Being of God as Love to the world's holy folk.

The tailoring of love to fill niches in individual psyches was familiar territory to Julia but she wasn't used to the endless giving and no receiving. She ruefully realized that this assignment would probably cure her obsession with the vagaries of love. She felt bereft without male admirers but at least she did not feel pinched with unfulfilled desires as the spiritual state had no arena for the experience of the sensual. She had almost no interest in Jimmy.

In fact, seeing him prompted a flash of irritation because she blamed him for her last demise.

Jimmy, on the other hand, was still in love with Julia. His love for her was born in ABOVE. The added sensual dimension he gained when he went BELOW to join her was extra icing on the cake. He had come to love her while in the spirit state and now once again in the spirit state, he still loved her. Julia found him a bother.

Dinah loved them both. She had no specific assignment upon her return to ABOVE but was given the choice to stay or to return to Earth. She contemplated the idea but soon word got out that she was back and her time was filled with many requests for help from family groups ranging from A to Z across the wide expanse of Guidance. She had a reputation for being able to contrive unique plans to help troubled Earthlings. Her strategies were nearly always successful. Soon the line of souls waiting to confer with Dinah was almost as long as the line of souls waiting to see Mick. As always, she thrived on helping others.

Jimmy had spells of sadness about not being able to fulfill his Earthly destiny. The fact that the current situation made it uncertain whether he would ever have the chance added to his depression. He went back to working part time at Sunset Productions but nothing really filled the lonely void within him. He vowed that if the current crisis passed he would immediately put in a request to go BELOW and try his hand again at love and family. This hope sustained him somewhat.

As with any state of emergency, except of course those in which blood and gore are a constant factor, after a while the sense of urgency cannot be sustained. The message from GOD wasn't forgotten but the fear diminished as time went by. Almost all souls were faithful in the execution of their duties but pockets of ease and relaxation could again be seen. The weekly lottery drawings were resumed and the little groups of card players reappeared. However, the feeling was far from that of old times. A hard attitude had replaced the former outlook of generosity and ease. A lot of manipulation was going down in the name of good deeds and this new mode of operation was having a bad effect on those ABOVE.

The belief that Earth people naturally tend towards positive evolution and only need a little protection and help, disappeared when permission was given to manipulate and overwhelm an Earth person's value system. The respect was gone and all regard for process was abandoned. The goal became the count of good deeds. The higher the count the more righteous the Guide felt. He could assure himself and others that if they **were** abandoned by GOD, it certainly wasn't his fault.

A pervasive feeling of distrust grew among the souls in Guidance. They suspected each other and were constantly trying to discern dishonesties. ABOVE became a somewhat wretched place with souls now quite stiff in their righteousness. The warmth was gone.

With the emphasis on statistical outcomes, there were new rules. The SuperArch became a businessman interested in output. As the Chief Executive Officer he was preparing to give a progress report to GOD. Now every guide had to keep case records and constantly fill out reports delineating the progress of his Earth charges. The Earthlings were given daily scores ranging from 1, which indicated no progress, to 10, which represented major growth. They were rated in numerous areas such as: personal behavior, public behavior, community improvement efforts, expressed attitudes, and unselfish acts.

New maxims were circulated. Banners flew over doorways and graced corridors. IT TAKES A 10 TO SAVE THE WORLD was a popular one and also, MAKE MORE HISTORY, MAKE 10'S. A Best Sayings Contest was established with the winner promised a trip to The Pines. The Pines was the name of the SuperArch's dwelling. It was rumored to have a huge bowling alley in which the thunder storms of Earth were created and to also have a giant maze that only the most advanced souls could navigate.

Being a Guard and thus not responsible for personal Guidance of any Earthlings and therefore not engaged in a competition for points, Jimmy could see the ugliness of what was developing around him. Also, being a jungle boy and attuned to intuitive reception, he could tell that they were on the wrong track to salvation. Jimmy was one of the few souls who was not surprised by the next blackout.

It happened just after Jimmy got off his shift and was on his way to visit Florabelle. A total darkness descended on ABOVE. Souls shrieked and screamed. The voice resounded from within.

NO, NO, NO! STOP MAKING THOSE RIDICULOUS REPORTS FULL OF TENS, AWAKEN YOURSELVES! YOU ARE BECOMING AS BLIND AND NARROW-MINDED AS THOSE EARTHLINGS BELOW. MY PATIENCE IS RUNNING OUT!

Slowly it became light again. There was an eerie silence. Every soul seemed lost in thought or shock, and then the general reaction seemed to be, *now what?* Following that reaction came a flood of personal defenses and even some angry accusations. *What does HE mean? Blind and narrow-minded? My Henry has collected over forty thousand dollars for needy children!* Another was heard to say, *My Sheila has single-handedly organized an entire city to clean up toxic wastes!*

However, many souls realized that they had been on the wrong track. Evidence of statistical successes was not going to impress the Supreme Being. A mood of depression descended upon ABOVE and as with any depression, less and less was accomplished. This was evidenced by a plethora of disasters on Earth. Car accidents increased dramatically as did all mishaps and the nightly news reflected a great rise in acts of violence. The guides ABOVE just weren't paying enough attention.

On Earth the phenomenon of increased problems, both accidental and premeditated, resulted in a lessening of faith in the established systems and the insecurity that accompanied that gave rise to the proliferation of more primitive belief systems. Astrologers and psychics were besieged and a few clever entrepreneurs made quick millions selling lucky charms. The first mass item was the rabbit's foot. Within a few months, despite protests from animal lovers, there could hardly have been a rabbit on Earth who was still in possession of four feet. Every citizen had at least one rabbit's foot in his pocket.

Another trend started when the Nightly News featured a young woman whose child had been diagnosed with a particularly virulent form of Leukemia. The mother bought a cat to keep her son company and the cat was apparently very affectionate and spent all day and night cuddling with the ill child. Miraculously, a month later the doctor found the child to be completely cured and the mother swore it was the cat that had healed him.

Other tales of cats attending miraculous happenings poured into television stations and filled the print media. There was an immediate rush for every household to have a cat. Cat paraphernalia became a big industry overnight: cat beds, cat toys, cat clothes for winter in cold climates, and gourmet cat foods. As with every run on the market, the supply of cats was unequal to the demand. Therefore, the next turn of events was cat kidnapping. When this affected even the rich and famous, police departments became involved and private detective agencies devoted themselves to cat protection and the return of stolen cats.

Photographers, who had formerly limited their clientele to famous or at least well-heeled personages, began to photograph cats. Many a family portrait was moved from over the fireplace and replaced by a large framed glossy of Tigger.

20

Jimmy's eight hour shift in the Guard Corps left him with a lot of free time. As Julia's Guide, he had been on the monitor at least fifteen Earth hours a day so he was used to having a consuming assignment. He asked Ludwig to assign him a second shift but he said it wasn't allowed. *One must be hyper alert and that state cannot be sustained for more than eight hours*, he bellowed. Jimmy knew it was useless to argue with him.

Small talk didn't come easily to Jimmy so he wasn't having much success making new friends. Dinah was his only real friend and she was so busy that they couldn't spend much time together. Jimmy had hoped that after her anger faded, Julia would become his companion. He was totally in love with her but she continued to avoid him. He hung around with Amesbury and Florabelle but they didn't want to go BELOW again so he couldn't fantasize with them about another lifetime. He often tuned in on Julia's kids and even on Mimi and sent down helpful vibes but he still felt useless, dead. Finally he decided that he should adopt an Earth person, someone who really needed him. He went to apply at Surplus. He was interviewed and his motives were determined to be sincere but when he mentioned his assignment in the Guardian Corps he was told that he couldn't adopt an active person because his charge would be left vulnerable for the eight hours a day that Jimmy was on duty. His only option was to pick someone from the Inactive Files. He was directed to a back room full of old scrapbooks. Each page detailed an available Earthling.

Jimmy loved looking through the scrapbooks. It soothed his soul. Handwritten entries and faded photographs filled the pages. The basic data: name, birthdate, locale, and other fundamentals had been put on disc but the homier facts only existed in the old scrapbooks. For instance, Pearl Brownley's favorite holiday was May Day, and Norman Lathof's joy in life was growing colorful gourds. It hadn't been thought worth the time to transfer the information. The assumption was that the people in the scrapbooks were nearly dead and would just die quietly with no further assistance needed.

After guard duty Jimmy went back to the Inactive Files Room and looked through a few more scrapbooks. Occasionally he tuned in on a person. Most of them were living nearly imperceptible lives, just creeping along, getting older and older. Some were in nursing homes and some lived with relatives who on a decency continuum ranged from nasty to nice. He decided to skim through the cases until he got to one that really struck him as needing a guide. Turning the torn and yellowed pages made him momentarily forget the highly mechanized and no longer pleasant world ABOVE.

On one of his visits to the Inactive Files Room, Jimmy read a case on a day that happened to be the person's birthday so he took the time to tune in on the monitor and sang her a fair rendition of Happy Birthday. The old lady was alone in a small grubby room in a welfare hotel in New York City. It was her eighty-sixth birthday. She heard Jimmy's song loud and clear and thought it was her mother and father coming to greet her on her birthday. She cried in happiness and called out, *I'm a comin', I'm a comin'....* Even this brief connection made Jimmy feel happy and strengthened his commitment to the search for a good prospect to adopt. He glanced over each page, especially the ones with photographs. He stared at the faces and could usually get a sense of the soul of the person. He was very drawn to a woman named Gertrude McTeal. A kindness radiated from her eyes that was even discernable in the small, faded photograph. After reading her specs Jimmy went on but felt pulled back to her each time he turned a page so he went back and gazed at her photo again. Her birth date was April 2, 1913. If she was still alive she would be eighty-seven years old. He realized that the odds were that she was senile and in an old folks home and he wouldn't be able to do more than just send her loving vibes but he couldn't get her out of his mind so he tuned her in on the monitor.

She was still quite alive. The picture that came up on the screen showed her sitting at a table reading a book. Her face looked the same as it had in the little picture even though the photo was twenty years old. As he watched, she adjusted her granny glasses and turned the pages of the book. Every few moments a blurry line moved across the screen. Jimmy went to a wide shot and could then see that the blurry line was a cat's tail. A cat was walking back and forth across the table, stopping momentarily in front of Gertrude so she could run her hand over its back.

Behind the old lady Jimmy could see a bed covered by a multicolored patchwork quilt and a window framing a view of trees. There were small braided rugs scattered on the floor and scrutinizing the walls, Jimmy realized that it was a log cabin. Through a door he could see another room with a big black cookstove.

Gertrude got up. She had a slight hobble but otherwise moved freely. She walked across the room and threw a couple of logs into the wood stove and then came back to the table. *Well, I guess it's time for supper,* she murmured. Jimmy was startled to hear her speak as he had somehow surmised that she lived alone. He adjusted the scope so he could follow her into the kitchen. He watched her as she stood by the counter making supper. Suddenly he realized that the sounds he heard in the background were meows and moving the scope so he could see the floor he had a view of many cats. The floor was covered with cats. The chorus of meows got louder. *Now, now, just hold your horses. It's almost ready.* Gertrude muttered. She stooped down and put a big pan of food on the floor. The chorus of meows was silenced immediately. Gertrude then went over to the stove and served herself some soup from a big black cast iron pot. She ate bread and soup and rocked and hummed as the room darkened around her.

Gertrude's life was so calm and slow, it was contagious. Jimmy felt better than he had in a long while. When it was time for him to go to work, he vowed to return later and tune in on her again.

From then on, Jimmy spent a lot of his free time watching Gertrude. He discovered that she lived alone, or actually with no other people, but with about fifteen cats, in a log cabin on a mountain road in New Hampshire. She took care of all her needs: chopped wood to feed her stoves, climbed up on the roof and shoveled off snow when it got too deep and heavy, and did everything else that needed to be done. One day a week she baked bread and on another day she did her laundry, washing the clothes in the tub and hanging them in the kitchen to dry by the big cookstove. Jimmy wondered how she got her groceries and other supplies but then he heard her mention that she wanted to get some peanut butter the next time Dottie took her shopping. He learned a lot about her life by listening to her talk to the cats. She had a running conversation going with them most of the time. They responded with meows. Everyday, in mid afternoon, after her nap, Gertrude went for a walk no matter what the weather. A trail of cats followed her.

It was beautiful in the mountains. There was a river next to the cabin and the sky was always lovely whether the day was cloudy or clear. It got to the point where Jimmy spent all of his free time on the monitor watching Gertrude. If she was asleep, he watched the cats.

Jimmy soon decided that he wanted to officially adopt Gertrude so he could legally intervene in her life. In actual fact he came more and more to believe that she had a perfect life and any intervention would be criminal but he wanted to have an official sense of belonging to her. He went to the Surplus Office to inquire about the specifics of the adoption procedure.

The sign above the door to Surplus Guidance read, ADOPT AN EARTHLING, CHANGE THE WORLD. Jimmy told the clerk behind the counter that he had picked someone and was ready to go ahead with the adoption process. He gave Gertrude's name. The clerk instructed him in the simple procedure. It was definitely a buyer's market. Surplus was teeming with unassigned Earth persons. The clerk went off to get Gertrude's file but soon came back and asked Jimmy incredulously, *hey man, why did you pick her? She's just some old bag living off in the woods. She doesn't need any help. Is this some kind of joke?*

Jimmy quickly explained that he couldn't take on a more active person as he was in the Guardian Corps but he did want to have some family on Earth to watch over.

The adoption was quickly processed and Jimmy went to a monitor and greeted Gertrude officially. He sent down the *I love you* message that he used to send to Julia only this time the feeling was familial not sexual. Gertrude stopped her chatter to the cats for a moment and stood quietly looking out the window towards the river. Jimmy could see a tear sliding down her old cheek. Then she seemed to regain her spirit and said, *Jimmy McTeal, if that's you teasin' me, watch out! I'll be up there to run after you soon!*

It was late afternoon and Gertrude set to feeding the cats and making her supper. Jimmy wondered if there was any way he could help her. His wonderings were cut short by an announcement.

ALL SOULS, EXCEPT THOSE ENGAGED IN GUARDIAN CORPS SURVEILLANCE ACTIVITIES OR FAMILY SENTRY DUTIES, ARE ASKED TO COME TO THE AMPHITHEATER FOR A SHORT MEETING.

Jimmy joined the crowds heading for the amphitheater. He could hear mutterings and questionings about what was going on but he didn't sense any fear as they all knew that whatever it was about, it was of their making, not GOD's.

The SuperArch stood on the central stage. He explained that he had called them together because after great soul searching, he had decided to resign. He felt that his inclinations in terms of statistics gathering were wrong and a new attitude was needed in the top job. He went on to say, *I've accepted a proposal from a wise old soul that seems to have a great deal of merit. I strongly recommend that this soul become the new SuperArch but, of course, his selection must be approved by all of us.*

A middle-aged man wearing a suit joined him on the stage. The SuperArch went on to say that he felt that the job could best be done by someone with experience in leading people through troubled times. The SuperArch then left the stage saying that they would now hear a few words from the nominee.

The crowd shifted. Speculations could be heard as to the identity of the candidate. He didn't look famous or memorable. He had the image of everyman. The hall fell quiet as he began to speak.

I have a dream that all of GOD's children BELOW can live in peace and harmony. We here ABOVE are the Guides and as such our job is to develop a conscience in those we guide and to help them clearly discern right from wrong. Our Earth peoples' brains have outrun their spirits and this perilous shift of power has brought us all to the brink of disaster. To survive we must devise a way to speed up the development of the spirit so it can take charge once again and keep the mind under control. However, as the mind is currently in the driver's seat, so to speak, we must awaken the spirit through the entrance of the mind as the spirit is severely atrophied through disuse in many of our Earth people, particularly those Wall Street types whose only gauge of value is money. What we need to do is to expose our Earthlings to their own truths. Let there be no more secrets. We here must all become whistle blowers and put our Earth people's deeds out in public. They will then be forced to contemplate their actions and feel remorse and the feelings of remorse will open the doors to the development of the soul. The second half of the formula will be as usual, to influence our Earth persons to self improvement and thus community and ultimately world improvement and to continue to provide them with opportunities for enlightenment as has always been our dictum. To differentiate my approach from that of our present leader's, let me say this very clearly. Do not manipulate but rather expose and let the public sense of morality rule the private. Also, I must ask you to restore a positive and communal attitude here ABOVE. And we must tighten our spiritual belts to eliminate the scourge of accidents that have recently happened BELOW due to a lack of attention paid here ABOVE. We cannot abandon our Earth people to chaos!!!

After a moment of silence there was a round of applause signaling a vote of confidence. The new SuperArch nodded in acknowledgement and then made a couple of announcements.

I have put a few lectures on video for your review and now we must disperse so we do not find ourselves meeting while the world BELOW explodes. However, let me first say to all of you, please feel free to schedule a meeting with me at any time.

Ludwig, who was not about to be outdone by anyone, held his own meeting for the Guards. He announced that this new dictum applied to them as well. Any imminent disasters should be managed in the usual way in terms of alerting the appropriate Earthlings so that corrective actions could be taken and, in addition, the guards should now make sure that the near crises were leaked to the press on Earth so the world's true instability would be obvious to all of its citizens.

The DO OR DIE banners faded and some of them blew away in tatters. They were not replaced. The new SuperArch had a different style. He was constantly seen in the sectors of ABOVE, mingling with the family groups in Guidance or greeting new arrivals in Admissions. He was very personable and in his strolls was constantly stopping to ask how a soul was feeling, and if there were any problems he could help with. He turned The Pines into a Community Center open to all and added to the environment by having an evening hour of gospel music broadcast throughout ABOVE. Things began to mellow out quite quickly in response to the disappearance of the regimentation and competition. Souls once again took time to commune with each other and give advice.

Once souls got used to the SuperArch mingling among them they would often ask him if he thought GOD would send another message. They closely scrutinized him to see if he seemed to be afraid. He didn't. He calmly commented that GOD lived within all souls. They simply had to pause when confused and their spirit would guide them to the correct action. These words caused souls to come to a feeling of peace. It began to feel beautiful in ABOVE and knowing such beauty, they were able to transmit it more effectively to their Earthlings.

The SuperArch was frequently asked if he thought that GOD would abandon the planet Earth. He always replied that he did not believe that GOD would turn HIS back on HIS children, each of whom contained HIS spark. HE had already put up with eons of wars and pettiness, why stop now? But souls questioned him further, *what about nuclear war?* The SuperArch became grave and could only say, *if the planet is destroyed, there will be nothing to work with.*

The SuperArch often met with the Guardian Corps. He usually attended the Sunday review meetings. He always congratulated the corpsmen on their unfortunately frequent interventions to avert disasters.

Earth life changed. The nightly news programs were now filled with revelations of the misdeeds of public officials and others whose inappropriate acts might have an effect on the citizenry. Companies that dumped toxic wastes were identified and their executives were forced to make public apologies and if it was proven that they knowingly dumped the poisons, they were sent to jail.

The realm of private life was similarly changed. There was no longer any quarter. All lies were revealed. Souls remarked that it was like a child's fear that people had x-ray vision and could read their minds like newspapers. The SuperArch said it was good preparation for ABOVE, where thoughts were heard. However, in ABOVE this feature was automatic. In order for it to be happening BELOW guides had to be on their proverbial toes, always arranging for so and so to find out what had been said or done

Jimmy was happy to feel the improved atmosphere in ABOVE. He enjoyed the friendly nods and waves. He had, however, given up on Julia. When their paths crossed she was pleasant but never more. He occasionally met her wafting along the periphery with Dinah but despite Dinah's warm greetings he could tell that Julia still blamed him for her death.

Jimmy did good work as a guard. He was very conscientious. In his off-duty hours he watched over Gertrude. He now communicated quite freely with her, gave advice about household problems and made suggestions about cat care, wood storage and other features of her daily life. Gertrude accepted his messages without question. She thought it was her husband Jimmy who had passed on fifteen years earlier but apparently had told her on his death bed that she would be hearing from him. She declared, *you finally figured out how to do it, Jimmy. Even if it did take you fifteen years!*

Jimmy didn't mind being taken for her husband. The name was right and after all, there was no way he would be found out. He sometimes wondered if he should try to track down the real Jimmy McTeal to see what he was doing and tell him how his wife was but the fact that Jimmy never felt anyone else sending vibes to Gertrude or even viewing her, (a discernible buzz happened when more than one monitor was tuned into the same person), made him surmise that Jimmy McTeal had probably gone BELOW again.

It got to the point where Gertrude even asked Jimmy questions. One day she couldn't get the stove to draw. It was her first wood stove fire on a cool fall evening. Jimmy advised her that birds had built a nest on top of the chimney, blocking the air. She thanked him and agilely climbed up on the roof and removed the nest.

Another winter passed BELOW. The constant revelations about misdeeds continued. Every night there was a series of exposes on the national and local news and similar happenings in everyone's private life. A state of paranoia pervaded the Earth.

In public statements criminals often used the word 'luck.' *By a stroke of bad luck my misdeed has been revealed but it is actually good luck because now I have a chance to right my life.* It was hearts and flowers stuff. The concept of good and bad luck reinforced the trend of believing in the power of good luck charms and cat robberies became even more commonplace. Pet stores never had kittens anymore just great varieties of dogs, birds, and fish. Fortunes were made overnight by people lucky enough to have a cat who delivered a large litter of kittens. Jimmy was grateful that no one had discovered Gertrude in her mountain home with her many cats. It was fifteen when he first met her but now the count was twenty-two as two momma cats had litters in the fall.

Ludwig announced that he was going to reorganize the guards' assignments as he did not want them to become complacent and develop habits that would deaden their receptive abilities. He read off the changes at the next Sunday meeting. Jimmy was assigned to submarine surveillance in the Arctic. He and two other guards were the Arctic Team. They relieved each other after eight hour shifts.

Jimmy had to admit that Ludwig was right. He did feel a heightened sense of alertness taking on the new assignment. He had to learn to identify submarines. In his off-duty hours he studied charts to familiarize himself with the features of the weapons systems and other characteristics of each nation's submarine fleet. He took his paperwork to the Inactive Files room and studied there. He loved the stacks of old scrapbooks and the dim light and had discovered that no one ever came to the Inactive Files room. He set up his study materials on the old table and took breaks by looking down at Gertrude through the monitor. He sometimes forgot to take off the earphones and would mutter submarine jargon as he stared at the diagrams. Gertrude would stop short and ask, *cruise missiles? Jimmy, what are you talking about?* Jimmy would murmur a sweet nothing and Gertrude just accepted that her Jimmy didn't always make sense.

In fact, during most of his off-duty time, Jimmy paid full attention to Gertrude. When she was asleep he watched the cats.

21

After meeting the challenge of creating a Love and Compassion Curriculum for the Religious Studies Department, and even getting some feedback that her efforts were making a difference BELOW, Julia began to get depressed. She tried to stay busy. She checked on Mimi regularly and noted that she kept an unbelievably slovenly home but happily had become the mother of delightful one-year-old twins. Although Jens was initially overwhelmed by the twins and seemed to be edging towards the shoals of adultery, he had some flashes of insight, aided by Julia, and the family was developing well, for the moment.

Julia tuned in on her children at least once a day and found that they were doing as well as could be expected but in many aspects of their lives were not living the way they would have if Julia had been there. She found this very frustrating, even down to the detail that Elias was eating lots of candy and getting very fat. Julia sorely felt the limitations of being dead and definitely still blamed Jimmy. Her frustration peaked when she tuned in one day and found Nancy crying and a frightened Laramie asking her, *what's wrong?*

Julia knew the problem before Nancy even spoke. It was as she surmised. Harvey was having an affair. It was his old pattern and Nancy responded by announcing that she was moving out. Laramie was devastated. She had never gotten very close to Harvey but she had come to depend on Nancy. After tearfully informing Laramie of her plans, Nancy went to her bedroom to pack. Laramie dissolved into a heap. She curled up into a ball on her bed and cried with great, racking, silent sobs. Julia agonized ABOVE, sending down messages of love and hope while knowing that such messages did little to lessen the impact of another devastation on an eleven-year-old child.

Julia wasn't surprised by Harvey's behavior, she had lived with it for twelve years but still, she hadn't expected it. Her usually acute radar for such behavior had been overwhelmed by her fervent desire to believe that her children were safe and happy. After continually sending down her most inspired messages and seeing no effect on Laramie, Julia abandoned the monitor and ran off to find Dinah.

Hugo was the only one at the Frenn site but he knew Dinah's whereabouts and directed Julia to the W sector. Once there, Julia quickly spotted Dinah. She appeared to be deeply engaged in a conversation with an old woman. Julia communed to her, *Dinah, quick, I need your help!*

Dinah turned to her and patted her lovingly and said, *it will have to wait a minute, dear, this situation with the Wetmore family is an emergency also. Sit down. I'll be with you as soon as I can.*

But it's about Laramie! Julia shrieked. *Nancy, her stepmother, is moving out, and you know how Laramie feels about Nancy!*

Dinah looked very sad and concerned to hear the news but still said, *please sit down. I'll be with you soon.*

Julia sat down but she found herself in a rage. She noticed that her image was flashing as it had been when she first arrived ABOVE. She couldn't understand why Dinah didn't drop everything to aid a family member, her grandchild! *Who cares about the Wetmores! Let them find someone in their own family to help them!* She muttered.

Julia felt like she was waiting forever. Dinah and the old lady got up and moved to the monitor. They gazed down and continued their conversation. Julia approached again and asked if she could just tune in on Laramie for a moment to see if she was all right. She was shocked by Dinah's response. *Please Julia, go to another site. We cannot change the focus here at the moment.*

That was the final blow for Julia. She was being ignored by her own mother, Laramie's grandmother. She ran off, unsure of what to do but insulted and unable to wait any longer for Dinah's attention. In her distraught state, she couldn't think of anyone to go to for help. She greatly respected James but she didn't know him that well. She thought about the other souls who might be able to assist her. Finally she decided that Jimmy was the soul she needed and ran off to find him.

Finding Jimmy was not easy. He wasn't on duty and no one at the Guardian Corps Headquarters knew his whereabouts. She resorted to an announcement asking that James Cantor come to the Information Desk in the Central Meeting Hall. While she was waiting for him she used a public monitor to check on Laramie and found her asleep. Julia's momentary concern diminished but her general concern increased as she scanned Laramie's aura and found it a sick brown color.

Jimmy was in his usual spot in the Inactive Files Room communing with Gertrude. It took a minute for the announcement to penetrate his consciousness but as soon as he got it he said a quick goodbye to Gertrude and headed for Central. He was surprised to see Julia there. She was sitting on a bench out front. He stopped to explain that he'd heard an announcement and then he noticed her concerned expression and realized that she was waiting for him.

They went for a quick waft on the periphery and Julia explained the situation. Jimmy was saddened to hear that Laramie's life was difficult. He suggested that Julia talk with Dinah as she was an expert at helping Earthlings. Julia explained that she had tried to speak to Dinah but she wouldn't listen to her, she just kept talking to some old lady. Getting the whole story out of her, Jimmy explained that Dinah wouldn't mistreat any soul in distress and that Julia shouldn't expect that family ties supercede the general ties that bind all souls. He assured her that Dinah would have helped her as soon as she had settled the old lady. Julia accepted the explanation but decided that Jimmy knew Laramie better than Dinah anyway. She begged him to help her.

They tuned in on Laramie and found her sleeping fitfully. The dawn's light coming in the window illuminated the child's furrowed brow. Jimmy now shared Julia's sense of alarm as the vibes emanating from Laramie were sheer depression and overwhelming stress. For the immediate future, Jimmy suggested that Julia stay tuned in on the child constantly and continually send down loving and hopeful messages. Jimmy also proposed that they find a way to procure a kitten for Laramie. The belief that a kitten was a good luck charm would help the child have a positive outlook. Jimmy then apologized, explaining that it was time for his shift. He wafted away but called over his shoulder that he would be back after his work day and that he knew an Earthling who had kittens and cats to spare and he would try to figure out how to get one to Laramie.

Julia stayed on Laramie every second. It put her into a rage to see the insensitivity of some of her teachers. *Don't they have any background in child psychology? After all, the child's mother just died!* Julia stopped her muttering and suddenly realized that in Earth time, it had already been over a year since she had died.

During Laramie's afternoon, when she was home from school and flopped on the couch watching TV, Julia decided that it was safe to leave the child for a moment in order to go and check in at the Religious Studies Department. There were a bunch of messages for her but nothing urgent so she hurried back to the monitor. Tuning in, she was surprised to see Harvey's back. She could tell it was him by the familiar contours, one of his shoulders was higher than the other. She stared at this identifying feature for a moment and then noticed that his shoulders were heaving. He moved aside and Julia could see an ambulance. It raced out of the frame. Then Elias moved into the picture. He was sobbing. Todd was holding his arm and saying that there was nothing he could have done.

Julia frantically directed the monitor so she could see the various pieces of the scene. There were police cars with flashing blue lights and crowds of onlookers. She focused on Harvey and the boys again. Harvey had an arm around the shoulder of each boy. Elias was crying. *First Mom and now Laramie. Why?*

Julia finally realized that Laramie had been run over by a car. Dropping her wand, she ran to the Records and Statistics Department and brought up Laramie on the Be Computer. In a moment the printer clacked out the message, *LARAMIE MONTAGE IS DEAD. SHE WAS HIT BY A CAR, THE DRIVER COULDN'T AVOID HER.*

Julia wafted over to Admissions at top speed and waited at the edge of the field. In a moment she was joined by Sonny. *We got a message from the Destiny Committee that one of ours is about to arrive.*

Julia nodded sadly, *it's Laramie. I'll take care of her but thank you for coming.*

Laramie landed in the field. She lay in a crumpled heap. Julia went to her and stroked her. It was actually more of a mental stroking but it had the same affect that a mother's hand on a child's forehead has in life. Laramie moaned a little and flashed irregularly.

When the child opened her eyes she saw the young and beautiful, tall blonde that was Julia's new image and obviously did not recognize her as her recent mother. Julia asked her to close her eyes again and rest. Florabelle wafted towards them and a few notes of the Star Spangled Banner plinked but Julia sent Florabelle the message, *cut the music. It will just scare her. I've got this under control. You're not needed here.* Julia had not forgotten how mean Florabelle had been to her when she arrived.

Julia sat next to Laramie. She enfolded her in warmth and told her that there had been an accident on Earth and now she had come to a place like heaven and even though Julia didn't look the way Laramie remembered, she was in fact her mother in this last lifetime. In between phrases she reminded Laramie to keep her eyes closed and listen. At the end of Julia's explanation Laramie opened her eyes and said questioningly, *Mom?*

Julia indicated yes and with definite nostalgic undertones she communed the old story about why Laramie had been given her name. *Your father and I were on the way to Las Vegas for a vacation but the plane was forced to land at a small airport in Wyoming due to bad weather. We were put up at a motel in Laramie and the next day a charter bus took us to Las Vegas. I was sure you were conceived that night so I insisted on naming you Laramie.*

When she heard this story, Laramie accepted that this young blonde woman was, as she claimed to be, her mother. The child visibly relaxed to the degree that the flashing of her image slowed.

Oh Mom, I've missed you so much! She cried.

Until a soul becomes acclimatized and fully integrates the transformation to the spirit state, it doesn't have total recall of other lifetimes. The most recent life dominates the mind. Thus Laramie was only aware of her sad and painful last life and being reunited with her mother brought her to a state of peace. They sat huddled together.

They were soon interrupted by Florabelle. Julia tried to wave her away, annoyed that she was bothering them again but Florabelle sent Julia a warning that she had a message to deliver and Julia wasn't going to like it. Julia communed, *tell me what it is and then leave!*

Florabelle conveyed that the Destiny Committee had listed Laramie as a suicide and she had to report to the Suicide Ward. Julia stooped to whisper to Laramie, *don't worry honey, it's just a bureaucratic mix-up.* She then turned to Florabelle and communed in an outraged tone. *That is ridiculous. First of all she isn't a suicide and even if she were, she's only a child, a child whose mother died and whose father is such an ass that he alienates any good woman!*

Florabelle was standing by quietly with a patient expression on her face. *You know how it is, Julia. You can go over to the Suicide Ward and explain the situation and see if you can get them to take her off the rolls.*

Julia agreed but didn't want to subject Laramie to the dismal atmosphere of the Suicide Ward so she asked Florabelle to make an announcement requesting that Jimmy come to Admissions so he could stay with the child. Laramie was too confused to really understand what was going on and Julia decided to help her stay confused until things were cleared up. She continued to sooth her and reassure her by telling stories about her childhood, in essence continually reminding the child that she was with her mother.

Jimmy arrived. He dashed over to them. Laramie cried out, *oh, it's you, Jimmy! You're here too!* They embraced and the flashings in Laramie's image almost entirely disappeared. Julia quickly communed the problem about the Suicide Ward to Jimmy and he agreed to stay with Laramie. Jimmy intuitively knew that he should talk with her about her last life experience in order to slowly bring her to an understanding of what had happened. Especially with children who had suffered a sudden, unexpected death, the method of orientation to ABOVE had to be very gentle.

Laramie communed freely about the hard times in her life after Jimmy and Julia and the baby died. Suddenly she stopped and asked, *is baby Deirdre up here too?*

Jimmy said yes and then explained that a soul has many lifetimes and after each Earth death the soul returns to ABOVE. Following a period of meditation and work and study there would be another opportunity to go BELOW again. The baby she knew as Deirdre was a soul named Dinah who was a good friend of Jimmy's and was also her mother's mother, so she was Laramie's grandmother and also her baby sister. *Are you following me, Laramie?*

Yes, I think so....

At this point in their conversation Julia returned. She was sending out very flustered and frustrated vibes. *They say that Laramie has to come with me. I explained that she is only a child, an emotionally exhausted child, but they said she isn't a child anymore than I am. She has lived twenty-six lifetimes. So I guess we have to go over there. Jeez, it's so depressing! Will you come with us?*

Jimmy agreed to go. Laramie had been acclimatizing quietly by herself and tuned in on their last exchange, *twenty-six lives! I can't remember that many!*

Julia and Jimmy were pleased at this evidence of her adjustment. By the time they got there, she would probably even remember the Suicide Ward.

22

The Suicide Ward was located on the far side of ABOVE on a diagonal from Admissions so they had the option of going along the periphery or cutting across. In a quick exchange Jimmy and Julia decided to cut across in order to give Laramie a chance to get further oriented before entering the depressing realm of the Suicide Ward.

Laramie seemed to enjoy the journey. Jimmy and Julia placed themselves on either side of her. Their force fields eased her awkward newcomer coordination. Their path took them through interesting scenes. First they went by the site where Ludwig trained the Guard Corps. A small contingent was marching and reciting some operating maxims. They continued on and crossed through a corner of Guidance. There was the usual hubbub. Wafting through the Central Meeting Hall, they encountered a rehearsal of the Celestial Symphony. At that point they joined the Periphery Path in order to get a distant view of Sunset Productions. The little figures and the spots of vibrant colors made a lovely scene.

Suddenly the scenery fell away and they seemed to be on a path to outer space. Then they began to hear the screaming. The shrieking sounds were mixed with very soothing and very loud music but it was nearly impossible to tune out the screaming and the combination was quite sickening. They went through a corridor and the howling increased until they were standing next to a large doorway.

At first it was hard to see into the vast space. It was so dark. When their eyes adjusted to the dim light they could see a huge space filled with shadowy figures. Most of the souls seemed to be perpetually milling around but some were banging their heads against the walls and others just lay on the floor and wailed. When one passed by the door Jimmy and Laramie and Julia could see it was a soul with discernable features but the gray pajama-like suit and the gray aura made the individuality hard to discern.

The Suicide Ward was the only dark place in ABOVE and it was a shock to someone who was not a regular. For some unfathomable reason there were always enough volunteers to run the ward and the site kept a very low profile in ABOVE. No one visited the place for pleasure.

In a moment a guard was at their side. *What can I do for you?* He asked.

They explained their mission and he directed them to the office. The door was locked but when the clerk behind the counter saw them, they were buzzed in. The office was brightly lit because the back wall was open to the sky and blessedly the room was soundproof. Looking across the counter and out the window and listening to the lovely harp music made it easy to forget the wild ward behind them.

Julia explained who she was and gave Laramie's name. The clerk consulted her list. *Oh yes, are you dropping her off? Come right through here, Laramie.* The clerk opened a door next to the counter and came out and took hold of Laramie and started to pull her in.

Julia protested. *It's all a mistake! She isn't a suicide!*

Then Laramie spoke up, *I just didn't look when I crossed the street. I was really depressed and I thought about dying but I didn't walk in front of that car on purpose!*

The clerk calmly responded. *We picked up a signal from you quite a while ago, dear. You have been on our list of potentials since, let me see…* she pushed a few buttons on her keyboard and scanned the screen, *since October of last year.*

Julia interrupted, *that's when I was killed! I was her mother. Anyone would have suicidal thoughts, any kid that is, if her mother was suddenly killed and her father was a jerk!*

The clerk tried to sooth Julia. *I understand that you are trying to help but think about it, it says right here,* she pointed to a place on the screen, *this soul, currently known as Laramie Montage, has lived twenty-six previous lives. I think she can speak for herself. And you know that when you take on a life assignment you are aware of what will happen in the first 27 years so she accepted the assignment knowing you would die.*

I don't think so. You see, I met Jimmy and then my life changed. It was probably an act of free will that got me killed. It probably wasn't in the life description she signed on for.

Well, that's possible, but still she can speak for herself.

Laramie took the cue and tried to explain. *Ok, Ok, it's true. I know the ropes around here but I really think an exception could be made in this case. I didn't commit suicide. I just didn't use adequate caution in crossing the street. When's the last time you were down there? The confusion down there now is unbelievable. And the way people drive!*

The clerk was clearly not convinced. *It has all the earmarks of a suicide. The only possible loophole I see for you,* the clerk was leafing through an official looking manual, *is that you were underage. You were only eleven, right?*

Laramie and Julia both nodded. Jimmy stood behind them looking hopeful. The clerk read from the manual, *in the case of underage suicides, the responsibility for the act can be judged by conducting a review of past lives to discover if there were any prior suicide attempts. Only when the person was under twelve years old and the present act can be determined to be an isolated incident for a soul with at least ten other lifetimes can the sentence of natural life in the Suicide Ward be lifted and a pardon issued.*

The clerk instructed Laramie to accompany her to a monitor in order to scrutinize her past lives. Julia was told that she couldn't go with her and Laramie assured her that she didn't need her help. When Julia turned around she saw Jimmy on the phone. He appeared to be engaged in a serious conversation. Julia then noticed that a gray figure on the other side of the window was talking on a phone also. A few souls had drifted up to the window and began to make signals to Julia, motioning that she should come in. Their auras were the colors of pain and suffering and she was drawn to go in and talk with them.

At that moment Julia heard a strange squeak and pulled herself away from the window and went to check on Laramie. It was Laramie making the squeaking sound. She was half talking, half communing. *I forgot about that one. It was a hard life. I had ten children! And how could I have forgotten about Nils! He was fantastic and we lived in that wonderful rose-covered cottage by the sea. Oh, and my daughter Cassandra, is she up here now?*

The clerk consulted a list and indicated affirmative.

Laramie looked up when Julia appeared next to her. *Mom, it's fantastic to see all your other lives!* Laramie's attention was redirected to the screen.

Julia decided to go into the Suicide Ward. She quickly wafted through the office and out the door into the ward. At first the sound was again overwhelming but soon she got used to it. The walls were lined with telephones. Many were being talked into by the gray spirits. Other souls were drifting around, but often in twos, something Julia had not noticed at first. A guard approached her and asked if she needed help. She said, *no, I'm just visiting.*

The guard looked startled and asked if she had ever been there before. She said no.

Let me explain, he said. *The suicides have to stay in this ward until the Earth time of what would have been the length of their lifetimes has elapsed. Thirty years Earth time in this room is quite a sentence. I doubt you will find a soul who has done suicide more than once. The only way to get out early is to be judged to have redeemed oneself by serious soul searching. They use these phones...* he pointed to the phones on the walls, *to talk to counselors to try to rectify their thoughts. True rectification resulting in Early Release is a very rare occurrence but everyone strives to be the one in a million.* He stopped his tour guide spiel and asked if she would be coming back again to visit. Julia said she doubted it as she had a job. She explained that she had accompanied her daughter in order to help her straighten out a particular situation. Both Julia and the guard seemed poised on the edge of telling a confidence. Julia indulged herself and asked him if he thought that someone in Laramie's position, accused of being a suicide but not actually being a suicide, could be taken off the rolls. He immediately responded that he had no way of knowing. *I'm not a claims examiner, I'm just a guard.* But as if wanting to offer her something, the guard leaned towards her and in a low tone imparted the confidence that there were only three counselors. *See all those phones, must be three hundred of 'em but there are only three counselors. What happens is that the three counselors talk to whoever gets connected with them and all the others talk to each other, but they don't know it because they don't listen to each other. They just talk non-stop. And no one identifies him or herself with names here. That's another thing they have to leave behind when they enter the Suicide Ward.*

One of the gray suited wraiths had settled at Julia's elbow and began to push against her as soon as the guard stopped talking. It communed a loud, *HELLO!* Julia turned towards it. Staring at the image, she perceived a woman. The face had a feminine inclination and long gray hair hung down from under the gray cap.

I think I'm doing better. I talked to a counselor for almost the whole day yesterday. I watched the clock. I talked to him from two to twelve midnight. She pointed to a place high up on a wall and when Julia squinted her eyes to adjust to the dimness, she saw a clock.

We like to follow Earth time here because our sentence is in Earth time and following a clock and a calendar makes it seem to go faster.

Looking around, Julia saw a calendar hanging by the door. The month was December, the year 2000.

I've figured out that I was always alone but that wasn't the crux of the matter. The problem was I didn't think I could handle what was going to happen in my life. I didn't want to make decisions. It was all too hard for me but I didn't expect this, not even life out there in ABOVE. She pointed to the doorway. *I thought it would be like never waking up again. I got more peace down there just sleeping at night!*

So you don't feel that you accomplished what you wanted when you committed suicide? Julia tried to turn it into a conversation.

Hell no! Being here is worse than anything on Earth ever was. I was only forty, in pretty good shape, no complaints about my health or anything. I just couldn't face the shame of being fired from my job for stealing. Now that I think of it, what a waste! I stole five hundred bucks. I didn't even really steal it. I just signed up for a trip and never paid for it. I was a travel agent. I guess I was also upset because I'd broken up with my boyfriend. Oh, it all seems so stupid now. I would never do it again. She turned towards Julia and asked, *do you know anyone important? Someone who could get me out of here early?*

Not really. How long have you been here?

Six years.

How long do you have to stay?

I was supposed to live to sixty-three. Thank god I wasn't having one of those ninety-nine year lifetimes!

So you have seventeen years to go?

Ya, on the record. But I think I can beat the odds. I talk to a counselor every day, for hours.

Julia noticed Jimmy heading towards her. He only wafted a couple of feet before he was approached by a wraith, and then another. Julia began to feel claustrophobic and decided to go and see how Laramie was faring. She was convinced that anything was better than staying in the Suicide Ward. She vowed to argue from every angle to get Laramie released.

She found Laramie sitting next to the counter. She looked terrible. The clerk was beside her. Julia asked Laramie, *what happened?*

Laramie looked up and seemed not to recognize Julia for a moment but then said, *all those lifetimes… all that trying to get it right…. It's so hard. What's the point? An exercise towards what mastery? Little pats here and there, a few diseases, heart attacks, once shot in a fight, once drowned in a lake, now run over by a car, why?*

The clerk commented that a Viewing of Lives Session sometimes put souls into a state of existential questioning. *It passes*, she said. The clerk then told Julia that Laramie had been struck off the rolls. After a review of her lives' tendencies it appeared that the car accident in this last life was just a matter of diminished perception due to stress which resulted in a crucial lack of judgement.

Julia radiated happiness and communed to Laramie, *let's go! We can go!*

Laramie didn't respond. Julia went over to the office windows and signaled to Jimmy to come in. She told him the good news and then explained that Laramie seemed to be in a state of shock and they needed to get her out of there. They came at her from both sides and pulled her along between them. Laramie was still very subdued and they got no help from her. They sped along as Julia's first impulse was to get far away from the Suicide Ward. She eased the pace when they got to the overlook by Sunset Productions. She asked Jimmy what the procedure was when someone was reassigned. He suggested that they go see Mick to formally register Laramie and find out how to proceed.

As usual, the line at Mick's desk was long. They waited. Jimmy and Julia were relieved to see that Laramie was coming out of her daze. They finally got up to the counter and Mick welcomed Jimmy and Julia but then sternly questioned Julia about why she wasn't wearing her rabbit ears. She mumbled that she'd left them at the site and explained that it wasn't a social visit. She introduced Laramie and told Mick about her escape from the Suicide Ward and asked, *should she just report to the family site?*

Mick reminded them that everyone now had a specific assignment unless there was a shortage in guidance personnel for the family. He brought the Frenn family constellation up on his screen and noted that the family was amply covered so he instructed Laramie to request an interview with the Destiny Committee. *And until you are called to see them, you should go to the family site.* Mick then turned to Jimmy and inquired about how it was going in the Guardian Corps. Jimmy told him the story of a recent near disaster. After a few minutes, some shouting about the delay was heard from the back of the line. Reluctantly, Mick said he had to get back to work.

They wafted off. Julia and Jimmy had to go to work also. Julia hurried off, leaving Jimmy to escort Laramie to the Frenn site. On the way to the Frenn's, Jimmy told Laramie about the changes in ABOVE and the switch in personnel at the top. Although the honeymoon period was over, the new SuperArch continued to get high ratings for his personal approach. He spent his days wandering through ABOVE giving compliments and advice to all he encountered.

Laramie listened intently and stared at the new décor. When Jimmy mentioned the recent problems ABOVE and that he'd heard the voice of GOD, Laramie at first thought he was joking but then noted the absolute seriousness in his tone. He described the regime under the former SuperArch and then told of the positive changes that had occurred both ABOVE and BELOW during the reign of the new one. He said that they seemed to be out of danger now but then admitted that he was worried that the Guardian Corps could not protect the Earth from all disasters as the possibilities for problems were so numerous. By the time they arrived at Frenn's, Laramie understood the situation and was radiating concern.

James and Hugo and Sonny were at the site. They warmly welcomed Laramie. Sonny offered to teach her how to use the monitor and suggested that she could be his replacement as he would soon be going BELOW.

Neither Laramie or Jimmy mentioned that the Destiny Committee might assign her to something else. They didn't want to upset Sonny. Jimmy left for work but promised Laramie that he would come back after his shift. *There's someone I want you to meet*, he said.

23

Doing surveillance work over the Arctic turned out to be much more difficult than Jimmy's former assignment. It was dull, or on Jimmy's better days, subtle. It was tedious. He had to constantly scan the seas and scrutinize the shadows under icebergs to detect and identify the submarines. The moving ice floes obscured and distorted their shapes and further visual confusion was added by disoriented whales whose sonar was apparently thrown off by the subs.

There were constant maneuvers and just as Jimmy got to the point where he thought he understood the pattern and who was who, something always changed and he would panic and prepare to put in a code D Alert as hostile acts seemed imminent. But then, once again, he would begin to detect a different rationale and ultimately a pattern.

When totally stymied as to identity, Jimmy observed inside the individual submarine. It was fun. He got a kick out of the sailors and the antics they engaged in to amuse themselves but he was also always worried about what else was going on out there with the other submarines. Looking down at the incessantly moving dim shapes he began to think of them as killer whales from warring pods.

Towards the end of his shift Jimmy always found it hard to concentrate. He thought about Gertrude and the cats and wondered what kind of day it was in the mountains.

After work Jimmy hurried over to the Frenn site. He stopped for a moment at a public monitor and tuned into Gertrude to tell her that he had to run an errand but would be back in a while and hoped to have someone to introduce to her. Gertrude, who by this time had become completely comfortable with the transmissions, responded as if Jimmy were in the room. *I hope it's my uncle Arthur or my grandmother!* She called out.

At the Frenn site Jimmy found Laramie and Dinah deep in conversation. They appeared to be old friends. He approached eagerly, always happy to see Dinah. She greeted him warmly as did Laramie. Jimmy happily realized that he was making progress, two souls loved him! After a wonderful but brief interlude between the three of them, Dinah was called away and Jimmy took Laramie to visit Gertrude.

Laramie was fascinated by the Inactive Files Room. Its mustiness was so reminiscent of Earth. Jimmy explained that he had adopted an Earthling and he wanted Laramie to meet her. He gave Laramie a pair of earphones and then tuned in Gertrude. She was just returning from her afternoon walk.

Hi Lambie, he communed.

Gertrude held open the door for the long procession of cats and said, *hi honey, it's a beautiful day. Spring is really comin'. There's a sweet smell in the air. It's so wonderful!! Oh, do you have someone with you?*

Laramie asked Jimmy, *why did you pick someone so old?*

Jimmy said to Gertrude, *I'll be right back, hon,* and quickly removed Laramie's earphones and turned off the monitor. He radiated anger. *Is that all you noticed, that she's old! Goddamn, she might have heard you!*

Laramie was appalled and quickly replied, *oh Jimmy, I'm so sorry. I didn't know she could hear me. She seems, ah, very nice! I promise, I won't say anything else.*

Ok. I'll tell you the details later. He turned on the monitor again and started up a conversation with Gertrude. *How are the cats, dear? Everybody OK? What about Lincoln's leg?*

Everybody's fine, just hungry as usual. Who's with you? I thought I heard something?

Oh, yes, it's my friend Laramie.

Laramie said, *hello.*

Did we know her from our life, Jimmy?

No, but she's a good friend of mine now.

Oh, I see. Hi Laramie, nice to meet you. Jimmy and I were married for fifty-two years. I guess I'll be joining you soon!

Laramie sent Jimmy a quizzical look but carried on a sociable conversation with Gertrude. *Oh, fifty-two years! That's quite an accomplishment. Did you live together there in the cabin?*

Oh, yes. When Jimmy was forty-three and I was thirty-nine we moved up to this cabin. The road didn't even go through in those days, ended just a mile up from here. We never saw anyone in the winter and not many folks the rest of the year. We had a very happy life.

I guess you were just meant to be together.

I guess so.

The three of them talked for a while and then Laramie called a fond goodbye to Gertrude and said she hoped to visit with her again soon. Jimmy stayed to commune with Gertrude in his customary fashion.

After feeding the cats and eating a bowl of soup, Gertrude loaded up the firebox and started in on her nightly routine. She filled a kettle and a big pot with water and heated it up on the wood stove. When it steamed she poured the hot water into a big copper tub. She was just about to take off her clothes and lower herself into the warm water when a voice surprised her. She quickly went to the door. *Why Dottie, what are you doing here? Is something wrong?*

No, I just wanted to stop by to talk with you.

But the roads are slippery this time of year. They freeze up again at night. At least you should stay the night with me and not try to drive home in the dark.

I'll be fine… the reason I came is to tell you that a decision has been made.

What kind of decision? Jimmy, I sense that something bad is going to happen.

Me too, Jimmy answered.

Dottie asked in alarm, *who is Jimmy? Is that the name of one of the cats?*

No, you know, my Jimmy, my husband. He talks to me now.

Dottie stiffened and said, *oh really….* This information seemed to diminish a sense of shame that was radiating from her. *You know I've always tried to do the best for you, Aunt Gertrude….*

Why yes, and thank you!

Well, I feel that I'm responsible for you because of your age and I'm really the only person who has any contact with you. Over the last year I've been noticing that you don't seem to remember things and only last week you tripped in the store. What would we have done if you had broken your leg?

Well, I didn't.

No, but you could have. Anyway, I've been talking to the visiting nurse about you and she said that I'm responsible for you. You remember you gave me that power of attorney so I could cash your Social Security checks?

Yes, dear, and I appreciate all your help and I hope that the money I give you from the checks helps you with your expenses. I know it's very expensive to raise children nowadays.

Gertrude abandoned her bath plans. Dottie didn't seem to have noticed that she was about to bathe.

Yes, it's very expensive and now both kids are on sports teams and I have to go to games or take them to practices nearly every day. I know it may be hard for you to fathom with all your free time, but it's difficult for me to take half a day to come up here and take you shopping every three weeks.

Well, I certainly don't want to be any trouble. Gertrude motioned for Dottie to sit down at the kitchen table and then went over and opened the stove and heaved in a big log.

Dottie cleared her throat. *We have decided that it's time for you to go to an old people's home. I found one with a vacancy and it's right in the middle of town so you can walk to the store and if you should get sick, and Aunt Gertrude, we have to be realistic, old people often get sick, they will take care of you. They have one wing that's a nursing home for people who become ill.*

Gertrude was beginning to look ill.

Of course, you can't take the cats, they don't allow animals, but you'll be sharing a room with a roommate so you'll finally have some company.

I never said I wanted any company. Is that why you drove all the way up here to see me, to tell me this?

Yes, first I was just going to come get you but then I thought you should have some time to digest the good news and to gather up your things.

When were you coming to get me?

On Friday, so that's why I drove all the way up here today and I also wanted to tell you that a real estate agent might be coming by tomorrow. If only you had a phone, I could have called you! Living alone out here is crazy, but I've heard that the land values have gone way up so this property might be worth quite a bit of money. You always said you wanted to have something to give me, so it's really a good solution for us both. I can't wait until I can just pick up the phone and call you to see how you are. You don't know how often I've been afraid I would find you dead up here.

Gertrude was reduced to silence. Jimmy just muttered, *oh no, oh no....* He tried to send down comforting thoughts but was himself so overwhelmed at this turn of events that he couldn't communicate much hope. Gertrude began to talk to him, ignoring Dottie who was sitting at the table with her. *Jimmy, we promised each other that we would live in this cabin until we died and you did!*

Jimmy said, *yes, yes.*

I can't see myself surviving anywhere else. I think all the noise and dirt in a city would be too much for me.

Dottie interrupted, *oh Gertrude, don't be silly. You're as strong as an ox for your age and you'll like it there. You don't realize how deprived you've been all these years. Even when Jimmy was alive! It's too confining to see only one other person and now you've been here alone for years. You must be depressed. Wait till you see how it feels to have meals with other people, talk over the news of the day, buy new clothes, all the regular parts of life you've been missing.*

Gertrude didn't answer her but again spoke to Jimmy. *I know I'll hate it, Jimmy. What can I do?*

Dottie got up and walked over to Gertrude's chair and put her arm around her shoulders. *See, being alone has got you talking to imaginary people. You know Jimmy is dead and gone.*

Jimmy muttered in disgust, *what an idiot!*

Gertrude agreed, *yes, she's an idiot.*

Dottie straightened up. *You aren't calling me an idiot are you?*

Gertrude quietly said, *no,* and then quite calmly told Dottie that she didn't want to go to an old people's home. She was very happy where she was. She went on to say that she could find a way to shop more efficiently and not need a ride to town more than every two months, and perhaps she could hire someone to come and pick her up so that Dottie wouldn't have to be bothered with her at all.

Now Gertrude, I've thought about this for a while and talked to quite a few professional people about it and we all agree that it would be best for you. We can't wait until you are seriously ill and expect that a nursing home will have an available bed. That's the reason you have to go now. There might not be another bed available for a year or two. It's very complicated, Aunt Gertrude. It has to do with Medicare and all kinds of other factors. I know you must be shocked but I think after you sleep on it you'll realize that it's a wise decision. Let me give you a kiss and I'll see you on Friday. Don't pack a lot. Remember, you'll be sharing the room. I'll plan to spend a couple of hours helping you with your packing. Oh, about the cats, Bill and the kids will come up Saturday morning and take them to town. The pet shop is willing to pay a hundred dollars for each one, and to think when I was a child my Uncle Nathaniel used to drown kittens because no one wanted them. Dottie awkwardly hugged and kissed Gertrude who sat like a statue, not responding at all. Dottie said goodbye and left. After the sound of her car roaring out of the dooryard had faded, Gertrude looked up and said, *Jimmy, what am I gonna do?*

Jimmy told her he loved her and wherever she went he would be with her. Gertrude sat in silence and Jimmy occasionally said, *I love you,* or, *I'm so sorry this is happening.*

Gertrude was quiet for a long time and then wearily stood up and said she was going to bed. *Jimmy, I'm gonna think about if I should just walk into the woods and disappear. I really can't bear to go to that place.* She climbed into her bed and was soon surrounded by the kittens and cats. Jimmy stayed at the monitor and watched her throughout the night as he often did. He was always entertained by the antics of the kittens and cats. They would usually sleep for short stretches and then run around batting at real and invisible playthings and romp with each other. But that night none of the cats left the bed. They must have sensed Gertrude's depression and didn't want to leave her side. Jimmy stayed with her until he had to report for Guard Duty.

24

Jimmy's shift was nerve-racking as usual but ultimately uneventful. As he was leaving the Guardian Corps headquarters he met Julia in the hall. He was suprisd to see her and felt a flash of resentment which bothered him. In a moment of insight he realized that he blamed her for the situation with Gertrude. If he hadn't been helping her with Laramie he would have been with Gertrude and he might have sensed something going on with that stupid Dottie and perhaps been able to influence her. But in truth, he realized that he would probably not have sensed anything but somehow it felt good to be able to blame Julia. He suddenly got it that she still blamed him for her return to ABOVE, so his blaming her for Gertrude's predicament made it feel even.

In fact, since Laramie had arrived ABOVE, Julia no longer felt the pull to her prior Earthly responsibilities. The boys were doing well with Harvey even though he was an ass. Finally, Julia was no longer angry at Jimmy, but he didn't know that.

Julia wafted along beside Jimmy sending him friendly vibes. *I think Laramie is doing OK now. Thanks for your help!*

No problem.

Laramie says you introduced her to an Earthling whom you've adopted. I didn't know you adopted someone.

Jimmy didn't want to talk about it. He remembered Laramie's comment about Gertrude being old and that, in combination with his worries about her, prompted him to respond curtly, *yes, I did.* He offered nothing else.

Julia looked at him strangely. *Did you have a hard time at work?*

Jimmy grasped at the excuse, saying yes and that he had to fill out some forms on a situation. Julia respected his mission. Everyone ABOVE knew how vital the Guardian Corps was to Earth's survival.

Jimmy hurried to the Inactive Files Room and tuned into Gertrude. She wasn't in the cabin and neither were the kittens and cats so he concluded that they must have all gone on a walk. But it was early afternoon and she didn't usually go for a walk until after her nap. He looked around the cabin and noticed a piece of paper on the table. He switched to a close-up shot. It was a note from Gertrude.

> **Jimmy, I have decided to go into the woods.**
> **I don't want to go to the old age home. If I can't**
> **stay here I want to be with you. I have a plan,**
> **Catch up with me. I'm on the river path.**

Jimmy arduously guided the monitor up the river path. On his usual walks with Gertrude he just set the monitor on her and it automatically followed her but without an image to latch on to, he had to move it step by step. He finally saw her, the cats were swarming around her. He called to her and she stopped.

Ah, Jimmy, you finally got here. I had terrible dreams last night. I dreamt that even though I was alive I was nailed into a coffin and buried. I've decided I'm coming to be with you. I'm going to jump off the falls. There's lots of water and I probably can't swim. I haven't tried for years. Anyway, the water is so cold that I figure I'll die very quickly.

Hearing Gertrude's plan brought visions of the Suicide Ward to Jimmy's mind. That was even worse than an old age home. He decided to tell her the facts. He explained that suicides had a tortured existence in ABOVE. They were trapped in a dark ward until the end of their natural lives. Gertrude responded by saying she was eighty-seven. How much longer could her natural life be? And surely it was better than an old age home. Jimmy told her emphatically that she was wrong about that. He said he would get an emergency consultation with the powers-that-be to see if it was time for her to come up anyway. He asked her to go home with the cats and have supper and settle in for the night and he would get back to her. She agreed but reminded him that Dottie was coming to get her in the morning. He assured her that he was aware of that and promised to get back to her before Dottie came.

Jimmy rushed off to Central Administration and told the clerk he needed an emergency consultation with the Destiny Committee. The clerk inquired about the nature of the problem and he explained that he was watching over an Earthling whose life situation was so difficult that she was contemplating suicide and he wanted to know if she could be brought up now. Perhaps her time had come?

The clerk informed him quite pompously that one's destiny could not be altered and if Jimmy exerted his best efforts and an Earthling still wanted to commit suicide, he should accept that suicide too could be part of one's destiny.

No, no, no, you don't understand. Please, at least tell me when she is supposed to be brought up according to her Lifespan Calendar.

The clerk remarked that it was an irregular request but as she wasn't busy she would look it up for him. She took the name and disappeared into a room full of whirring machines and came back a moment later. *She's due to come up in July.*

Is there any way the date could be moved up? The lady is eighty-seven. She's put in a long good one.

I'm only a clerk. You'd have to speak to a member of the Destiny Committee about that.

That's what I asked to do in the first place!

Hey Buddy, don't get excited. One of the judges is on call. You can contact him on that phone over there. She pointed down the corridor.

Jimmy went to the phone and after being put on hold for a few minutes, was connected to a judge. He explained the situation, emphasizing Gertrude's long life of self reliance. In consideration of her age and circumstances and the fact that she was to be called in within six months, the judge granted a Demise Variance and put through a request that she be brought up immediately.

Jimmy hurried back to the monitor in the Inactive Files Room and tuned in Gertrude. It was just after midnight and Gertrude was asleep. The cats were piled all around her on the bed. Jimmy called to her gently so as not to scare her. She woke up immediately.

Gertrude, I've made all the arrangements. You're going to be brought up here right away.

Oh good! She said. *But do you mean right now? I guess I'd rather be dressed than in my pajamas.*

Well, why don't you get dressed and then go back to bed. I really can't say if it will happen in an hour or if it will be sometime in the morning. I guess it depends on how many people are on the list for today.

Can I bring the cats, Jimmy? They haven't left my side for two days now.

No, animals are not allowed.

Oh well, we will be together again, Jimmy. I can't ask for more than that.

Jimmy said, *yes, my dear…* and suddenly realized that the jig was up and once she arrived ABOVE he would obviously not be able to go on pretending to be her husband. He told her that he would be waiting for her and that she shouldn't be surprised if he looked different. He would explain everything.

Gertrude carefully slid out of bed, attempting not to disturb the cats but they woke up and en masse accompanied her across the room to the closet. As she got dressed, they milled around her feet. She put on her best outfit, she called it her marryin' and buryin' dress, and then went back to bed and the cats settled in again. Jimmy assured her that he would be waiting for her, but said he had to run a quick errand. He wafted over to the Statistics Department to find out what had happened to the real Jimmy McTeal. He put in the request and in a few moments was handed a computer printout.

> *McTEAL, JAMES*
> *DECEASED NOVEMBER 10, 1984.*
> *DESCENDED ON OCTOBER 2, 1996,*
> *TO BE BORN AS A GIRL CHILD TO*
> *PHILLIP AND MARIE DeSALLE,*
> *RESIDING IN TOLEDO, OHIO.*

The clerk was watching him and asked, *you didn't want the whole soul profile did you? To get that you'll need a release from the Vital Statistics Department.*

No, no, Jimmy muttered. *This is fine.*

Jimmy headed for the Admissions Department. He thought he should alert a counselor that Gertrude was coming and apprise him of the situation so he could help her get oriented and help her understand that he was not her Jimmy. Halfway there he stopped and realized that he wanted to meet her himself and stay with her until he could explain everything. They had been together for a year now so they knew each other pretty well. Once he had settled this in his mind he wafted over to the Inactive Files Room to tune in on Gertrude so he would be available to help her in her transition.

25

BELOW

The first light of morning was coming through the cabin windows. The bed was a mass of lumps with the cats piled all over one another and Gertrude. She seemed to be sleeping.

Hi Lambie, Jimmy woke her up gently.

Hi hon, am I still alive? I guess so. At least the cats seem to be alive. She peered over the covers.

It should be sometime soon, dear. I'm staying with you and I'll be waiting up here to greet you. Don't be afraid. When you are actually dying it may feel terrible for a moment but then it will be fine.

Thanks Jimmy… I've been thinking, I'm gonna try to bring the cats. No harm in trying, right?

I guess not.

Gertrude started talking to the cats, calling them all by name and holding up the bedcovers, inviting them to come in. Many of them stood poised observantly as this had been forbidden territory in the past. Whenever one had tried to creep under the covers Gertrude had always said, *no, no, no, you're going to bite my toes.* But this time, after a few entreaties from her, they apparently believed the invitation and began to file in. Soon they were all under and Gertrude soothingly said, *OK my sweets, now we are going back to sleep.* The bed was a mass of movement and then they all settled down. Gertrude had a peaceful smile on her face. *I'm ready now, Jimmy,* she said, closing her eyes.

Jimmy watched the trees and mountains get bathed in the early morning light. It was a perfect day. Gertrude's wind-up clock ticked loudly. An hour passed and nothing happened. The cats started to get restless as Gertrude was usually up by then. They began to slip out from under the quilt. Gertrude pleaded with them to come back under the covers.

Jimmy wished he knew how she was going to die. Perhaps the plan was that part of her chimney was supposed to fall on top of her when she went out to bring in the day's wood supply. He realized that it was highly irregular for her to know of her impending death and to anticipate it by staying in bed. But after some thought he concluded that she was undoubtedly on the heart failure list. She had done nothing in her life to elicit a violent or bizarre death.

Jimmy, nothing is happening and I don't know how much longer I can stay in bed. Dottie is coming. Are you positive that I'm going to die this morning?

Yes, the reapers probably have a long list but I'm sure it will be soon. Look, why don't you just stay in bed. You don't want to be bothered with packing anyway. Just tell Dottie that you feel sick and can't get up right now. She can pack your clothes if she wants to.

Ok, but it's the first time I've ever stayed in bed this late. But I guess I'd better get used to it. I'll get a lot of rest up there, right?

No, not really. We work pretty hard up here. You'll soon see. It's difficult to explain. Throughout their relationship, Jimmy had said very little about ABOVE. He had just let Gertrude have her own thoughts on the matter. Most of their conversations were about the daily events of her life.

At nine o'clock a car roared into Gertrude's yard and then a knocking could be heard. When Gertrude didn't appear, the knocking got louder and more insistent. Jimmy asked Gertrude if the door was unlocked.

Gertrude said, *of course, I never lock it.*

Dottie called out, *Aunt Gertrude, are you all right?* She pushed open the door and immediately saw that Gertrude was not in the kitchen so she looked into the main room and saw that Gertrude was still in bed. She screamed, *OH! Auntie, are you all right?* She ran across the room to the bed. Gertrude played dead for a few seconds. She couldn't help herself, then she opened her eyes and said, *oh, hello Dottie. I'm not feeling well so I stayed in bed.*

But Auntie, we have to pack your stuff and remember I'm taking you to your nice new home today. Your roommate's name is Celia. She's very nice and is looking forward to your company. She's hoping you will like the same TV programs that she likes.

I don't watch television. I don't have electricity, remember?

You won't believe what you've been missing, Auntie!

Gertrude sighed and said she hoped she would feel well enough to get up in a while.

How are you feeling bad, Auntie? Does anything hurt?

Gertrude explained that she just felt weak, like she might drop dead at any moment. Dottie laughed and said, *oh, Auntie, I think you're just a little scared about your new life. Don't worry, I'm sure you'll love it and I'll be able to visit you more often because it's only a twenty minute drive from my house. I'm busy every minute though, but I'll try to make time.*

I can't get up right now, dear. Why don't you pack for me. Just take anything you think I'll need. Ah, could you bring me that bag of dry catfood, dear? I want the cats to have their breakfast.

Oh, I can do that for you. Is their bowl in the kitchen?

Yes, but please bring it here to me.

You want to feed them in here? Won't it make a mess?
Please Dottie, bring the food. It's my way of saying goodbye to them.

Hearing this, Dottie seemed to understand. She scurried off to get the food and then brought it to Gertrude with the empty bowl. Very methodically Gertrude sat up straight in bed and leaned forward to fold back the covers. This didn't seem to work the way she wanted it to because the covers were very bulky. On a typical winter night it was twenty below outside. Changing her strategy, Gertrude threw the covers on the floor and put the bowl in front of her on the bed. She emptied the bag into the bowl. It was a nearly full ten pound bag so the cat food spilled over the sides of the bowl onto the bedsheets. Dottie was watching and squealed, *isn't that too much?* Gertrude said, *don't bother me. I told you I'm sick.* She watched with delight as the cats leapt onto the bed and began to eat. Gertrude stretched out her arms to encircle them. Just then Jimmy saw the arrow of death arrive and he quickly communed, *Gertrude, touch as many of the cats as you can.* She said, *Ok,* and that was her last word. She fell over dead and, simultaneously, eleven cats fell over dead too. The rest continued to eat feverishly.

Dottie screamed and rubbed her eyes in disbelief. *Gertrude, are you all right?* Of course Gertrude didn't answer. Dottie stared down at her and all the dead cats and screamed again. Jimmy laughed quietly and turned off the monitor and headed over to Admissions.

26

When Jimmy got to the field it was apparent that the reapers had been busy as many figures were scattered throughout the area but he immediately recognized Gertrude because she was the only one surrounded by a bunch of prostrate cats. Two junior guides from Admissions were standing next to her. One said to the other, *would you look at that*!

Jimmy approached them and said, *she's a friend of mine. I'll take care of her.*

But what about the cats? They asked.

Is there a rule about it? Jimmy asked.

Well no, I don't think so. But there aren't any up here.

Let's not worry about it, Jimmy said.

Gertrude and the cats were beginning to stir. Gertrude was groaning a little and trying to sit up. The cats seemed to get the hang of it immediately. As soon as they became conscious they began to waft. Jimmy heard a building chorus of voices. *This must be the place they go to… it seems pretty neat up here. It's so easy to move around!* Jimmy realized he was receiving the cats' thoughts. It sounded identical to any other soul to soul transmission.

The cats were rubbing against Gertrude who still seemed unable to wake up. Jimmy stood next to her and murmured, *Gertrude, hi Lambie, I'm Jimmy.*

Hearing this she opened one eye and stared at him. *You don't look like my Jimmy.*

Jimmy gathered his wits about him, preparing to give her an explanation but she noticed he was radiating concern and said, *oh, don't worry, Hon, I've known you weren't my Jimmy almost from the start but I thought I would scare you away if I said anything. Thank you. I've been so happy with your company this last year. Jimmy and I never got along as well as you and I do. Where is he anyway?*

Jimmy was so relieved and also impressed by her apparent grasp of the situation that he blurted out, *he's a baby girl in Toledo, Ohio.* Gertrude was not quite that assimilated and a very bewildered expression settled on her face but then instantly disappeared and was replaced by radiant joy when she saw the cats. *Oh my darlings, you are with me. How wonderful!* Gertrude seemed to get energy from them. Jimmy perceived them telling her to just think herself upright and once she was standing they coached her on wafting, cheering when she got it right. Admissions Guides who were ministering to the other new arrivals had a hard time concentrating on their duties as Gertrude and the cats were so entertaining.

Jimmy said, *Lambie, I'm so glad you're doing well.* She responded by communing that she was very happy and then, staring at him, she said, *I hope I'm not that frumpy old lady I was. Are there any mirrors around here?*

Jimmy told her she did still look like she last looked on Earth but she could request a change of image. She sadly replied that she supposed she would have to stay that way, after all that was the way she was.

Oh no, Jimmy said. *Most of us have changed what we look like. Why not?*

Gertrude happily digested this information and then echoed, *why not?* Jimmy led her and the herd of cats to the Admissions building. The clerk at the Information counter informed them that because of the great expansion of his counseling duties, Mick no longer did image changes. They were directed to an office down the hall.

Luckily, there was no line and they got to see a counselor right away. However, word got out about the cats and soon a crowd gathered.

Now, you won't wander away will you? Gertrude asked the cats.

In a chorus they answered, *no, we will stay with you for eternity*. Hearing this she relaxed and let them play and commune with the many souls who hovered about, taking delight in them.

Gertrude decided to remain a woman. She just asked to be nice looking and about thirty-five. She requested that her dress be slightly updated but she wanted a minimal change so the cats would be able to identify her. They did scurry away when the mist descended around her but immediately returned when the vapors cleared, and then seemed to find her essentially unchanged.

Jimmy asked her if she would like to accompany him on his daily round of duties or if she would like to go to her family group. She said she was very eager to see her grandmother. Jimmy requested directions and was told that the Sweetzer family was located at S-16. Gertrude said excitedly, *yes, my grandmother was a Sweetzer!*

With the cats' assistance, Gertrude quickly learned to waft perfectly. She moved through the corridors of Guidance effortlessly. Her passing caused quite a stir as the cats wafted along behind her. After stopping a few times to ask directions, they arrived at the Sweetzer site. A young lady dressed as a Rockette from Radio City Music Hall was standing beside the path.

Gertrude ventured uncertainly, *Grandma, uh, Beatrice?*

The young woman stared at Gertrude questioningly and then asked, *Gertrude, is that you?*

They wafted together in a joyous souls embrace and the grandmother asked, *have you been in that cabin all these years, dear? I haven't checked on you for quite a while as you didn't seem to need any help and I've been very busy guiding my great, great grandchildren who are fearless and wild....*

Witnessing the beginnings of a long communication, Jimmy gently interrupted and told Gertrude that he had things to do before reporting for guard duty but he would come back later. He was radiating small vibrations of concern and fear, worrying that he had lost his friend. Gertrude picked up his concern and interrupted her conversation with her grandmother long enough to reassure him that she would be eagerly waiting for him and that she too was used to spending her days with him. He wafted off happy.

Gertrude settled in. She became the chief Guide for the Sweetzer family because her grandmother needed a well deserved rest. Jimmy spent most of his free time at the Sweetzer site. He got along well with Grandma Sweetzer and his close relationship with Gertrude continued. The cats accepted him as a regular.

Grandma reveled in the company and in the visits of the many souls who stopped by to observe and play with the cats. She eventually had to make a rule that no more than fifteen souls could occupy the site at one time as some neighbors, the Swindells, protested that the many souls visiting the Sweetzers were spilling over into their site. The Sweetzer site was quite small as throughout history it had been a small family.

Offers to adopt the cats poured in. Gertrude refused them all but souls weren't discouraged, the offers just became more ingenious. One soul even appealed to the SuperArch to find a way to distribute the cats equitably throughout ABOVE. In response, the Super sent out a memo stating that the cats, without question, belonged with Gertrude and any changes would be determined by her or them.

This proclamation led to a round of appeals made directly to the cats. Constant pleas of, *here kitty, here kitty...* were heard around the site. Gertrude, Jimmy, and Grandma Sweetzer learned to ignore them. The cats seemed to enjoy the attention but they never strayed.

Julia noticed how happy Jimmy was in Gertrude's company and she seethed. It amazed her as it seemed to be the vagaries of love all over again. She didn't know such emotions were possible in the spirit state and resolved to talk it over with Dinah.

27

A herald transited ABOVE announcing that the SuperArch was going to make a speech about the State of Spirituality. All souls who were not on duty were instructed to gather in the Great Hall and all others were advised to listen to the speech over the Public Address System.

As wafting about with the cats created pandemonium, Gertrude decided to stay at the site. Jimmy wanted to stay with her so Grandma Sweetzer went off to the Great Hall.

The speech was inspiring. The SuperArch informed them that progress was being made both ABOVE and BELOW. He commended the Guides for their unrelenting exposure of truth to their Earthlings and the resulting improvement in the general morality and social conscience of all BELOW. The Super went on to state that he knew that GOD was pleased with the improvements, but unfortunately all the revelations of untruths had not affected the armaments situation. There had been some exposure of lying but the basic belief in security through ever-increasing armaments had not diminished. SECURITY IN PREPAREDNESS AND STRENGTH was the most commonly held maxim on Earth. Rogue countries were a particular concern. Despite efforts to contain the sale of missiles by Russia, the appeal of the cash offered by angry third world countries was too much for them. Proliferation of armaments was ongoing. The Guardian Corps had difficulty keeping track of the missiles as they were moved in the dark of night.

The SuperArch declared that he thought they had gone as far as they could go in their Guidance efforts. He emphasized that he was not suggesting any slackening in the efforts to influence Earthlings to positive deeds but rather he was now announcing an additional effort, a pilgrimage to Earth. He said that this type of endeavor had never been undertaken before in the manner that he was about to propose but he was sure that the move was appropriate for the perilous circumstances. He then asked for volunteers who would be willing to go down to Earth for a one week stay to eliminate the weapons of mass destruction. The volunteers would be clothed in the images of all the peoples of the Earth, all colors and all religions. They would spend the first three days making themselves known, talking with people in whatever quadrant of Earth they were assigned to. When the media began to pick up on them they would declare that they were soldiers in God's Army and had come to Earth to do away with weapons of mass destruction. The Super assured them that they would be taught to identify the weapons systems before they went BELOW and that they would certainly get cooperation from all nations once their powers were recognized. Anticipating the question, he clarified that the volunteers would not take on functioning bodies for their one week stay but would just be clothed in an appropriate image. In fact they would be invulnerable as they would not actually be alive. He concluded by saying he realized that such a maneuver had never been allowed before, however, the rules were now different since GOD had issued his warnings.

The end of the speech was hailed with resounding cheers and then the crowd rushed to Processing to sign up for God's Army. Soon after, an announcement was made that no more volunteers were needed. The number of volunteers far exceeded the quota, so many souls were turned away. But they were told that a communication center would be set up in the Great Hall for the duration of the onslaught and souls would be needed to monitor the progress of the Army and to convey messages to and from Mission Control. *ALL THOSE INTERESTED ARE ASKED TO SIGN UP FOR A SHIFT.*

Grandma Sweetzer returned to the site in a state of extreme disappointment. She said she had just missed being chosen. There were only two souls in front of her when it was announced that the quota was filled. Jimmy suggested that they sign up for monitoring shifts so they could be part of the excitement. Grandma was cheered by the idea. She did a few Rockette style kicks and then wafted down the path to sign up.

Jimmy wondered if anyone from the Frenn family was among the volunteers. He went over to Frenn's and found Sonny on the monitor and no one else at the site. Jimmy waited until Sonny took off his earphones and then asked him if anyone in the family was going down as a volunteer. Sonny told him that Hugo and Amesbury were going and Julia too. The three of them happened to be at the Processing Department during the speech so they were nearly the first in line when the mission was announced. Jimmy asked about Dinah. Sonny said she had been chosen to assist with the training. Apparently she was an old acquaintance of this new SuperArch's.

The training sessions were conducted in the Great Hall. The trainees could be seen trooping in each morning. They were put on an Earth time schedule to familiarize themselves with the times of day.

Ludwig taught the classes on disarmament. He described in exacting detail how to disengage all manner of weapons, ranging from nuclear warheads to agents of chemical and biological warfare. They practiced on models provided by the Research and Development Department. At the end of a long and extremely detailed workshop on nuclear warhead identification and disassembly, Ludwig passed out workbooks and had the trainees divide into pairs to test each other on the particulars. He announced that at the end of the training program he would be administering a test to make sure that they all had sufficient knowledge to carry out their task.

After the first day of the Descent Preparation Course, Julia and Hugo and Amesbury returned to the Frenn site in a state of exhaustion. There was a great deal of information to be taken in and all three of them admitted that it had been a long time since they had attended school. They moved three chairs into a small semi-circle and quizzed each other. Amesbury and Hugo quickly lapsed into the familiar truncated communication shortcuts that often develop between old friends and Julia began to feel slighted, although they made gallant attempts to include her. She decided that it would be best if they were partners in learning and she found another partner for herself. She went over to the Sweetzer site to ask Jimmy to be her coach. She figured that Gertrude wouldn't mind as there was no doubt that the mission was a noble endeavor.

As usual, the Sweetzer site was jammed with souls marveling at the cats but Julia managed to push her way through the crowd to reach Jimmy. Gertrude and Grandma stood by his side. They welcomed her and when Jimmy hesitated in response to her request, Grandma jumped in and volunteered to coach Julia. She said it would lessen her disappointment about not getting the chance to go down herself. This was not the outcome Julia had hoped for. She had wanted to spend some private time with Jimmy, but she readjusted her expectations quickly and accepted the offer graciously.

From then on, after the training sessions, Julia went directly to Sweetzer's and Grandma helped her go over the day's facts, quizzing her from the training manual. Characteristically, Julia had little patience so Grandma alternated the fact sessions with dance lessons, teaching Julia the Rockette routines. In order to practice they had to clear an aisle through the cat admirers and then they kicked their way from one side of the small site to the other. Occasionally, when Julia's feet got all balled up with the cats, she would curse, *oh blast,* and that reminded her of the facts she was supposed to be memorizing. She would lose her rhythm for a moment but then resume her kicks and recite names and numbers of parts. Grandma would dance alongside her and exclaim, *good, good,* when Julia got it right. It sounded like an unrecognizable jumble except for an occasional word like 'warhead.' Jimmy and Gertrude found Julia and Grandma very entertaining as did many of the neighbors and the cat groupies.

After the sessions with Ludwig, Dinah presented an all day workshop on the Powers of Persuasion. The SuperArch gave the introductory lecture. He said that although the troops were engaged in an exercise to eliminate nuclear, chemical, biological, and assault weapons from the planet, that was only one half of their mission.

Your other goal is to affirm peace as the posture of individuals and nations. This mission is not going to become an annual event. It is a one time show and as the technology for manufacturing nuclear, chemical, biological, and assault weapons will remain, your most important task is to convince the peoples of Earth to live in a climate of mutual respect and to recognize that their choice is either nonviolence or nonexistence.

He ended his talk by saying that when they were asked from whence they came they should reply that they were soldiers in God's Army. A profound silence filled the hall.

Dinah allowed time for a short period of reflection and then divided the volunteers into smaller groups. She conducted numerous exercises to sensitize them to individual differences and promote the development of insight. In the late afternoon she had them practice the speech about elimination of deadly weapons. Ludwig convinced Dinah to use a videotape camera to have her students record their presentations and then make informed criticisms of themselves.

The last two days of the training session were run by the Descent Orientation Committee. The first day was a lecture session of general information needed by all volunteers. On the second day, small groups of trainees met with a staff member who oriented them to the particularities of their assigned locations. On the last day Ludwig administered his weapons exam. He made a florid declaration that no cheating would be tolerated and marched up and down the aisles during the test. He had certainly been a German schoolmaster in at least one Earth lifetime.

Since five hundred souls were going BELOW, the day before departure a descent order was announced. Hugo and Amesbury were told to present themselves at the staging area at 10:30 a.m. and Julia was given the time of 4:30 p.m. Hugo and Amesbury were being sent as partners to the United States. Julia was assigned to Peru. Each enlistee was taught to be fluent in the host languages and was dressed in local garb.

Families accompanied their volunteers to wave goodbye and wish them Godspeed. Throughout the entire day there was a huge crowd around the elevator. The SuperArch had anticipated this and had an observation deck constructed. Family members gathered there to view their loved ones entering the elevator.

In normal descent situations one person might be going down, or rarely two, so the elevator was not constructed to carry a crowd. Six souls was the maximum that could fit comfortably and the elevator could do about six trips an hour. It took fourteen hours to get them all down to Earth. Throughout the entire day the SuperArch stood by the elevator and personally wished each soul a successful journey.

28

BELOW

The re-entry site was a large field. It was April and the grass in the meadow was just turning green. The sun was high in the sky. Many figures strolled about acclimatizing themselves.

After a brief orientation period they were ordered to follow the signs to the Reception Center and then told to go to the dining hall for further instructions. The dining hall was built to hold only four hundred people but rows of extra chairs had been set-up around the edges of the room. It took quite a while for everyone to gather. When the seats were filled the lights were dimmed and a screen was lowered from the ceiling. The program began. The narrator said in warm tones, *Welcome to Earth!* There was beautiful music and a lovely picture of a cascading waterfall. The video was quite short and at the end a serious young man announced that they should go to the table that had a sign with the name of their assigned country hanging over it and they would be individually counseled and instructed on their identities and their tasks. He ho-hummed a few times and then said he was very proud to be part of such a noble effort.

When the assignments were first given out Hugo had traded with someone in order to be Amesbury's partner. They were both given the image of middle-aged men and dressed in suits. Amesbury was tall, dark and handsome and Hugo was lean with white-hair and a distinguished look. The two of them headed for the table under the USA banner.

Julia now had the image of a South American Indian woman. She was attractive and lithe and dark-skinned. She strode across the room with the grace of a dancer. About half way across she did a few Rockette kicks.

After Julia was briefed she was sent to her destination. It was the city of Cusco in the mountains of Peru. She was disguised as a Ministry of Health worker, an Indian woman trained as a visiting nurse. Unfortunately, she was working alone because one of the trainees had flunked Ludwig's armaments exam and the Super decided that Julia could handle the assignment on her own because of her experience implementing the Love and Compassion Curriculum.

At first Julia was a little lonely but she was also enthralled with the beauty of the small city. The climate was wonderful, warm and sunny during the day, and the air was incredibly clear. Cusco was at an altitude of 11,000 feet above sea level so the air was very thin but Julia had no problems with that as she didn't have a real body. She got into her role and soon found herself enjoying it. She was able to speak Spanish and Quechua and all the dialects befitting her incarnation. She went from house to house introducing herself and asking if there were any health problems. She was usually given tea and told about the family. Julia asked each family about their ancestors. She mentioned that she sensed the presence of Indian spirits hovering over Cusco. She was always told that her perceptions were correct. Many Indians had been killed at the time of the Spanish Conquest in 1533. Despite the long interval of Earth time since the massacre, the rage had not dissipated and there were frequent bizarre happenings such as steeples falling from the roofs of churches and piercing the heads of visiting priests and rocks falling from seemingly nowhere to crush Catholic tourists.

Julia quickly understood that her ultimate task was to harness the spirits of the Indians of Cusco and bring them on line to help in the disarmament task. Their spirits had remained over Cusco for hundreds of years. These Inca souls were the most developed souls on Earth and had somehow empowered themselves to stay BELOW after they died. They were the only souls who had ever managed to stay on the Earth plane except for the Floaters, which was the name for those spirits who stay BELOW because they do not know that they are dead. The Earth's seas are littered with them, hence the name Floaters. They have no bearings to convey the passage of time and believe that it was only a moment since they fell into the sea. They wait for rescue. Their relatives ABOVE beg and plead with them to look up so they can be guided HOME, but they never do. The Inca spirits hovering over Cusco knew full well that they were dead. They had somehow managed to continue to drift on the planet instead of rising to ABOVE.

During the next three days Julia worked twenty-four hours a day and met people from all walks of life. After the introductory chat she would ask about their ancestors and was always told tales of attending spirits. She found out that the spirits went to Machu Picchu for gatherings at the time of the full moon. Julia began to spread the word that there would be a meeting of the whole Indian community at Machu Picchu on Saturday night, the eve of the full moon.

On Saturday, Julia took the afternoon train to Machu Picchu. She was gratified to see that the train was filled to overflowing with Indians wearing traditional garb. Everyone greeted her as she moved from car to car throughout the three hour train ride.

They arrived at Machu Picchu at dusk and boarded the last buses of the day. The buses had to return to the train station five times to bring all the people up to the site. The bus drivers were Indians, otherwise the people would certainly have been told that the historic site closed at five-thirty. The Swiss hotel manager ran through the crowd saying there were no more rooms at the hotel and that people should leave. He was ignored.

As the last rays of sun faded behind a mountain peak and the full moon was rising in the east, Julia signaled to everyone to sit down. She entreated the spirits to join them, to come to the assistance of the planet, to help insure that the human race would not be extinguished and the planet abandoned. A chanting began to run through the crowd. Julia sat back and listened as the volume rose. Some of the men began to dance and slowly the group evolved into a circle with the dancing men in the center.

All vestiges of the sunset had disappeared but the scene was well lit by the full moon. After an hour or so, winds began to play about the field. A woman's hat was blown off and here and there skirts and shirts began to fly up under little gusts. Julia knew this signaled the arrival of the spirits. She noticed that some of the women had gathered fire wood and started a bonfire that after a moment of being tenuous small flames, turned into a big blaze casting eerie shadows. The chanting continued and the dancing men seemed tireless. Suddenly a force seemed to descend into the middle of the dancers and the men stumbled backwards and fell to the ground, kneeling in a praying position while facing the center of the apparently empty circle.

Julia could make out dim images in the middle of the circle. As she stared she began to clearly see lithe dancers with spears. First just a few but then more joined in. The praying men began to move backwards, increasing the size of the circle. The apparitions danced on and then began to break out of the circle and form a long line that snaked around the bonfire. Everyone focused on the bonfire and the chanting became louder and had an insistent tone. Julia tried to figure out if the Indians could actually see the spirits or if they could only sense their presence. It was hard to tell.

After what seemed like hours of the spirits dancing and the people chanting, the moon had moved across the sky and Julia had become as mesmerized as the others. Suddenly everything became quiet. The people sat down in a circle around Julia and they were joined by the spirits. Julia realized that it was her time to speak, to introduce the mission. She rose awkwardly and was grateful that she had practiced her presentation. She talked about the peril of nuclear weapons on Earth. They represented the capability for instantaneous and permanent extinction of all life on Earth. She explained that some of the spirits who had risen from the dead were coming back to Earth as an army to eradicate these weapons and to educate the populace to embrace peace. As a result of this action and education the world would become much safer. Without threat of annihilation, life on Earth could proceed as it always had.

One of the spirits stood and approached Julia. He asked why she thought that nations would not immediately produce more weapons as soon as God's Army had retreated. After all, he had been promised by the invading Spanish that he could live peacefully on his land after they had taken the spoils. Instead he had been summarily killed as had all his brothers. After this comment, many other spirits stood and spoke in support of his concerns.

Julia responded by saying that she realized that the course of human history on Earth was full of broken agreements, particularly with the natives of the planet. She agreed that mankind was not known for being trustworthy and keeping his word and that was why the world had evolved into this modern state where peace was kept only by the mutual threat of total annihilation. The plan was to destroy all existing nuclear weapons and agents of chemical and biological warfare and during the process it would be demonstrated that God's Soldiers were invulnerable. This knowledge would intimidate the citizens of Earth. They would believe that their every action was being monitored even after the soldiers had disappeared. *I'm here to ask you Inca spirits who hover perpetually over the Earth to make contact with the spiritual world ABOVE. You will not be coerced to come up but rather are being asked to monitor the Earth people's future actions and immediately identify any abuses by nations who begin to again produce weapons of mass destruction.* She informed the Inca spirits that they were the only spirits, other than the lost

Floaters, who had not ascended to ABOVE immediately after their Earthly deaths and no one was trying to force them to do so now. *However, it is hoped that you will act as guardians of the peace.*

Julia went on to talk about the state of the world and told of the warnings they had received in ABOVE from GOD. *We must all work together to preserve the planet Earth and demonstrate to GOD that humans are a worthy species and can control their self destructive tendencies.* By the time she had finished speaking and answering questions, the light of dawn was tinting the eastern sky.

The Inca spirits agreed to guard the Earth. They headed off in many directions to follow the disarmament process and become familiar with the weapons and the men who made the policies. Julia accompanied them. She had completed her assignment in Peru and wanted to know how the efforts were going in the rest of the world.

29

Amesbury and Hugo had spent their first few days on Earth walking around the Pentagon trying to get appointments with the important people and using the rest of their time to talk with anyone who would listen. They discovered that there were quite a number of people who realized that the presence of many thousands of nuclear warheads capable of destroying the planet thousands of times over was a very perilous situation. However, most people felt that there was no option.

Hugo and Amesbury repeatedly said that they had come to end this Earthly peril. *We're here to wake you people up to the fact that the existence of nuclear weapons means certain disaster. It is only a matter of time until an irreparable mistake is made or a lunatic leader gets hold of some warheads and destroys the world.*

There were so many people at the Pentagon that Hugo and Amesbury couldn't get a sense of whether their speeches were having any effect. At the end of the third day they decided to get some media coverage by beginning the disarming process. All the soldiers from ABOVE had been instructed to wait three days before storming the weapons arsenals.

Hugo and Amesbury went to Sandkit Naval Base. They told the guard at the gate that they had come to inspect the nuclear warheads. They appeared legitimate in their well-tailored suits. They were asked for identification. They said they had none and told the guard that he could let them in or they would let themselves in. Hearing this, the guard picked up his machine gun and pointed it at them, saying they would have to get past him first.

Amesbury and Hugo walked through the gate. The guard shouted at them to halt but they didn't. He threatened to shoot them if they didn't stop. They continued. The guard shot over their heads and shouted another warning. They proceeded. The guard yelled to his supervisior on a walkie-talkie. He was instructed to shoot them and told that the Military Police were on the way. The guard ran up to them shouting that if they didn't halt he would have to shoot them. Continuing to walk jauntily towards him with obvious determination, Amesbury began to lecture him. *My good man, do you realize that everyone will be dead. It's only a matter of time and a short time at that! A world with thousands of nuclear warheads cannot be considered safe and with liklihood for continuance.*

The guard grabbed at Amesbury in an attempt to stop him. He stumbled and paled as his hand went right through Amesbury. He screamed and aimed his machine gun and fired off a round. Nothing happened. Amesbury and Hugo kept walking. The guard screamed again and headed back to the gatehouse at a run.

Throughout the next four days, all around the world, God's Soldiers destroyed the stockpiles of nuclear weapons and agents of biological and chemical warfare. They were aided by the crews at Mission Control ABOVE who guided them to weapons caches and reminded them if any details were forgotten. After numerous attempts to stop them, it became clear that no Earthly power could affect them. Thanks to CNN, after just a couple of hours the whole world knew that God's Army had come to Earth to show man that nuclear war must never happen. Churches were filled to overflowing and in cities and small villages around the world banners were hung across streets, spelling in every language, WELCOME MESSIAHS.

Everything came to a standstill. People stayed home and watched TV to keep abreast of the miraculous happenings.

A GROUP OF MEN AND WOMEN WHO APPEAR TO BE NORMAL PEOPLE BUT CANNOT BE KILLED, HAVE INVADED THE EARTH. THEY ARE DESTROYING ALL THE NUCLEAR WEAPONS AND AGENTS OF CHEMICAL AND BIOLOGICAL WARFARE AND ADDRESSING THEMSELVES TO THE TASK OF EDUCATING THE PEOPLES OF THE EARTH ABOUT THE PERILS OF NUCLEAR WAR.

People left home only to go to their houses of worship and always left one family member on guard to listen to the news.

The disarming went on for three days and three nights. Presidents and members of Senates and Congresses and Parliaments made statements. In the first few hours of the onslaught there were questions in every country about whether these radicals were from an enemy country. But after souls emerged unscathed from machine gun fire, chemical warfare, and all other manner of offense, a click seemed to happen in the collective mind of the Earth's peoples, and the invaders were perceived as Messiahs.

Through the equalizing power of television and the Internet, people all around the globe were brought to the same mind-set. It was a religious experience. Looking down at the Earth from ABOVE, the whole planet seemed to have a new, healthy, green aura.

On day seven of this momentous week on Earth, Mission Control sent down the message that the job was done and the soldiers would be recalled over the next few hours. They were advised to inform the Earth people around them that they would be leaving soon but would continue to watch over things from ABOVE. The Soldiers of God answered questions until they were recalled and, often in mid-sentence, instantly disappeared.

Jimmy was on a monitor in the Great Hall during the recall. He followed along, going from one scene on Earth to the next. He was watching when Julia and Amesbury and Hugo were brought in. The three of them were holding hands. In Julia's last instant on Earth, she executed a series of Rockette kicks. Grandma, who was on the monitor, clapped and cheered. *Her technique is flawless*, she raved.

Jimmy loved catching the moment when the actual disappearances occurred. There were always gasps and an exclamation from the crowd and then a moment of silence before the business of life resumed, like a motor momentarily faltering and then roaring into full throttle again.

The SuperArch welcomed each returning hero personally. He stood at the edge of the field all day long telling each returning soul, *good job! Well done! Thank you! Welcome home!* There was a mood of excitement and jubilation in ABOVE. They had a grand ceremony celebrating the success of the mission. Each volunteer was presented with a citation of merit.

Soon everything was back to normal.

CPSIA information can be obtained
at www.ICGtesting.com
Printed in the USA
JSHW010123040423
39790JS00003B/145